"Send that man away!"

Thea Maxwell stared at her father without understanding. "Who...you mean Rafe?"

Her dad nodded. "He's the law."

"What's that got to do with anything?"

"He'll be investigating Bobby's accident." Robert Maxwell closed his eyes for a moment. "If one of those boys dies, it's going to be all we can do to keep your brother from being tried for murder. This deputy you're so set on getting friendly with will be the one making the arrest, gathering the evidence. And he'll be the one pushing to convict."

He looked straight at Thea, his face haggard, his eyes as cold as stone.

"Are you willing to let your *boyfriend* send your *brother* to prison?"

Dear Reader,

In the midst of writing *Married in Montana*, I made a major change in my life: I bought a horse. After taking riding lessons for a few months, my daughter fell in love with a spotted saddle horse named T-Bone, a sweet guy with whom she could learn the ropes of riding and showing horses. I was horse crazy when I was a teenager, so I've enjoyed encouraging her equine adventures.

I suppose my early romance with horses explains, in part, why I love to write about the people who make ranching their life. The vacation I would choose is a couple of weeks spent on a working cattle ranch—in Montana, of course— riding out with the crew every morning, coming in tired and dirty and hungry in the evening…and then getting up the next morning to do it all over again!

I get to live a bit of that cowboy life when we go to the barn to ride—and when I write books like this one. My heroine, Thea Maxwell, is living my idea of the perfect life. All she needs is the perfect man with whom to share it. Deputy Sheriff Rafe Rafferty fits the bill…except for the fact that he's on one side of the law and she, thanks to family complications, is on the other. Working out Thea's and Rafe's problems, against the magnificent backdrop of the Montana Rockies, gave me a great deal of pleasure. I hope their story does the same for you.

All the best,

Lynnette Kent

P.S. I should mention that once I finished *Married in Montana*, I took the horse experience a step further…I bought one for me!

Married in Montana
Lynnette Kent

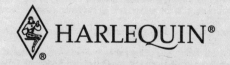

TORONTO • NEW YORK • LONDON
AMSTERDAM • PARIS • SYDNEY • HAMBURG
STOCKHOLM • ATHENS • TOKYO • MILAN • MADRID
PRAGUE • WARSAW • BUDAPEST • AUCKLAND

ISBN 0-373-71002-X

MARRIED IN MONTANA

Copyright © 2001 by Cheryl B. Bacon.

Visit us at www.eHarlequin.com

Printed in U.S.A.

For Roxanne and Ellen,
who mined the Maxwells
and their story with me.
Thanks for all the hard work.
We make a great team!

CHAPTER ONE

SETTING HIS JAW, Rafe Rafferty stepped out of his truck into the driving rain. He turned immediately to open the rear passenger door. "Okay, son, you're home. Get out."

Sprawled across the back seat, a nineteen-year-old troublemaker rolled his handsome head from side to side. "Don' wanna be home." Each word puffed out a rich aroma of beer.

"Doesn't matter what you do or don't want." Rafe reached in and caught the boy by one wrist. "You're not spending the night in there." He gave the connected arm a jerk. His passenger flowed into a sitting position, held it for a second, then slid to the floorboard like a rag doll.

Rafe glanced at the water running an inch deep around the soles of his boots. "This is gonna hurt you a hell of a lot more than it hurts me." He braced a foot on the running board of the truck, grabbed the boy's ankles, one in each hand, and thrust backward with all the force his legs would generate.

A second later, Bobby Maxwell, heir apparent to the Walking Stones Ranch near Paradise Corners, Montana, landed on his butt on the driveway in the rain.

Rafe ignored the boy's cussing. "I'll wake them up inside," he told Bobby. "And then I'm leaving. You want to sleep out in this weather, that's your business. Getting you home before you killed yourself or somebody else was mine."

His heels struck loudly on the floorboards of the wide porch as he crossed to the ranch house's front door. The brass knocker had been fashioned as a bull's head—an Angus, no doubt, the specialty of Walking Stones Ranch— with a twelve-inch horn spread and a ring through its nose. Rafe grabbed that ring and slammed brass against brass five times, good and loud. Then he backed up a step, propped his thumbs in the pockets of his uniform slacks and waited.

Soon enough, the porch lamps flashed on, the dead bolt turned and the big double doors swung backward. Just over the threshold, a woman stood silhouetted against the glow of interior lights. According to what he'd heard, there was no Mrs. Maxwell. So this would be Bobby's older sister, Thea Maxwell, the one who, so rumor had it, could give most cowboys in the area a run for their money when it came to ranch work.

"Hello?" Her voice was deep, husky, questioning. And totally feminine. Hearing it, everything inside Rafe—his pulse, his breath, his thoughts—stopped for a second in surprise.

"Is something wrong?" Worry edged the words as she stared at him, waiting.

He pulled himself together, freed a thumb and tipped his hat. "Good evening, ma'am. I'm Deputy Sheriff Rafferty. I brought Mr. Bobby Maxwell home."

She raked a hand through her short hair. "Let me guess—you caught him tipping Fred Byron's cows again." Now her voice held a smile, inviting him to smile, too.

This was business, though, so he didn't. "No, ma'am. I broke up a fight at the Lone Wolf Bar up in Paradise Corners and found him in the middle."

She stiffened. "Is he hurt?"

"He's beat up a little. But mostly he's too drunk to run around loose."

"Dammit, Bobby!"

"Don' yell at me, Tee."

The Maxwell boy stumbled up the three steps onto the porch, swayed and wrapped an arm around a stacked stone column to keep from falling over. His clothes were soaking wet, plastered to his skin. "Don' yell, okay? No harm done."

"This time." Brushing past Rafe, Thea Maxwell crossed the porch to pry her brother from his prop. The drape of her blue pajamas hinted at some very nice curves underneath. Rafe liked women with curves. And voices like hers.

At the moment, though, this woman wasn't thinking about impressing him one way or another. She was fussing over her brother. "You'd better get into some dry clothes before you get sick. How'd you get so wet?" She pulled his arm over her shoulder, turning him toward the front door.

As they passed Rafe, Bobby gave him a wink and a good-natured grin. "Can't 'member."

"Do you remember promising you'd stay out of trouble?" Still holding him up with an arm around his waist, she propelled Bobby down the length of the palatial great room. Rafe could hear her scolding as they disappeared through an arched doorway. "When are you going to grow up?"

Bobby laughed, but his mumbled reply was lost in the distance. Duty discharged, Rafe turned away from the warmth of the house to start the long drive back to town.

"What the devil is going on here?"

He pivoted back to face the growling question. Now a man confronted him from the doorway, tall and broad-shouldered, still dressed in the working clothes of a hands-on rancher. This would be Boss Maxwell himself. Robert Maxwell Senior.

Another respectful tip of the hat. "Sorry to bother you, Mr. Maxwell. I brought your son back from town—he was too drunk to drive. He can pick up his truck in the parking lot where he left it."

Maxwell's temper vibrated in the air. "Who asked you to butt in?"

Rafe refused to be baited. He didn't want to tell Maxwell that his son had started a bar fight—why cause the boy any more grief? Especially with an old man as hard as Maxwell was reputed to be. "I thought Bobby could use some help getting home, that's all. Now, if you'll excuse me—"

"You'll leave when I say so, and not before." Maxwell stepped into the porch light. His lined face testified to years in the harsh Montana weather, his red hair showed streaks of white at the temples. "My boy doesn't need a baby-sitter, especially not some wet-behind-the-ears deputy still breaking in his boots." The rancher didn't have to raise his voice to make a point—his sharp tone did all the work.

"I may be new to Paradise Corners, but I've been wearing these same boots for six years now." The grin he tried got no response, so Rafe abandoned the effort. "I was just doing my job, sir." This last "sir" came out through gritted teeth.

"Your job is to stay out of decent people's business. The folks of this county will let you know when they want your help. As for the Maxwells…" The older man sliced the air with the side of his hand. "We don't need your help. Just stay clear. I've got connections all over this state. I can get you run out of town so fast—"

Thea arrived in time to hear the threat. "Calm down, Dad."

Both men jerked their heads to stare in her direction. They'd been so involved in their argument, they obviously hadn't noticed her return to the doorway. Arms crossed, she surveyed them in turn, reminded of mature bulls staking a claim on the same herd of cows. Both big, both strong, both stubborn.

She put her hand on her dad's arm. "Deputy Rafferty did us a favor. There's no telling what would have happened if Bobby had tried to drive home. Why don't you just say thanks and get to bed? It's 1:00 a.m., and you wanted an early start in the morning."

Robert Maxwell didn't give in, but she hadn't expected him to. With a sound somewhere between a snarl and a grunt, he turned on his boot heel and stomped back into his wing of the house.

Shaking her head, Thea looked at the deputy. "We haven't treated you very well, considering how helpful you've been. I'm Althea Maxwell—Thea to most people." She held out her hand to shake his. "Would you like some coffee before you head back?"

His warm palm closed against hers, comforting, safe. "That would be great. I'm Rafe, by the way. Well…" He shrugged. "Actually it's Owen, but I got tired of the teasing by about the second grade." He grinned and took off his hat.

Thea blinked twice. Hard. With Bobby in such a state, she hadn't had time or opportunity to notice the deputy's looks, but she sure was noticing now. Deep brown eyes under thick lashes, a proud nose that might have been broken a time or two, dark brown hair that kept its wave even with a regulation short haircut. And then there were his shoulders…

A cold draft through the open door brought Thea to her senses. "Oh…good. The kitchen's this way." Only as she led him through the dining room did she remember she was in her pajamas. Flannel pajamas, true, in a conservative dark blue. She might as well be wearing jeans and a shirt.

But standing across the kitchen from the gorgeous deputy as she made a pot of hot, sweet coffee, she couldn't help feeling...exposed. She should have put on a robe, at least.

"Thanks for leaving out the part about the fight," she said, filling a mug for each of them. "Especially since Bobby probably started the whole thing." She glanced at the deputy, who nodded. "He's not in any shape to deal with Dad's temper tonight."

"I'd imagine that requires a clear head."

She waved him to the kitchen table. "Nerves of steel help. As well as not having done anything wrong to begin with." She sighed. "With Bobby, we hardly ever get all three at the same time."

Considerately, Rafe Rafferty left that comment alone. "These are good," he said after a minute, gesturing with one of the oatmeal cookies she'd set out. Thea looked up from her coffee and saw that, like a little boy, he had a crumb at the corner of his mouth. Such a nicely shaped mouth...

"Did you make them?"

Startled yet again, she laughed, hoping he hadn't noticed her staring. "Coffee is my only kitchen skill. Our housekeeper, Beth, is the genius."

He nodded. "Genius covers it. I hear you work the ranch with your dad."

"That's right." She said it with the warm surge of pride she always got when she thought about her job. "I wouldn't do anything else."

"It's beautiful country, that's for sure." A fifth cookie left the plate. "But hard work for a woman, I'd imagine. I've done some climbing since I got here a few weeks ago—this terrain can be tough."

Eyebrows lifted, Thea sat up straight. "You think it's easier for a man?"

He stared at her a second, his jaw hanging slightly loose, then laughed. "So you do that, too."

"Do what?"

"Your dad doesn't have to yell—he can cut like a bullwhip with just a whisper. And your voice just did the same thing."

Her cheeks got hot. "I didn't intend to go after you with a bullwhip. Still, if you assume that because I'm female I can't—"

He finished the cookie and dusted the crumbs from his big hands, shaking his head the whole time. "Sorry, my mistake. It's just hard to imagine a woman as pretty as you out there castrating calves all day." His smile was a clear invitation to flirt back.

But Thea had seen that smile—heard the line that went with it—too many times. She wasn't about to fall for another slick maneuver, wasn't about to be used to curry favor with her father.

Especially not when she felt so…so vulnerable to this man. After just ten minutes of his company, no less.

"I can castrate with the best of them, thank you very much, Deputy. I've delivered breech calves by myself and spent three days alone on horseback rounding up cows lost in a blizzard. There's nothing on Walking Stones I can't or won't do." She stood up. "Now, if you've finished your coffee, it's late and I'm going to be at work before sunrise."

He got to his feet and picked up his hat. Under the bright kitchen light, his cheeks were a dull red. "I apologize yet again, Ms. Maxwell. I seem to be stepping in it whichever direction I turn." Without waiting for her guidance, he made his way to the front of the house, fast enough that Thea had to hurry to keep up with his long strides. Before she quite reached the door, he'd crossed the porch and started down the steps.

The cold rain had gotten worse, whipping across the driveway like bullets. Rafe Rafferty drew up his shoulders as he jogged out to his truck. The engine roared to life, the lights blazed, and for a second she could see him through the water-glazed windshield as he wiped a hand over his bare head. He glanced her way, and his mouth tightened.

Then the tires squealed against the stones of the driveway and the truck disappeared into the night. Heedless of the damp chill, Thea stood there for a while, knocking her forehead against the edge of a door.

I can castrate calves, she mocked herself in a prissy voice, *and deliver breech births and round up cows in a blizzard.*

But she didn't know jack when it came to men.

ROBERT MAXWELL WAITED to check on his son until the upstart deputy had left and Althea had gone back to her bed. Standing in the doorway of Bobby's room, he shook his head at the sight of his boy, spread-eagled on top of the blanket. In the dim light, he looked so much like his mother...the same thick, wavy black hair, the same dark sloe eyes, the fair skin and curved lips. Helen had given beauty to all of their children, but especially to their son. If only she had lived to give them her good sense.

Instead, his three daughters seemed determined to flout his authority at every turn. Jolie, the eldest, now a doctor in California, had gone as far away from home as she could just as soon as she graduated high school. Cassie, their middle girl, had married the first wastrel she'd set eyes on and was now raising her seven-year-old son on her own. Althea, on the other hand, had turned down every man who looked her way—including the governor's boy, a fiasco that had nearly quashed an important land deal requiring his dad's approval. Damn, the girl was stubborn. Wouldn't even agree to get the sale papers signed first, before she booted him out.

As for his son, his hope, his pride…the next generation of Maxwells and the future of Walking Stones Ranch depended on a boy who did everything he could think of to shirk the work, escape the responsibilities. Robert knew that time and trends were against the individual rancher these days—without constant and diligent work, without cunning and education and insight, a man's property could be taken from him by one bad season, by an unexpected epidemic, by a few unlucky investments.

But Bobby didn't give a tinker's damn. One hundred fifty years of Maxwell sweat and blood stood in serious jeopardy, unless something changed the boy's attitude and bound him to the land.

Only once in his life had Robert Maxwell failed to get what he wanted. He had not been able to save his wife's life 15 years ago, not with prayers, or money, or even with the force of his will. He'd accepted that defeat as a circumstance beyond his control.

But as long as he lived, he would not tolerate the loss of even a square foot of Walking Stones land. The ranch would remain intact, no matter what it took in terms of time, cash and determination. This was the legacy Maxwell men labored under from birth until death, a legacy Bobby *would* come to understand. To embrace.

He simply had no other choice.

WHEN RAFE FINALLY reached the questionable shelter he'd been calling home for the past few weeks, Jed waited by the door. "Not even a dog should have to go out in this," Rafe told him. But Jed just heaved a heavy bloodhound sigh and headed into the dark. By the time he got back, Rafe had changed his clothes down to the skin and started a fire. After he toweled the dog off, they both settled down near the blaze.

"You'd think I wouldn't be so surprised," Rafe commented after a swallow of beer. "I've seen folks like this before. The Maxwells own more of Montana than God. Which, at least in their opinion, puts them above the law."

Jed thumped his tail twice. "Yeah, I know it's bull, too. But they don't. And it's gonna get worse. Bobby's a nice kid, I'm thinking, who's got a serious problem with alcohol. If his family has a clue, they're not doing anything about it."

Rafe finished the beer and settled into the lumpy couch he was using as a bed until the moving company found his furniture. "Princess Althea almost had me fooled into thinking she was different. That smile of hers could keep a man warm through the worst Montana blizzard."

He pictured her as she'd looked across the kitchen table—her greenish-blue eyes wide and friendly, her mouth deep pink and richly curved, the crisp layers of her shiny black hair begging to be played with. He'd admired her stamina, her patience with her little brother, the fact that she didn't get flustered about sharing cookies with him at one in the morning in her pajamas. She was far and away the best part of Montana he'd come across yet.

Then, in a split second, the mask had crumbled, leaving him with just another Maxwell, arrogant and totally out of reach.

"Doesn't matter." Rafe punched the couch pillow and pulled the mothball-scented blanket over his shoulder. "This town—and the family that appears to own it—may not want a deputy who does his job." The guys in the county office had warned him about his likely reception in advance. So far, the locals had lived up to expectations. Strangers of any kind were greeted with suspicion by the citizens of Paradise Corners. A deputy of the county sheriff automatically represented an attempt by somebody in far-away Big Timber, the county seat, to assert control over local affairs. And if that deputy hailed fron somewhere foreign—say, Los Angeles, California, as Rafe did—then he was guaranteed a hostile reception at best. "Unfortunately for Paradise Corners, I'm here and I'm planning to stay. The Maxwells and everyone else might as well get used to having me...."

Jed lifted his head and gave him a soulful, understanding stare.

Grinning, Rafe reached out and rubbed the wrinkled head of his best friend and only real family in the world. "The Maxwells had better get used to having both of us around."

TWO SILENT MEN sat the breakfast table when Thea came into the kitchen the next morning. Her father glanced up and nodded, then returned to his eggs. Herman Peace, manager of Walking Stones, gave her his usual lopsided smile. "Lazybones."

Thea returned the smile and stepped to the coffeemaker on the counter. "Guilty as charged."

Déjà vu—pouring a mug of coffee brought back last night's interlude with Rafe Rafferty. She'd regretted everything about those minutes—what she had said and what she hadn't—through the remainder of a mostly sleepless night.

"'Morning, Thea." Beth Peace, Herman's sister, bustled in from the hallway leading to the pantry and laundry room. "I'll have your plate ready in a flash. Your dad needed some more juice." Standing beside his chair, she filled his half-empty glass to the brim.

"Thank you, ma'am." Robert Maxwell's smile was

sweet when he chose to use it. Which was seldom outside of Beth's kitchen.

"Take your time." Thea shuddered as she swallowed her black coffee. She preferred sugar and cream, but with the day ahead, she figured she needed a straight shot. "I won't starve."

But Beth was already cracking eggs into the big iron frying pan with one hand, punching slices of bread into the toaster with the other. Never hurried or flustered, but always busy, she'd been running the household as long as Thea could remember, even before their mom died. Bobby had been four at the time—Beth was the only mother he really remembered.

"Did you wake up your brother?" Her dad set his plate in the sink. "We're already late getting started."

"I knocked on his door, and he said he was coming." Not a lie, exactly—her dad didn't want to hear what Bobby had actually said, or the vocabulary he'd used to say it. "His shower was running as I came down the hall."

"Get him outside by six, with or without breakfast. You coming, Peace?" Opening the door to the mudroom, he asked the question without looking back for an answer.

"Right behind you." The manager gulped down the last of his coffee. As the door shut behind Boss Maxwell, Herman cocked a thick gray eyebrow and grinned at Thea. "Man's just a bundle of sunshine in the morning, ain't he? Have a good one," he told his sister, planting a kiss on the woman's cheek. "I'm hoping for stew tonight."

Beth pretended to push him away. "You'll take what you get and be satisfied." But she smiled and lifted her hand as he backed through the door. Then she dished up Thea's eggs and bacon and toast, set the plate on the table, and poured another glass of juice.

"Thanks, Beth." Thea sat down to her meal, hoping the

housekeeper had something important to do besides ask questions.

No such luck. "The deputy sheriff brought Bobby home last night?" Mug in hand, Beth sat in the chair her brother had vacated. "Drunk?"

Chewing, Thea just nodded.

"Fighting?"

"Uh-huh." She gulped down the orange juice.

"What are we going to do with that boy?" A worried frown creased Beth's smooth, plump face. "He's getting wilder every day. Your father should have let him go to California to college. Jolie would have looked out for him."

"But Bobby would never have come back." Thea had given up trying to figure out why. All her brother had to do was show some interest and he'd have Walking Stones and everything it stood for handed to him on a platter. While she, who would give her right arm for the privilege of tending the land...

She shoved the thought out of her mind. There was no time for bitterness this morning. Bobby had less than five minutes for breakfast. She scooted her chair back from the table. "I'd better go see if he's on his feet."

Beth nodded. "I'll make him a sandwich to eat as he rides."

The door to Bobby's room was still shut. Thea knocked, got no answer, and turned the knob, dreading to see her brother still in bed. All hell would break loose if Bobby had gone back to sleep.

But the situation wasn't quite that desperate. He was awake and dressed, more or less, though his shirttail hung outside his jeans and the cuffs were unbuttoned. He sat on the bed wearing one boot, with the other lying on the floor between his feet. Head propped in his hands, elbows on his knees, he didn't look up when she stepped into the room.

"Dad said to have you outside by six. We're pushing the deadline."

Bobby drew a deep breath. "Tell him I'm sick."

"Hangovers don't count, you know that."

"Tell him I'm dead."

"I'm not sure even death would be an excuse for you not showing up for work this morning."

That got her a ghost of a chuckle. "Damn, my head hurts."

"Maybe you could remember that feeling *before* you start drinking?"

"Maybe." With a sigh, he pushed his hands through his thick, wavy hair and reached for the other boot. "I must've been totally plowed last night. I don't remember driving home."

"You didn't." Thea kept her mind blank. "The deputy brought you."

Bobby looked up, his sleepy eyes a little wider. "Yeah?" He thought a second. "Oh, yeah. He pulled me out of the truck and dumped me in the rain."

"He what?" Being furious with Rafe Rafferty felt really good—like Christmas and the Fourth of July rolled into one. "That's why you were so wet? I thought you'd just climbed out of the truck cab." If she ever saw that deputy again—which she would avoid if at all possible—he would get a sharp piece of her mind about trying to drown teenage boys who'd had a little too much to drink.

"I wasn't climbing anywhere if I could help it." He jerked on the right boot, eased to his feet and tucked his shirt into his jeans. Tall, like their dad, narrow of hip and wide of shoulder, Bobby had the looks of a movie star. Or a model.

Good thing he'd never expressed any interest in being either. Thea didn't want to think about Robert Maxwell's reaction to those ambitions. "Ready to ride?"

Her brother just looked at her. "Are you a sadist?"

From the back of the house came a bellow Thea recognized as their dad calling Bobby's name. She grabbed her brother's arm and pulled him after her into the hallway. "You tempt me, boy. You really tempt me."

RAIN-WASHED, Paradise Corners looked fresh and clean when Rafe started for the office on the morning after his visit to the Maxwell ranch. The business district covered a square of about twelve small city blocks—mostly independent merchants, a lawyer or two and the post office, plus the courthouse and four churches, one on each corner of the main intersection, which gave the town and the street their names.

Most residents lived south of Main Street, in tidy houses under old pine and cedar and oak trees. The Methodists, late arrivals to this part of Montana, had built their church to the south, in the lower foothills, rather than downtown with the Baptists, Mormons, Catholics, and Lutherans. Bars and gas stations clustered at the western end of Main, around the road heading toward the mountains. East of town, the north-south state highway ran toward the two-lane road leading the unwary out to Walking Stones Ranch. Rafe didn't plan to make that trip again any time soon.

On the north side of town, rough lanes wound high into the foothills of the Crazy Mountains and the Gallatin National Forest, with isolated houses tucked into corners here and there. Rafe's rented house sat north of Main Street, too, but closer in—a brisk three-block walk brought him to the bustle of Saturday morning in a ranching town. To his right stood Grizzly's Diner, the only decent place to eat if you didn't want to cook. Leaving Jed posted just outside the door, Rafe stepped into a wave of friendly chatter that suddenly lulled as customers reacted to his arrival.

In a couple of seconds the talk resumed, quieter than before, as if people didn't want to be overheard. Sitting at the counter, Rafe fought to ignore the fact he was being stared at and studied the menu.

"Coffee, Deputy." Mona Rangel, the owner, set a mug down at his right hand, already mixed with sugar and milk, the way he liked it. "Something to eat?"

Rafe grinned his appreciation. "Let's try something really wild today—scrambled eggs instead of fried. Think we can stand the shock?"

Her gray eyes flickered with humor, but she didn't break a smile. "Three scrambled with bacon and toast, coming up." She turned toward the kitchen, cutting off his only friendly contact in the place.

Halfway through his second mug of coffee, somebody actually joined Rafe at the counter, on the very next stool, no less. He glanced to the left and caught the eye of Judge LeVay, his ostensible boss and the main representative of the law in Paradise Corners, besides himself.

"Good morning, sir."

"Deputy." LeVay nodded. He looked the part of a wise old western judge, from his thick white hair and mustache to the black suit and vest and string tie. "Just coffee," he told Mona when she appeared.

The judge said nothing until the coffee arrived and had been sampled. Rafe endured the silence without comment—he had no illusions that this was a chance encounter. Or an invitation to join the local shooting club.

"Got a call early this morning," LeVay said finally. His voice barely carried over the noise of the crowd.

Rafe didn't comment.

"Robert Maxwell seems to think you exceeded your authority in dealing with an incident last night."

"Mr. Maxwell's perceptions are a little…skewed."

One white eyebrow lifted. "The man is a close friend of mine. I believe what he says."

"The drinking age in Montana was twenty-one, last time I checked." The judge glanced over his shoulder, a clear warning for Rafe to keep his voice down. "And DUI carries some stiff penalties…at least on paper."

LeVay drained his mug and wiped his mouth with a napkin plucked from the stainless-steel cube between them. "I appreciate your concern. I'm sure Mr. Maxwell does, too. However, I believe he can handle this…situation…without outside interference."

Rafe dropped the oblique approach, but kept his voice quiet. "That boy's going to hurt himself. Or somebody else. He's out of control."

For a second, the judge's pale blue eyes met his, and Rafe knew they were in agreement on that fact. But then LeVay slid off the stool.

"Leave it alone," he advised. "You've got enough trouble on your hands in this town without getting the Maxwells riled up." With a nod of greeting to a couple of men in a nearby booth, the older man made his way to the door. Through the glass, Rafe saw him stoop to talk to Jed. The bloodhound squirmed gratefully as the judge scratched the sensitive spot on the back of his neck. If Jed liked the man, Rafe decided, he couldn't be all bad.

But if Maxwell owned him, he couldn't be completely trusted, either. Better not look for help from that quarter.

Rafe turned back to finish his eggs, and found Mona standing opposite him.

"Take the judge at his word," she suggested, swapping his cold plate of food for a steaming hot portion. "Maxwell owns this town and most of the people in it, one way or the other. You land on his bad side, you won't get an ounce of cooperation from anybody." She smiled. "Except me. Maxwell doesn't like me, either."

"Why not?"

"I taught in the county school system for close to two decades. Bobby was one of my sixth-graders. Bright kid, spoiled rotten. He didn't do a lick of work in my class all year. I wouldn't promote him, no matter how many fits his daddy threw. Maxwell got me fired, but Bobby still had to repeat the sixth grade, and he didn't pull the same stunt again. Graduated in the spring with pretty good grades, I heard."

"And you're working in the diner?"

Mona shrugged. "My husband built the place and ran it until he died last year. I figured keeping Grizzly's open would give me something to do and pay my respects at the same time." Her smile was rueful. "Anyway, watch your step. The Maxwells are about as safe to be around as timber rattlers. A little more predictable, maybe—you threaten them or theirs, you can be sure they'll do their best to take you down."

She moved away, and Rafe thought for a second about calling her back for one more question.

What about Thea Maxwell?

Did she take after her old man? Did she follow his orders straight down the line? Was she just one more piece of property her father owned?

Did it matter? Boss Maxwell had practically threatened him with bodily harm for interfering. The lady herself had brushed him off like yesterday's dust. And there was little doubt that her brother would keep to the straight and narrow *exactly* as long as it took him to pick up his truck.

Any more trouble with Bobby would put Rafe on the side of the devil, as far as all the Maxwells were concerned.

Didn't he have enough trouble in this town already? Was his sense of self-preservation so weak?

With a silent sigh, Rafe acknowledged that the same two words answered both of those questions—plus one more…

Could he really be crazy enough to consider going after this woman?

Remembering Thea's voice, her smile, the light in her eyes and the strange peace he'd felt when he first saw her, Rafe nodded and took a sip of coffee. Three simple questions, one simple answer.

You bet.

CHAPTER TWO

ALL DAY SATURDAY—sunrise until sundown—Bobby worked on getting his big sister to drive him to town to pick up his truck. Successful, as usual, he now sat beside her in the front seat of her Land Rover, beating a tattoo on his knees in rhythm with the tune screaming from the CD player. They'd rolled the windows down, though the night air blew cold. Between the big starry sky and the miles adding up between him and the ranch, he was beginning to feel he could breathe again.

Thea pressed a control on the steering wheel and turned the volume down.

"Hey!" Bobby reached for the button on the console. "I like that song."

This time she punched the music off. "We need to talk."

Here we go again. "No, we don't."

She ignored his protest. "What are you trying to prove with the drinking and the fighting and the stupid stunts? I have to tell you, nobody is impressed with your maturity and sense of responsibility."

"I'm only nineteen years old, for God's sake. I don't have to be mature or responsible."

"It would be nice if you were still alive when your twentieth birthday came around."

He rolled his eyes. "Give me a break. The most life-threatening thing I do is show up for work every day, give the old man another chance to run me into the ground."

"It's your ranch…your life…we're talking about here. Dad wants you to be prepared to take over when he retires."

The words were out before he could stop them. "If he'd listen to me—just once—and realize I don't want the damn ranch, we'd all be better off."

Thea took her gaze off the road to stare at him. "Why not?"

Bobby dropped his head against the back of the seat and closed his eyes. His head still ached from last night. "When did I ever say I did?"

"You loved the place when you were little. We couldn't convince you to come in for dinner some nights, at least not until it got too dark to work."

"Yeah, well, I grew up." He didn't have the words to explain how the ranch, the old man…Thea herself…smothered him. And even if he could find the words…no way could he hurt Thea like that. She'd taken care of him since he was four years old.

"I'm not so sure." She braked at the intersection of the ranch road with the main highway, then turned left toward town. "Adults acknowledge their responsibilities."

He ground his back teeth. "Damn, I'm tired of that word."

"Don't swear at me."

"Don't tell me what I can and can't do." Now he sounded like a four-year-old even to himself.

They rode the thirty miles to Paradise Corners without saying anything else. Thea took the shortcut, which brought them to the Lone Wolf Bar without going through the main part of town. His truck sat right where he'd left it last night, reflecting the neon lights of the bar in its bright red finish.

Bobby pulled in a deep breath. "Thanks, Tee." He used his childhood name for her to apologize. "I appreciate the ride." He opened the door and dropped to the ground, then turned to give her a grin and a wave through the open window. The night was young, and there was a girl he knew…

Thea evidently had other ideas. "You're going to follow me home, right?"

He stared at her in disbelief. "Uh…no, I hadn't planned on going home yet."

His sister could swear with the best of the cowboys, and she did it now as she slammed the door and strode around the Land Rover to face him. She was only a couple of inches shorter and ten years older than he. That made her a strong woman, even when she wasn't spitting mad.

Like this. "You are not going to spend tonight carousing and fighting, buddy." She jabbed a finger into his chest. "I'm not having you brought home by the deputy again. Or an ambulance. You get your butt in that truck. I'll follow you."

"Tee—" The problem was that he wanted to laugh. He never could get mad at his big sis. "It's Saturday night. You don't really want me sitting at home on Saturday night."

"I believe we'll all survive the experience."

The urge to laugh faded. "Look, I promise I won't get plowed again. I'll stay sober as a judge."

"You know as well as I do how much LeVay likes his scotch." Her eyes had lost their fierceness. He was gonna win this one, too. "And you promised the same thing before you left home last night, as I recall."

"Cross my heart." He suited action to words. "Look, I told Megan we'd go over to Bozeman tonight. She's supposed to get here about eight—" A beat-up Jeep rolled into the parking lot. "See, that's her right there."

Thea had all her antennae up now. "Does Mr. Wheeler

know you're taking Megan to Bozeman? Why didn't you pick her up at her house?"

"Uh…sure, he knows." He hated to lie, but he didn't want to continue this fight in front of Megan. "I thought I'd be in town earlier than this, so she got her friend Racey to drop her off."

The Jeep stopped right beside him, and Megan scooted out. "Thanks, Race. See ya'." She straightened up and smiled at him. "Hey, Bobby."

"Hey, honey." Something about Megan's smile, about the worship in her brown eyes and the pout of her full lower lip, glazed tonight with some kind of sparkly pink lipstick, simply took away his ability to think. "Ready for a night on the town? You look great."

She blushed, and smoothed a hand over her short jean skirt. As if he hadn't already noticed those long bare legs. "I'm ready." She looked toward his sister and smiled. "Hey, Thea. How are you?"

"Just fine, thanks." She shoved a hand through her hair and blew a breath off her lower lip. "Listen, can you get this rascal home at a reasonable hour tonight? He dragged in late and you can't begin to imagine what kind of commotion that makes with Dad."

Megan didn't have it in her to lie. Bobby took her arm and stepped into the breach. "I promise, Ms. Watchdog. I'll hit the door at midnight on my own two feet. Will that do?"

Thea drove her hands into the pockets of her jeans. "I guess it'll have to. I didn't bring along a rope to tie you down."

"Great. See you later, then." He walked Megan to the truck, thanking God that he'd bought the biggest pickup on the market, because he couldn't wait one single minute more to kiss that pink frosting right off her sweet mouth.

In the shadow of the cab, out of Thea's line of sight, he backed Megan against the door, braced his elbows and leaned his body into hers. She was a slender little thing, yet she fit him just right. "We didn't get a chance to say hello properly out there. Want to try again?"

For an answer, she smiled, wrapped her arms around his neck and pulled his face down to hers.

FROM THE DRIVER'S SEAT of the Land Rover, Thea watched until Bobby got into his truck and headed east toward the highway. She didn't wonder why it had taken him a good ten minutes to get Megan in on the passenger side. His eyes had glazed over the minute the girl set foot on the ground. He'd have stepped on his tongue if he'd tried to walk.

She smiled slightly and sighed at the same time. Her dad had been tough on Bobby all day—not just his usual silent observation, but heavy disapproval coupled with a level of expectation his children could never meet. Robert Maxwell didn't suffer mistakes or fools. Thea had learned over the years how to avoid both. Most of the time.

But Bobby enjoyed courting disaster. He didn't look ahead and he didn't look behind, and he never seemed to notice what havoc his behavior wreaked in other lives. Her own, for example. She'd been his shield, his defender, for half her life. Jolie and Cassie had taken off, leaving her to fill the role of mother/daughter/sister/ranch hand. Sure, she loved the job. She worked hard every day to earn her dad's respect, because she loved him, too. And, of course, she loved Bobby to distraction.

"So why am I sitting here whining?" She watched folks she knew heading into the bar, but couldn't hunt up any enthusiasm for joining them. The stores in town closed down by six on Saturdays, so she couldn't go shopping, not that there was anything she needed to buy. A drive back out to the ranch, a check on a couple of the cows she and her dad were worried about, and then that romance novel she'd gotten in the mail but hadn't had time to open…

"Is this your night for trouble?"

The one voice she hadn't wanted to hear came from just outside her window. Thea turned slowly. "Well, hello, Deputy. Somebody already started a fight in there?" He had not, unfortunately, grown hairy warts or developed a squint since last night. The man was inhumanly attractive.

And his grin could melt granite. "I'll give it a couple more hours. Most of them have to be really tanked to start hitting. Speaking of which, I notice your brother picked up his truck."

Thea clenched her teeth. "How observant of you."

Hands on his hips, he stared at her a second, then shook his head and tipped his hat back slightly. "My fault. That comment was uncalled for and unfair. I apologize."

Again unfortunately, Thea could tell he meant what he said. Something cold inside of her started to thaw. "That…that's okay. Bobby's hard to handle. But he's not mean."

"I guessed that. Makes it hard to stay firm with him, I bet."

Damn his insight. She tried to be flippant, to hide an inclination to melt even further. "Easy enough to see, since we've obviously spoiled him rotten."

Rafe Rafferty didn't move, but he withdrew as completely as if he'd stepped back three paces. "You said it, not me." With two fingers, he resettled his Stetson. "Have a good evening, Ms. Maxwell."

Thea refused to watch him return to his nice silver truck—she didn't want to know how he looked from behind or how he walked, with those long legs and narrow hips.

She made a big production out of getting the Land Rover started and into gear.

But she looked up just as he drove past. For a second she thought he had a woman in the passenger seat...and then realized that a dog sat straight and tall beside him, floppy ears blowing lightly in the breeze through the open window, sad and wrinkled face about as contented as a bloodhound ever could look.

Thea put her head back against the seat and groaned. Was anything ever more calculated to get and hold a woman's attention than a gorgeous single man and his totally ugly, totally lovable dog?

That might, she decided on the quiet drive back to the ranch, be the point. A man as handsome, as polished, as Rafe Rafferty had no doubt sampled his share of girlfriends. Just last night, he'd shown how quickly he could turn to flirting. And if flirting didn't work, a man that smart would no doubt determine the quickest, surest way to get what he wanted—including a girlfriend. A dog ranked up there with diamonds, as far as Thea was concerned. No...above diamonds. How could a cold stone compare to the unfailing love of your best friend?

But she didn't intend to fall for the ploy. She'd learned from experience that men, especially flirtatious and handsome ones, made more trouble than they were worth. She had enough to do keeping Bobby in line—*trying* to keep Bobby in line—and doing her job to her dad's satisfaction. So what if she was lonely sometimes, if her bed...her life...seemed cold?

Maybe she should just get herself a dog.

FOR FOUR GENERATIONS, the Maxwell family had occupied the same pew every Sunday in the First—and only—Methodist Church of Paradise Corners. This week was no exception.

Even though Bobby hadn't come in until after three. Even though Thea had lain awake for the next hour, listening to her dad's sharp reprimands and her brother's sullen protests, cut off, in the end, by a slamming door.

They drove to town in the dark blue Cadillac Robert Maxwell had owned for almost twenty years now, with Thea in the front passenger seat and Bobby slumped in the back behind the driver. His eyes were closed, but he didn't look as if he'd spent the night before drunk. His blue shirt, yellow tie and khaki slacks were practically an apology in themselves.

But no one said a word. Thea considered making conversation, but decided she didn't have anything to say to either of the stubborn men she lived with. As far as she was concerned this morning, the entire male sex—including and especially Deputy Sheriff Rafferty—could kick itself into that deep gorge out behind the church's cemetery and stay there. How much simpler her life would be then.

The fall morning was gorgeous, with the foliage nearing its peak of color. A small grove of aspens beside the white-sided church building quaked in the breeze, their gold leaves like little pieces of sunlight drifting to the ground. Thea stood for a minute, appreciating the view. As she resumed her progress to the door, a tall, broad-shouldered shadow fell onto the brick walk ahead of her. Her skin prickled and her breath shortened—she didn't have to wonder whose shade she'd stepped into. Next thing she knew, Rafe Rafferty was walking beside her.

"Do you think," he said without looking her way, "that if I kept to the weather and the scenery, we could possibly get through a whole conversation without some kind of insult?"

She barely held in her chuckle. "Depends on what you have to say about the scenery. I'm not making any guarantees ahead of time, if you're planning on insulting Paradise Corners."

He heaved a loud sigh. "I was just thinking how green Montana is. Even with the leaves turning, there's some kind of green everywhere you look."

"That's the evergreens—white pine and lodgepole pine, the cedars and junipers and spruces. Even when the last leaves fall, there's still color in the trees." She watched him out of the sides of her eyes, noticed his nice-fitting chocolate-brown suede jacket and dark green corduroy slacks. She caught herself admiring him and administered a mental slap. Of course a Los Angeles playboy would have a sense of style. "I guess you don't have as many trees in southern California."

"Palms and eucalyptus, avocados and scrub junipers. They're technically trees, technically green. But—" he gestured at the foothills "—not nearly this rich. The air here smells like Christmas every day."

"Wait until summer. A lot of the time between last July and September all you could smell was smoke from the wildfires."

They'd reached the church door, where a couple of deacons shook hands in welcome and passed out bulletins. The first, a short, spare man, reached up for his usual kiss. "Howdy, Miss Thea. You're looking pretty this morning."

"Thanks, Uncle G." He wasn't really her uncle, but she'd practically grown up with him, since he supplied Walking Stones with feed of every kind. "Have you met the new deputy? Deputy Rafferty, George Dillon, of Dillon's Feed and Tack."

The deputy held out his hand. "Good to meet you, Mr. Dillon."

Uncle G. took it with the enthusiasm of a man reaching under a rock and expecting a snakebite. "Deputy."

Rafe saw Thea Maxwell's straight black eyebrows draw together as she noticed George Dillon's cool welcome. But after three weeks, Rafe was used to the town's cold shoulder.

The next greeter Thea introduced him to was a woman. "Miss Barbara, this is the new deputy, Rafe Rafferty. Rafe, Miss Sentry owns the beauty salon."

Distracted by hearing his first name in Thea's husky, musical voice, Rafe almost missed the salon owner's lifted eyebrow.

"Deputy." Her tone could have shriveled lemons. She did not extend her hand.

He bowed slightly. "It's a pleasure, Miss Sentry."

At the door to the sanctuary, Thea glanced back toward the gauntlet they'd just run, her honest eyes troubled.

"Don't worry about it," Rafe advised, setting a palm to her waist to draw her inside. "Can you sit with me?"

But that was a mistake. She stiffened under his hand and stepped away. "I...thanks, but no. I'm sitting with my dad and...and Bobby." With a nod, she left him standing in the middle of the aisle and wove her way through the crowd until she reached the safety of the front pew, where she planted herself between Robert and Bobby Maxwell.

Good thinking, Rafe told her silently. *If you weren't protected, I might attack you right here, right now.*

He recognized his own bitterness. And he recognized that meeting Thea Maxwell had done a number on his equanimity. He coped with the distrust, the dislike, of people like George and Barbara, understood that he would have to earn their acceptance. That was okay—he would rather prove himself than simply weasel his way into the job and then not be able to handle it.

But Thea appealed to him, and his pride demanded that she reciprocate the feeling. Every time he tried to approach her on a man-to-woman basis she spooked. Rafe had broken his share of horses, and he'd had more luck with kindness and patience than with force. This time, he couldn't seem to make the right move. He only wanted to be friends, for God's sake.

He thought about the inviting curve of her mouth, and amended his intention. Friends to begin with. What could be so threatening about that?

At the end of a service he didn't pay much attention to, he shook the preacher's hand at the front door, then stepped a few yards off the walk to examine the small, walled cemetery beside the church. Maxwell headstones stood and leaned everywhere he looked—most members of the family for the last hundred years must have been buried in this spot.

A glance back at the doorway showed him Robert Maxwell greeting the minister, with Bobby and Thea in her bright red jacket just behind. Rafe approved of the straight black skirt she wore, the strong but slender legs her blue flannel pj's had hidden. Each glimpse he got of her added something positive to the overall picture. The smile she sent him now was downright friendly. Even encouraging, he decided, and went back to try again.

"Good afternoon, Mr. Maxwell, Bobby."

The rancher turned a rock-hard stare on him. For a second, Rafe wondered if Robert would shoot first and ask questions later. That kind of threat hung in the air.

But the older man settled for a solemn nod. "Deputy." Then he turned his back on Rafe and strode toward the parking lot, obviously expecting Thea and Bobby to follow.

The boy stared after his father, shaking his head. "You'd

think an hour in church would have reminded him that he's not God.''

"Bobby!'' Thea's cheeks flushed as bright as her jacket, but she laughed. "Maybe we just don't realize that the Almighty delegated Montana to him.'' She glanced at Rafe. "Sorry.''

"No problem. Do you have plans for lunch?''

"Lunch?''

"Both of you, I mean.'' The wariness in her eyes had him backing up, slowing down. Make it a family affair first. "Grizzly's serves pretty decent roast beef on Sunday. I can't offer home cooking—I've only got one plate and one mug.''

Thea looked at Bobby, hoping for some help, but he was surveying the crowd, searching for Megan, no doubt. That left her to deal with the deputy on her own. "Um…why only one plate?''

Rafe Rafferty's grin should have been a controlled substance. "The moving company has 'temporarily misplaced my shipment.' Meaning that they lost my boxes and furniture and haven't figured out where they are yet.'' He shrugged. "I'm trying not to replace any more than I have to.''

"Makes sense.'' Which was more than she could say for the butterflies in her stomach. He was going to repeat his invitation. And she would have to turn him down. He would take it wrong, which was a good thing, because she really didn't want him to think she was interested….

"So, are you free for lunch?''

Bobby had disappeared. Thea gathered her wits. "I—I'm afraid not.'' As expected, his eyes cooled. He took a physical step back. "M-my sister Cassie and her little boy are coming over this afternoon. They'll be there by the time we get home.'' And in any normal world, she'd invite him to join them. As a neighbor. As a possible...friend.

But this was Robert Maxwell's world, and she knew what kind of reaction such an invitation would receive. The situation with Cassie and Zak was strained enough. They didn't need an outsider looking on. No matter how nice, no matter how gorgeous he might be. ''But thanks for the offer.''

She tried a smile, and got a slight one back. ''Sure.'' Then the deputy took off, leaving her with the agonizing pleasure of watching him walk away, his shoulders straight, his head high.

You're out! she thought. He'd given her three chances and she'd blown him off each time. There wasn't much hope that he'd try again.

Swallowing down regret and disappointment, Thea joined her dad in the Cadillac.

His impatient stare informed her he'd been waiting. ''Where's your brother?''

''I saw him with Dan Aiken and Racey Taylor.'' And Megan. But if she told him that, there would be hell to pay. Bobby wasn't here, so that would leave the accounting to her. And she was in no mood for the hassle. ''I didn't catch him before he drove off with them.''

''He's supposed to come home for lunch with your sister, dammit.'' Despite the anger in his voice, he drove as calmly, as efficiently, as he did everything. As if his emotions didn't affect his actions at all.

''We'll ask them to stay for dinner. I bet Bobby will be home by then.''

Her dad cracked a laugh. ''That's a bet you're likely to lose.''

Thea put her head back and closed her eyes. ''I know.'' *Boy, do I know.*

CASSIE MAXWELL WARREN'S five-year-old Toyota was parked in the front driveway when they arrived home. Pulling around to the garage behind the house, they could see Cassie standing by a corral near the horse barn across the ranch road, her arm around little Zak as he balanced on a fence rail, staring at the horses.

"The boy likes it here," Robert Maxwell commented.

Thea unhooked her seat belt. "I was looking at that yearling foal of Misty's the other day, thinking he could make a good ride for Zak in a couple of years. He might even be able to help with the training, when the colt's ready."

Her dad nodded, his eyes still on his grandson. "Cassie would need to bring him over more than once a month."

He never came much closer to admitting that he missed his middle daughter, or wanted to see more of her and her son. Thea smiled. "Maybe you could mention the colt while they're here today. We can ride out after lunch and show him to Zak."

"Maybe." And that was as much enthusiasm as he'd ever given one of her suggestions. "Guess I'll go over and say hello."

"I'll check in with Beth to see if she needs help." The chances of their housekeeper needing help with Sunday dinner were about the same as getting a "Great job!" out of Robert Maxwell.

But Zak was still getting used to the family he hadn't known he had. Cassie had crowned her adolescent rebellion with marriage to a man their dad had refused to allow on the property. And while he'd been proven right—Cassie's ex-husband hadn't had the strength or commitment to support a wife and baby—the rift between father and daughter had taken several years to bridge, years in which Zak didn't meet his grandfather, or his aunts and uncle. The little boy tended to shy away from contact if too many of them approached him at the same time. Thea figured she could wait until they all sat down at the table for her own greeting.

But even then, Zak flinched away from her smile, hiding his face against his mother's arm. Cassie laughed, but her cheeks reddened. "Thea won't bite, silly," she told him, ruffling his bright red hair. "Can't you say hello?" Zak shook his head without looking up.

"Don't worry about it," Thea said, taking the bowl of mashed potatoes from her dad. "Zak and I can take a walk after lunch, see if we can spot some deer prints down on the creek bank. We had a doe and two half-grown fawns down there several mornings this week. The mountain snows are starting to push the wildlife to lower ground."

"Deer season starts next weekend," Herman commented. "Bobby and me were talking about heading out Saturday morning. You coming, Boss?"

"Too much work left to take off hunting." Across the table, Zak sat up wide-eyed, staring at his granddad. He was young, but not too young to understand the conversation.

"The work'll be here when we get back. The season only lasts a few weeks."

"I'll think about it."

"How's work, Cassie?" The two men raised their eyebrows at Thea's abrupt diversion. She shook her head at them, with a pointed glance at Zak. They wouldn't be the ones who had to explain deer hunting to a little boy who still liked to watch *Bambi*.

Her sister gave Thea a grateful smile. "I saw one of my cases settled just this week—the court gave full custody of three little girls to their mother, after the dad had refused, several times, to return them once his visitation period had ended."

"Father ought to have some rights to be with his children," their own commented.

"Then he shouldn't have walked out in the first place and taken up with a girl nearly young enough to be his daughter!" Cassie's sharp reply earned her a stern stare. But even as a teenager, she'd never backed down from a confrontation. "The fact that he shares genes with those little girls doesn't make him their father. Time and attention and affection are the contributions of a real parent."

Robert Maxwell's fierce hazel gaze clashed with Cassie's equally furious one across the table. The tense silence might have lasted all afternoon, but Beth cleared her throat, got to her feet and picked up the empty chicken platter. "I've got blackberry cobbler and ice cream for dessert. You girls help me clear the table and we'll bring in coffee."

In the kitchen, Cassie set the plates she carried by the sink, then went to stand at the window of the back door. Thea could read a desperate battle for control in the ramrod straightness of her sister's spine.

"I don't think he meant to argue with you," she ventured after bringing in a second armload of dishes. "That's just his way of asking a question. Like…'Couldn't they work out some compromise?'"

Cassie's shoulders shook on a little laugh. "Thanks for the interpretation. Maybe what we all need is a dictionary of Maxwell-speak. 'Drive safe' means 'It was good to see you, come back real soon.'" She rubbed the back of her neck. "Where's Bobby this afternoon?"

"That's a very good question." Beth placed saucers and coffee cups on a tray. "I make that boy his favorite lunch and he doesn't show up to eat it. He'll be hearing about that this week, especially when he comes around trying to sweet-talk me into fried chicken again." She pushed the door into the dining room with an ample hip and carried the dessert tray through.

Thea opened the freezer and pulled out the ice cream. "Bobby went off with Jerry and Dan after church. And Megan Wheeler."

"Is he crazy?" Cassie turned sharply to face her. "Dad hates Mr. Wheeler almost as much as Mr. Wheeler hates him back for buying that farm out from under him. Bobby doesn't really think he'll get away with dating Megan, does he?"

"I don't know what he thinks. I haven't talked to him about it. Maybe you can." Cassie and Bobby were alike in temperament, if not in looks. Both of them possessed a streak of stubborn wildness that drove their dad crazy. Not to mention making life eventful for everybody else living in the house. Thea had moderated a thousand arguments over the years...mollified a thousand hurt feelings and short tempers. No wonder she'd grown into a prickly, suspicious woman. She'd taken on everybody else's thorns.

"We've got a new deputy in town these days." She bit her tongue. What had possessed her to share that information, from out of thin air, no less?

"Beth said he brought Bobby home the other night because our dear brother was too drunk to drive. Is he drinking a lot?"

"Yeah, he is." Dread welled up in her chest. Putting the thought into words made it so much more real. "Two or three nights a week, he's in town at one of the bars. He says it's no big deal."

"Denial." Cassie took the ice-cream scoop out of the drawer. "You'd better talk some sense into him before it's too late."

The command didn't sit well with Thea. "I talk to him all the time. I'm the only one who does. Why don't you shoulder some of the responsibility for what's going on? He's your brother, too.''

Just like that, they launched into yet another echo of fights from days gone by. Cassie crossed her arms over her chest. ''I have just about as much as I can handle these days, working full time at Child Protective Services and taking care of Zak. It seems to me that you have more opportunity—''

Thea chopped at the air with the side of her hand. ''Only because nobody else will take the time or make the effort—''

''Excuse me.'' Beth's sharp voice jerked them out of their squabble. ''If you ladies don't mind, the rest of us would like ice cream with our cobbler. Not to mention a little peace and quiet.''

Without looking at her sister, Thea picked up the slightly soggy ice-cream box and the scoop, then stalked through the door the housekeeper held open. Aware of Herman's amusement and her dad's frown, she ladled sloppy vanilla cream over each bowl of cobbler and took the box back to the freezer before sitting down to her own portion. No one at the table said a word. They finished their desserts in record time.

But only little Zak, happily smearing himself, his shirt and the tablecloth with purple berries and sticky cream, actually enjoyed the food.

CHAPTER THREE

BOBBY BOUNCED into the back seat of Dan Aiken's truck, dragged off his jacket and tie and unbuttoned his sleeves. "Man! I thought that sermon would last till sundown. Preachers must get chosen by how long they can talk."

"You're telling me." Dan fired the engine, backed through a mud puddle and left the church parking lot with a squeal of tires. "I was about to stand up on the pew and start crowing like a damn rooster, just to get him to stop."

In the passenger seat, Racey laughed, coughing out a lungful of cigarette smoke.

"I thought the sermon was really good." Beside Bobby, Megan had a holier-than-thou look on her face. But her eyes laughed.

"You little liar." Grinning, Bobby caught her wrist to pull her over for a kiss.

At his touch, she winced and gave a hiss of pain.

"What? What's wrong?" He opened his fingers and looked at her arm where it lay across his palm. A bracelet of dark red bruises circled her delicate wrist. "Damn. Did he do this to you?"

Megan had turned toward the window.

"Did your dad do this, honey?" Hand on her chin, he made her face him. Tears filled her big brown eyes and dripped onto his thumb as she nodded.

Bobby fell back against the seat, swearing under his breath. "Somebody ought to put that bastard in jail. Or maybe just take him out and shoot him like the rabid dog he is.''

Megan's soft fingers touched the back of his hand. ''It's okay, Bobby. Really. He woke up when I came in last night, is all. He didn't like that it was so late, and he…he took me to my room.''

''Dragged, you mean.'' She didn't have to draw him a picture. ''Did he know you were with me?''

''He thought I was with Racey.''

''I guess that's a good thing.'' Megan's dad would've killed her if he knew she was seeing a Maxwell. He would've killed her if he knew about the little motel in Bozeman where they'd spent the better part of the night. ''How'd you get out this morning?''

''Mama told him I had to go to church. Then she said I was going to Aunt Sara's to baby-sit.''

''Are you really?'' What good was a long Sunday afternoon off without Megan?

She smiled when he looked at her. ''Sara and Rick are taking the kids to see his mother down in Red Lodge. I don't have to be home until six.''

''So what are we gonna do?'' Dan reached out and pulled Racey closer. ''And where are we gonna do it?''

They stopped at the Quik-Save in Mitchell for some sandwiches and chips, colas and beer. The girls stayed in the truck; when Bobby and Dan stepped outside again, they found a cowboy, elbows propped on the driver's-side window frame, with his head and shoulders inside the cab. The black pickup with a double gun rack across the parking lot identified Hank Reeves—Megan's ex-boyfriend, sometime wrangler for local spreads and full-time pain in the butt.

Bobby stepped up to the rear door of the truck and opened it into Reeves's shoulder as if he hadn't noticed anyone standing there.

"Hey!" Reeves staggered back a stride, called Bobby a foul name.

Putting the bag of food down beside Megan, Bobby turned to face the cowboy. "You talking to me?"

"Not if I can help it." Reeves tried to lean in the window again, but Dan had him blocked. "You're in my way, kid. Beat it."

Dan had a very short fuse. "Get away from my truck before I kick you away."

Reeves grabbed Dan's Sunday-shirt collar. Fists tight, Bobby tensed up for some action, and then he heard Megan say his name.

"Don't fight him, Bobby. Not here, not on Sunday."

"Was he bothering you?" Megan had dated Reeves until Bobby asked her out last spring. The guy still hadn't gotten over being replaced by a Maxwell.

She shook her head, and her shiny hair bounced. "No, he was just saying hello. Please…let him leave. Don't cause any more trouble."

Dan and Reeves were still scuffling for purchase, trying out holds to test each other's strength. With a sigh, Bobby circled around and pulled his friend back from Hank Reeves's grip. "Break it up. Come on, settle down." His hard shove sent Dan stumbling up against the front fender of the truck. Bobby turned to Reeves. "Just hit the road. It's Sunday, and the girls don't want to watch a fight."

Reeves started forward, hesitated, and glanced at Megan. Finally, he swore and picked his hat up out of the dirt. "I'll see you about this later," he promised Dan. Glancing into the truck, he actually smiled for a second at Megan. "I'll see you later, too, sweet thing."

Bobby gritted his teeth and kept his hands at his sides. Barely.

Once Reeves's truck left the parking lot, Dan gave

Bobby a shove as good as the one he'd received. "I shoulda just beat him up once and for all. Why'd you get in the way, man?"

Bobby climbed into the back of the truck cab, set the grocery bag on the floor and pulled Megan into his arms. "Because the lady said so." He lifted her face to his for a kiss. "And as far as I'm concerned, what Megan says goes!"

RAFE FOUND the first carcass about a mile into the forest.

He'd taken Jed out for a hike Sunday afternoon, hoping to work off the extra helping of roast beef Mona had piled on his plate at lunch, trying to outwalk his irrational disappointment at being blown off—again—by Thea Maxwell. At least this time she'd had a good reason. But that didn't make him feel any more optimistic about the future.

Walking at a good pace, Rafe left the last isolated houses behind and entered national forest land. Jed wandered ahead, in his usual dopey way, snuffling at the carpet of needles shadowed by tall pines and cedars, the bases of trees, the crevices of rocks. Though he frequently disappeared from sight, the noise he made carried. He sounded like a miniature steam engine chugging up the hill.

Suddenly, the huffing stopped. The forest went still, too quiet. And then it came—the long, baying call of a hound on the scent, and the snap of branches as Jed crashed through the underbrush on the slope high above. Breathing hard, Rafe followed.

He used his hands to climb a couple of the steepest ridges. As he levered his body over the rim of a nearly vertical ledge, he saw his dog about a hundred feet ahead, frozen in place, ears stiff. On his feet again, Rafe approached carefully, soundlessly. If the damn dog had cornered a grizzly, their day was about to turn crazy. The hunting knife Rafe carried wouldn't be any good against a hungry bear.

But when he reached Jed's quivering black-and-tan flank, he realized that the whitetail buck lying only six or so yards away wouldn't be any kind of threat at all. He was already dead.

Not only dead, but decapitated.

Sickened, angry, Rafe crouched a few feet from the carcass, surveying the gory scene. This was a shameful waste, however he looked at it—good venison left to buzzards, wolves and coyotes, or a magnificent animal destroyed. Hunting for sustenance was one thing. Hunting solely to capture a set of antlers to decorate the family-room wall was something else altogether, at least in his book.

But this particular kill was also a crime. Deer season didn't start for another week, and taking an animal before that date constituted poaching, as did taking an animal without a license and without tagging it to indicate the hunter had stayed within his quota. The Fish and Wildlife guys would want to know what had gone down, so Rafe mentally cataloged the details to include in his report. Whoever made the kill knew what they were doing—one round, straight through the buck's chest to his heart, had dropped him like a stone.

As Rafe walked a circle around the dead deer, Jed stepped close enough to sniff at the body. If he'd been part of a pack, he might have taken his share of meat.

"But you've got good manners, right?" The dog came back to his side and Rafe rubbed his ears. Then he snapped on the leash. "Got any ideas what direction this guy took off in, Jed? We might as well see where he went."

They circled again, with Jed's nose close to the ground. At a point almost directly opposite the way they'd come up, the dog veered away, following a scent. Rafe let him lead, hoping this wasn't a wild-goose chase. Jed didn't always choose the right trail to follow.

The slope in this direction was easier, the tree cover thinner. Jed followed a trail back down into the foothills, onto the bank of a creek running through an aspen grove. He put one paw in the water then backed up, with a low whine in his throat. Rafe saw the marred ground on the other side of the stream, where the hunter had landed his jump. "Good job, buddy. We'll get over there, too, see if we can track the bastard down."

They crossed farther upstream to avoid confusing the hunter's prints. Not that they'd be any help—the guy had slid backward when he landed, smearing whatever pattern was on the bottom of his shoes. Jed picked up the scent again and bounded forward, leaving Rafe nothing to do but follow.

The aspen grove bordered a wide meadow filled with pungent sagebrush and the windblown arcs of tall, gray-green grass. Now the hunter's path was visible as a dark line of crushed plants. Rafe released Jed's lead and pursued the trail on his own.

The line gradually curved to the west, where a thick stand of pines edged the open field. When the tall brush ended, the trail seemed to end as well. Jed zigzagged between the trees, doing his best to pick up a scent, looking more and more worried as the minutes passed.

But Rafe, listening to the wind, had picked up voices. He called the dog to heel. "Which way, buddy? Where are they?"

In response to his whisper, the bloodhound headed roughly south. Signs of human intrusion appeared—a soda can against the foot of a lodgepole pine, a paper napkin blown into a spiny shrub's branches, a circle of burned grass where some idiot had built a fire. Rafe cursed the stupidity, and moved on.

By the time he and Jed reached the voices—and the pair of trucks parked in a clearing just off the road—Rafe had collected beer bottles and empty condom packets in a discarded plastic bag, along with food wrappers and paper products. He didn't need to evaluate the assembled company to realize that this was a popular teen hangout. And somehow he wasn't surprised to find Bobby Maxwell in the center of the group.

They'd heard him coming, because he made no attempt to be quiet. About half a dozen faces were turned his way when Rafe stepped into the clearing.

Bobby raised a soft-drink can in greeting. "Fancy meeting you here, Deputy! Come join our picnic." A pretty girl sat by his side on the tailgate, trying and failing to hide how nervous she was.

In the next truck bed, a towheaded boy leaned back against a silver metal toolbox. He glanced at Jed, who was still casting around the clearing, investigating scents. "Nice-looking dog, Deputy. What are you hunting?"

"A trash can," Rafe said, holding up the bag of refuse. "This where you spend your Sunday afternoons?"

"Sometimes." Bobby swung his legs—still in his Sunday pants and shiny boots—back and forth from the knees. He'd ditched the tie and folded back his starched shirt cuffs. "You might've noticed, we're not exactly living at the center of the social world."

"Who are your friends?"

"Megan Wheeler." Bobby touched the top of her head with his drink can. "Dan Aiken, Racey Taylor, Jerry Heath, Kim Rawlins. Anything else you need to know?"

Rafe reached into a juniper shrub and pulled out a recently emptied beer can, still wet with condensation and scented with yeast. "I might like to know who sells beer to underage kids on a Sunday."

Bobby's angelic expression wasn't intended to fool anybody. "I wouldn't know. I'm a decaf diet-cola man, myself. Dan swears by guava juice."

"Makes my hair shine," the boy said, rubbing a hand over his head. Bobby and friends laughed...except for Megan, who still looked worried.

Straight answers from this crowd were unlikely, but Rafe decided to take one shot. "Seen anybody else around this afternoon?"

"No, sir." Bobby leaned back on his elbows. "Nobody but us nature lovers."

They were being careful to avoid giving him any concrete reason for suspicion. Without probable cause or a bona fide warrant, he couldn't search the vehicles for alcohol, an illegal kill or anything else. And Rafe didn't doubt that Judge LeVay and Robert Maxwell would, between them, discount even the strongest probable cause.

"Enjoy," he said, approaching Bobby as he lounged in the truck bed. He set the bag of trash on the tailgate, between the boy's knees. "And rub up that shine on your halo by dumping this where it belongs." Whistling for Jed, he turned his back on the group and headed for the trail that would take him back toward town.

"You can count on us," Bobby yelled after him.

Rafe heard the triumph edging his tone. "I know I can," he called over his shoulder.

The important question being...for what?

DURING THE NEXT WEEK, the game warden got two more reports of poached bucks farther up in the mountains. Bobby Maxwell came into town every night about eight-thirty and drank until the bar closed or the bartender threw him out. Dan Aiken was with him, more often than not. Eavesdropping in the diner, in the general store, in the grocery market, Rafe learned that those two, along with Jerry Heath, hung out together like the Musketeers. And got into almost as much trouble.

He heard them himself, racing their trucks down Main Street at midnight between Thursday and Friday. They roared past him just as he reached the intersection in his own truck. Bobby gave him a grin and a salute as he flashed by. Then, with a squeal of tires that dragged sparks from the asphalt, the three vehicles wheeled off into the darkness in three different directions. Rafe was tempted to drive up to Walking Stones and wait for the Maxwell kid to come home, then arrest him for drunk and disorderly, DUI, and any other infraction that came to mind along the way.

But another wee-hours confrontation with Robert Maxwell would be as counterproductive as the last. Judge LeVay would hand out the same warning to keep clear of Maxwell business, while the folks in town would chalk up yet another win to Boss Maxwell, and their respect for Rafe would drop another notch. He knew a no-win situation when he saw one.

The solution to his problem came to him at breakfast Friday morning. Sitting in his usual spot at Grizzly's, Rafe picked up his coffee mug, stared at it for a second, then grinned. There was still one person concerned about Bobby and his friends whom he could approach without risking his health or his job. In fact, getting her on his side might raise his status around town, help him settle the Maxwell kid down and improve his personal life.

He made the call when he went home for lunch. A voice he didn't recognize answered the phone. "Walking Stones Ranch, Beth Peace speaking. May I help you?"

Rafe cleared his throat. "This is Deputy Sheriff Rafferty. Could I speak to Thea Maxwell, please?"

A silence followed, and he didn't think he was imagining the disapproval pulsing through the line. "Miss Maxwell is at work, Deputy. Can I take a message?"

"Sure." His disappointment was way out of proportion to the situation. "Please ask her to call me at the office before six, or at home afterward." He dictated the numbers. "It's important that I talk to her. Not urgent." No need to cause a panic. "But I'd like to get in touch as soon as possible."

"I'll tell her. Goodbye." Beth Peace disconnected briskly. Secretary or housekeeper or whoever, she'd taken on the familiar Maxwell attitude.

The phone rang a total of eight times before he left the office that afternoon. Rafe jumped each time, picked up the receiver with his breath a little short…and dealt with two traffic complaints involving tourists, three questions about the start of deer season, a report of vandalism to an abandoned cabin in the woods, a hang-up call and a wrong number. No word from Thea Maxwell.

By nine that night, he'd decided she was going to ignore him. That realization, coupled with a message on his answering machine that said his furniture remained lost on the highway between Los Angeles and Paradise Corners, shortened his temper to the point where even talking to Jed was too much of an effort.

When the phone rang at nine-thirty, Rafe had just dropped his only coffee mug, which left a zillion pieces of pottery scattered across the kitchen floor plus one long and extremely painful shard embedded in his foot.

"Hello." Not his friendliest tone. Receiver clutched between shoulder and cheek, he tried to ease the ceramic splinter out of his arch.

"Um…Deputy Rafferty? It's Thea Maxwell."

He jerked as she said her name. The splinter burrowed deeper. Rafe swore.

"I beg your pardon?" Glacier mode.

"Damn, here we go again." Rafe gave up on the splinter. "I'm sorry. I wasn't talking to you."

"That's just your usual phone manner?"

"I have a piece of glass in my foot and was trying to get it out when you called."

"Are you okay?" Her question carried a current of laughter. And maybe a hint of concern?

"I'll live." He dabbed gingerly at his bleeding foot with a paper towel. "I think."

"I'm sorry, too, for calling so late. We worked past dark, bringing some cows down from the high country. A few of them spooked, detoured through a steep gorge, and the only way out was back into the mountains. That added about five hours to the process." Weariness roughened her voice.

"I've had those kinds of days. You need a meal and a bath and a bed."

"Yeah." She sighed. "So why did you call? Our house-keeper said it was important."

Rafe pulled his thoughts back from a mental picture of Thea Maxwell soaking in a tub of warm, sweet-smelling water. "Uh…yeah. It's about your brother."

"Oh, really."

"But I don't want to get into anything tonight." He'd expected the sudden change in her tone, but it bothered him anyway. "I wondered…is there sometime in the next day or two that you could come into town?"

"You want to interrogate me at the jailhouse?"

He sighed. "I want to buy you a cup of coffee, maybe a piece of pie, and talk this situation over like reasonable people."

Thea recognized Rafe Rafferty's exasperation. She couldn't blame him—he didn't have a clue that her question was purely defensive, an effort to get control of the excitement his invitation provoked. "I, um, I usually come in on Saturday mornings to pick up groceries. Do you have time…tomorrow?"

"Sure." How could he sound so calm when she felt as if she was standing in the middle of an electrical storm? "How's ten-thirty sound? Too early?"

"Th-that's fine."

"I'll see you then."

Was he hanging up? "Rafe, um, Deputy? Wait a minute. Deputy?"

"Rafe will be fine." She practically heard him grin. "What's wrong?"

"Where do you want to meet?"

"Oh, yeah. Good question. Is Grizzly's okay with you?"

"Great. I…I'll see you at Grizzly's at ten-thirty."

"Sounds good." After a long pause, he said, "Well, then…good night. Get some rest."

"You, too." There was some kind of problem here, saying goodbye. "Um…good night."

"Sure." He pulled in a deep breath. "'Night." After yet another hesitation, Thea heard the phone click off. Rafe Rafferty was finally gone.

Unless you counted the way she thought about him as she showered. The way he got between her eyes and the book she tried to read while eating the warmed-over plate of chicken and dumplings Beth had made. The way he got all tangled up in her dreams.

THEN THERE WAS the problem Saturday morning of what to wear. Nothing special, of course. Just the usual jeans and boots and a shirt, with a jacket against the cold wind sweeping down from the mountains. So what if the shirt was new, hanging in her closet since her trip to Denver last summer? The bright red would be cheerful on this gray day. And, yes, the black jeans were new, too. A woman didn't have to look like one of the boys when she drove into town. There was such a thing as self-respect.

But she got a sharp glance from Beth. "You're awful dressed up. What's going on?"

Thea picked up her coffee cup. "Nothing. Just driving in for the groceries, same as usual."

"What can I fix you for breakfast?" Saturday was short-order day—you could ask for strawberry waffles or ostrich-egg omelettes and Beth would do her best to oblige.

But Thea couldn't imagine putting food on top of the jitterbugs in her stomach. "I ate late last night. I'll just get something in town."

"With that deputy?"

Trust Beth Peace to know everything. "He wants to talk about Bobby."

The housekeeper puffed out like a threatened hen. "What's there to talk about?"

"I don't know." It was too early to leave, but she couldn't face any more questions. "I'll tell you when I get home." She put her cup in the sink and started out the back door. Her work jacket hung there—dusty worn denim with a tear in the sleeve from yesterday's argument with a fallen branch.

Beth followed her as she reversed directions and headed for the coat closet in the great room. "You might want to put on some jewelry for this date of yours. Earrings, at least."

Shrugging into her black wool blazer, Thea thought about it. Then shook her head. "It's a business meeting, Beth, that's all. He wants to talk about Bobby. I don't need to get all dressed up. See you later.'' She left by the front door, preferring to walk all the way around the house in the cold rather than go through to the back with the housekeeper at her heels, teasing.

But she didn't get away fast enough to avoid hearing Beth's comment.

''Of course you shouldn't get dressed up.'' The older woman crossed her arms over her full breasts. ''And I'm the queen of the monkey house.''

Thea looked back just before she rounded the corner. ''I'll add bananas to the grocery list,'' she called, and heard Beth's laugh carried off on the wind.

Instead of heading straight out to the state road, Thea turned the Land Rover toward the work buildings, the cattle barns and the pastures beyond. Backing onto the foothills of the Crazy Moutains, the Walking Stones Ranch claimed terrain from water meadows all the way to subalpine mountain peaks. Most of that land was as familiar to her as her own bedroom.

And she loved to examine it the way other women might admire their jewelry. Even on a cloudy day, Walking Stones showed its riches, in the dull gold of cut hayfields, the fading green of frosted grass, brilliant yellows and reds from the aspens and oaks, the velvet black of fat Angus cattle grazing for breakfast. Wood smoke, wet leaves and a hint of snow colored the wind, its moan the only sound in an otherwise blessed silence…

Until it was broken by a rifle shot.

Thea jumped, then sighed and shook her head. Deer season opened today. Herman and Bobby and her dad had left before dawn for the start of their annual male-bonding ritual. She'd never been invited to go along, but she'd never wanted to. Venison steak didn't hold a candle to range-fed Angus beef, as far as she was concerned. Culling the deer population made sense, she supposed, although she had a strong belief in nature's ability to handle its own problems. There were, after all, coyotes and wolves.

Mostly, though, she liked looking at the deer alive, liked the alert shine of a doe's eyes, the sweetness of the fawns, the power and majesty of a heavily antlered buck. Why destroy something so beautiful?

Turning into the wooded hillsides, she headed up a dirt track toward the fence line dividing Walking Stones land from the national forest. The winding mountain road beyond the back gate was the long way into town, guaranteed to take up enough time that she wouldn't look stupid arriving early for her meeting with Rafe Rafferty. Or, worse, eager. Just because she wanted the chance to see him again, maybe have a decent conversation, didn't mean he had to know how she felt.

Thinking of his dark eyes and the humor she'd caught there a couple of times, Thea stopped at the gate, climbed down from the Land Rover to unlock the chain, drove across the cattleguard, stopped again and got out to refasten the lock. She pulled hard, to be sure the snap had caught, started to turn away, and realized her brain had recorded an image she hadn't quite processed.

Easing between two of the fence wires, she walked carefully over the rough ground, uneven with clumps of grass and rocks and dirt. About a hundred feet along, she came upon what her eyes had seen without her mind knowing. A deer. A doe.

Or what was left of one, anyway.

CHAPTER FOUR

ON SATURDAY MORNING, Paradise Corners was crowded with just about everybody Thea knew. She identified them by their trucks, just as they did her, and returned their greetings—the truly friendly ones, the wary ones, and the ones designed to make points with Boss Maxwell by sucking up to his daughter. For those, she smiled through gritted teeth.

Outside Grizzly's Diner, the deputy's bloodhound posed with the regal attitude of a conquering lion. Thea crouched to meet him at eye level. "You're in control, aren't you? Got your eye on the whole town from right here." He let her stroke his baggy jowls and crinkle his ears, but didn't give up his watchful pose. Reluctantly, she straightened up and pulled on the diner's door. Time to meet the man waiting inside.

First she had to meet and greet at every other table in the place, saying hello to the folks she'd had as teachers and church leaders, school-trip chaperons and sports coaches. There were others, too, who gave each other nods and shrugs and deliberately ignored her as she moved past them. All the time, shaking hands and smiling, she was aware of Rafe Rafferty in the booth at the back, watching and waiting. For her.

When she finally got there, he stood up. "Good morning. Thanks for coming."

She'd forgotten how tall he was. How tanned. How gorgeous.

"Hi." Completely inadequate as a greeting, but she couldn't do any better at the moment. Just to have something to do, she took off her jacket and slid onto the seat. A glance out the window gave her something to say. "I met your dog outside. He's a good guy."

Grinning, Rafe sat down across the table. "Jed's the best. What would you like to drink? Want something to eat?"

The memory of the slaughtered doe, on top of the tension twisting her stomach, made facing food impossible. "Just coffee, thanks."

He signaled Mona Rangel behind the counter. Before the pause between them could get too awkward, the former teacher set two heavy white mugs down on the table. "Good morning, Thea."

Yet another reason for nerves. Thea had always regretted that she hadn't been able to talk her dad out of his fury over Bobby's sixth-grade failure. "How are you, Mrs. Rangel?"

The older woman nodded. "Just fine, thank you."

"Glad to hear it." Thea emptied the usual three packets of sugar and a good dollop of milk into her cup, stirred furiously, then looked up to find the deputy watching her.

"Something wrong?"

Great...he could read her like a book. She picked the least embarrassing reason for her edginess. "Um, nothing major. I...I found a poached deer on the property as I was leaving. I guess it shook me up a little."

"The season started this morning." He doctored his coffee, then took a gulp. "Maybe the hunter hadn't got there to collect the carcass yet."

"This was an old kill. The coyotes had been at it."

His straight eyebrows drew together. "What else?"

"The head was gone. And it was a doe." Thea cradled her mug in both palms, waiting to be teased for her squeamishness. "I know, I know, it's inconsistent to raise cattle for the market and balk at hunting."

"Maybe a little," Rafe agreed. His tone was almost gentle. "But this wasn't an animal taken for food, was it? Just a trophy for somebody's wall. That's the wasteful part."

She stared at him, amazed at his perception and his attitude. "You're exactly right, it's the waste that bothers me."

He smiled. "Don't sound so surprised. Not every man on the planet likes to spend his time in the woods killing game."

"Every one I've ever met."

"Well, then," Rafe drawled, "I'd say it's time to broaden your experience."

The look in his eyes—half smile, half challenge, all male—robbed her lungs of air. He was flirting again.

But Thea didn't know beans about that game. Anyway, she was here for a different reason. After a sip of coffee, she found her voice. "You said you wanted to talk about Bobby?"

Rafe sat back, and the warmth in his face faded. "He's been in town every night this week."

"I know."

"Raising hell."

Thea squeezed her eyes shut.

"Probably drunk more often than not."

She didn't say anything.

"He's got a problem, Thea. You have to see that."

"He's only nineteen."

"But he's been drinking for years. Right?"

She lifted her chin, trying to deny it. "How would you know something like that?"

"You mean, because there aren't any records? Because LeVay makes sure the law stays away?"

The word Thea muttered under her breath would have horrified Beth Peace. "You're guessing."

"Am I wrong?"

"No, damn you." A sudden lull in the hubbub around them told her she'd been too loud. She lowered her voice. "But what, exactly, do you think I can do? Or anybody else, for that matter?"

Rafe leaned his elbows on the table. "Talk to him? Better yet, get your dad to talk to him."

"You're assuming Robert Maxwell would admit to himself or anybody else that his son wasn't the finest specimen walking the earth today."

"He's a successful rancher. He has to be a realist."

"About everything but Bobby." She heard her own comment, realized how jealous and petty she sounded. Hands flat on the table, she tried to retrieve her self-respect. "Look, Bobby's always been a handful. He's not real happy being at home right now—that youthful desire to see the whole world, you know?"

He grinned. "I've been there."

She stiffened her spine against the urge to melt. "So, he's got to get this out of his system. Better here in Montana, where there aren't so many people, than Los Angeles or San Francisco. He'll settle down." She knew how naive she sounded. "Start taking the work and his place in it seriously. We just have to wait for him to grow up a little."

Rafe's gaze acknowledged her wishful thinking. "I can't cut him that much slack. I have other people to consider." He reached out, ran his knuckle along the back of her hand from wrist to fingertip. "You're one of them. I can see you're caught in the middle."

Thea knew better than to fall for such an obvious line. She'd recognized Rafe Rafferty as a ladies' man from the beginning.

But, oh, she wanted to believe. Something inside her ached with the need to believe that touch, to accept the concern in that handsome face, those dark brown eyes.

While she was still battling herself, Mona came back to the table with the coffeepot. "Refills?"

Grateful for the diversion, Thea pushed her mug to the edge. "Sounds good." Rafe did the same and they all watched the process in silence…until Thea's stomach produced a loud and unmistakable growl. She felt her cheeks heat up, wished the earth would open and swallow her whole.

With only a half smile, Rafe glanced at his watch. "It's after eleven. That's close enough to lunchtime, isn't it?"

The other woman wiped a cloth over the table between them. "Far as I'm concerned. I made a big pot of chili this morning and there's corn bread baking. Want me to bring you each a bowl?"

Thea managed to meet Rafe's eyes for a split second, found his eyes kind. Maybe even hopeful. "Sounds really good."

Mona nodded. "Back in two shakes."

Rafe added sugar and milk to his fresh coffee, wondering how to get the woman across the table to relax. He'd had his own nerves about this meeting. He cared way too much about what Thea thought, about the way things between them turned out. But she seemed almost paralyzed. And Rafe really didn't think he was that intimidating. At least, not without a gun in his hand.

So he set himself to calm her down, with as innocent a topic as he could come up with. "You must have quite a few dogs on the ranch."

She grinned, and her flush faded a little. "Cow dogs, sure. And strays the hands feed, who never leave again. Seems like each cowboy has his own mutt to take care of."

"Don't you have a mutt of your own?"

Her black hair bounced as she shook her head. "I guess it seems weird, but we don't have house dogs at all. Our housekeeper got bitten when she was little, and something like that tends to stay with a person, I think. She's been running the house since forever, so what she says pretty much goes. The dogs stay outside."

There was a wistfulness in her eyes that prompted him to ask, "What kind of dog would you choose if you could get one?"

She grinned easily, for the first time. "Well, I think I'd want a big one…"

The chili arrived while they talked about dogs. With their second helpings, they moved on to horse breeds and training.

"I didn't realize you had ranch experience." Thea crumbled corn bread over her chili. "More than just summer camp, I'd say."

Rafe decided to take that as a sign she'd been wondering about him. "I grew up on a spread in southern California. Nothing even a tenth the size of Walking Stones. But I learned the business."

"Do your folks still run cattle?"

"The ranch belongs to my aunt and her husband. My parents died when I was six."

She looked up at him, her eyes dark with pain. "I'm sorry. That's really hard."

"I didn't mean to make a play for sympathy." He shrugged. "I grew up okay."

"Most of us do. That doesn't mean it's the best way. Bobby might not be such a…a problem if our mom hadn't died when he was four." In one of the lightning change of moods he was coming to appreciate, Thea chuckled. "Who knows? Maybe Dad wouldn't be such a pain in the butt, either."

Rafe laughed with her. "There's a thought."

Mona's apple cobbler with ice cream and more coffee took them into movies and books. Rafe surrendered to impulse and recounted his one run-in with a Hollywood star while on the L.A. police force. "We spent four hours combing every inch of Rodeo Drive, looking for this crazy lady's dog. You haven't felt like a fool until you've crawled through an alley on your hands and knees yelling for Horatio."

He got another one of Thea's deep chuckles for his efforts. "Where'd you find him?"

"In the back room of a jewelry store. The dumb dog had slipped through security and curled up on a workbench in the middle of a few hundred thousand dollars' worth of diamonds. They had to brush the stones out of his fur."

"Not your standard impression of police work in Los Angeles." She was still laughing. "Drug busts, gang wars, high-speed chases—that's what I would expect to hear about."

"I did that, too." Rafe shook his head. "Sometimes I think maybe I should have stayed, tried to improve the place. I guess you could say I bailed out." Damn. Something else he hadn't meant to say. The woman didn't want to hear about his personal doubts.

"You can't be responsible for saving the whole world, or the state of California, or even a neighborhood." Her quiet tone respected his frankness. "I tend to think most people have a purpose in life, something they were meant to do. Maybe your responsibility lies somewhere besides L.A."

"God knows there are enough troubles in the world to

go around.'' The woman had a way of making him feel good without even trying.

She nodded at his observation, and from there the conversation veered toward resolving world hunger, whale hunting and the destruction of the rain forests.

The lunch crowd came and went and they were still sitting there, trading philosophies. Rafe accidentally caught sight of the time. ''Jeez, I didn't mean to keep you here all day.''

She glanced at the empty tables around them and got a guilty look in her eyes. ''You were probably supposed to work this afternoon.''

''Everybody knew where to find me if something went wrong. A little place like this doesn't present all that many law enforcement challenges.''

Her eyes changed. ''Except for Bobby.''

''Well, yeah.'' Rafe couldn't lie to her. ''But he's not too far gone. Like you said, he needs to realize it's time to grow up.''

Thea sighed, then slid out of the booth. ''I'll see what I can do.'' She bent to pick up her jacket, shook it out and started to stretch one arm into a sleeve.

Rafe took the soft black wool out of her hands. ''Let me help.'' She looked startled, but turned away so he could slip the coat over her arms. Surrendering to temptation, he straightened the collar and smoothed the cloth over her shoulders before he stepped back. ''There you go.''

''Thanks.'' Her voice sounded breathless, the way he felt. A grown man, especially one reasonably experienced with women, shouldn't get a big charge out of such a simple touch.

But Rafe knew that right this second he wouldn't trade places with anybody else in the world.

They said goodbye to Mona and stepped out to where

Jed had waited patiently all this time. Thea crouched in front of the dog and ran her palms over his shoulders. "He's been here for hours, just sitting. I thought bloodhounds had a tendency to bolt."

"Jed's not your ordinary hound."

She glanced up at him with a smile. "No bias there, of course."

Rafe grinned back. "Of course not. But he was the runt of the litter, and he was so grateful to be the center of attention when I took him home that it's really rough getting him to stay by himself for very long. The tradeoff is that I keep him with me and he behaves himself. Works pretty well."

"That's the kind of dog to have." She straightened up from her crouch without a wobble or a creak—just smooth, controlled movement. "Well, thanks for lunch. And…and for caring about Bobby. That's really above and beyond the call of duty for you."

Her hand was extended and Rafe took it, anticipating the feel of skin against skin. He wasn't disappointed. There was a warmth between their palms that had nothing to do with body temperature.

Before he could stop her, she was backing away. "Um, I'll see you later. Maybe church tomorrow?"

Rafe nodded, because he didn't trust his voice. Thea smiled, looked worried, then outright scared. She bolted for her big black Land Rover, and was gone.

"YOU FORGOT the groceries?" Beth's brown eyes widened. "How could you forget? That's what you drove into town for!"

With her coat hanging off her elbows, Thea slumped back against the wall. Since leaving Rafe Rafferty, she hadn't thought about groceries even once...until she walked through the door into the kitchen.

"I...I'll go back and get them." She shrugged her coat on again. It had started to sleet, and she could hear ice bouncing off the wide window over the sink. But facing a slick highway would be preferable to facing Beth's disappointment.

"It's after four o'clock, young lady. By the time you get back to town the market will be locked for the weekend. What am I supposed to fix for Sunday dinner tomorrow?"

"Um...we could eat in town. At Grizzly's."

Beth crossed her arms. "As long as I've worked here, your father has never had to eat his Sunday meal anywhere but at his own table, unless he chose to do so. I am not going to tell him I can't make him a decent meal."

Tired from a day of tension, wanting to be by herself to think over the time with Rafe, Thea kept her temper with an effort. "Well, this is a cattle ranch. There have to be steaks or a roast in the freezer. Bake potatoes, make a salad, grill a steak. If you fix some of your buttermilk biscuits," she wheedled, "Dad will be perfectly satisfied."

The housekeeper drew a deep breath. "I suppose so. But what in the world possessed you—"

Thea left her coat on as she backed out of the kitchen into the dining room. "I'll get your groceries first thing Monday. Promise. And I won't forget again. I...I guess I just had my mind somewhere else." Before Beth could ask where, Thea hightailed it across the house to her bedroom, where she shut and locked the door.

She hung her coat over the chair at the dressing table, then sat down and propped her elbows on the table's edge, staring at herself in the mirror and wondering if Rafe saw the same face she did. Kind of ordinary, really—good enough skin, maybe a little too tanned, cheeks that got too red in the cold, a mouth too wide, a chin too square. Definitely not beautiful.

And he was a man who was surely used to having beautiful women in his life.

But he had talked with her for hours, as if what she said really mattered. Was he that good at the game? What did he think he would win?

Or was the rapport…the sense of connection…real? Could she trust it? Was this going to be the one?

A fist pounded on her door. "Hey, Thea, we're back. Open up."

She dropped her head into her hands. "Give me a couple of minutes, Bobby. I just got back myself and I'm bushed."

"You can't be as tired as I am. Man, we sat out there till I thought my knees would crack when I stood up."

"Did you get anything?" She almost dreaded asking.

"Nah—they're still pretty shy. We found a few scrapes, and some tracks, but it's early yet. Another couple of weeks, there should be deer everywhere."

"Great." Thea sighed. "Go away, Bobby. I'll talk to you after dinner, okay?"

"Yeah, sure." He went on down the hallway to his room, whistling. When Bobby was good, he was very, very good. And when he was bad—

Yet another knock on her door. "Althea, I want to talk to you."

When her dad used that tone there was no putting him off. Thea opened the door. "Yes, sir?"

"We'll go to my office." He turned on his heel, and she followed him, as he expected her to.

Robert Maxwell's office suited a man of his importance, his interests. A huge oak desk stood in the center of the room, surrounded by a bank of file cabinets and a wall of books. Not novels, of course, but bound professional journals, textbooks on cattle and agriculture and business. Two comfortable armchairs rested in front of the desk, but Thea wasn't asked to sit.

"I spoke with Hal LeVay on my way through town." Her dad filled his pipe, tamped it, lit the tobacco and puffed. "He said you spent most of the day in that woman's diner, talking to the deputy sheriff."

Thea put her hands in her pockets. "I was there for a few hours, yes."

"Talking about what?"

"Different things." At twenty-nine, she considered herself past the age of interrogation, and her dad should, too.

He regarded her over his pipe. "What was the reason for this meeting?"

"We had coffee together, then lunch."

"He asked you to meet with him?"

"Yes."

"This was a date?"

She wished she could say yes, if only to be defiant. "He wanted to talk to me about Bobby."

"Dammit, I told him to stay out of our business."

"Bobby makes that hard, Dad. He's been raising hell in town. Rafe…Deputy Rafferty has a responsibility to keep the peace."

"His responsibility stops where my authority begins. And that means my children."

"Then maybe you need to exercise more of your authority over your son." Her dad's eyes narrowed, but it was too late for Thea to turn back. "Bobby's drinking way too much, has been all summer, and even before. He needs to recognize that he has a problem with alcohol and deal with it."

Robert Maxwell's response was short and rude.

"Dad, you know this is true. He can put away a six-pack

between the end of work and dinnertime. He has no idea of moderation or control."

"So you're going to let this deputy interfere in your family? Is this the way you were raised?"

"I was raised to think Maxwells were damn near as perfect as a human being could get. But I figured out the truth. We're no better than anybody else, maybe not even as good as most."

Thea saw her dad's fingers tighten around the bowl of his pipe, recognized his impulse to physical expression of his anger. He'd administered her last spanking when she was twelve—the point at which her mother had forbidden him raise his hand to her children ever again.

But then their mother died. The girls had been too old for corporal punishment at that point, but Bobby had received his share, and then some. Would he be in better shape if their dad had abided by his wife's decree even after her death?

"Look, Dad." She closed the distance between them and put a hand on his rigid arm. "Think about this. Ask yourself if Bobby is really in control of his drinking, of his life in general. Maybe there's something we can do to help him settle down. That's what you want, isn't it? For Bobby to take up his part of the ranch work and love it the way you do?"

He shut his eyes for a second, then looked at her again. "I want your brother to be a part of the team that runs this place. Bobby and Herman and I should be working together, keeping Walking Stones strong." Still puffing on his pipe, he stepped out from underneath her palm and went to stare out the window. "If I see Bobby's having trouble with that…I'll figure out what to do about it."

Thea stood where he left her, coping with the sensation that a bucket of cold water had been dumped over her head.

The team—Bobby and Herman and her dad. She'd worked full-time for the Walking Stones ranch since she was old enough to sit a horse by herself. She loved the place with every ounce of her strength, every piece of her soul.

But she didn't have a place on the team.

"Sounds good, Dad," she said heavily. "I'm sure you'll handle the situation." Turning, she made her way almost blindly to the door.

"Althea."

She stopped, but didn't turn. "Yes, sir?"

"Stay away from the deputy. Getting involved with him will just make trouble. You can do better than that."

Thea took a deep breath against the words that came to her lips. What good would it do to argue?

But when she took another step, she found herself turning around, striding back to the big desk in the middle of the room, confronting the man behind it.

"I don't mean any disrespect, Dad. But this is not *Romeo and Juliet*. I am not sixteen, or even twenty-six, years old. If I want to date Rafe Rafferty, or any other man on the planet, I'll do so. I don't need your permission. And I surely don't need your help—the Maxwell name is enough to screw up most relationships all by itself. Just ask your son."

He said her name again, but Thea didn't stop this time. She let herself out of the office, crossed the house and locked herself behind her bedroom door again, wishing for once that she could be the one getting drunk in town and raising hell.

CHAPTER FIVE

"I'M GONNA SHOOT! An' you better believe I can hit what I'm aimin' for."

Rafe heard the querulous warning as he got out of his truck. Approaching the sturdy cabin across a clearing, he saw old Mr. Walters standing on the porch in his brown flannel pajamas with a shotgun braced at his shoulder.

The click of the bolt sliding back was loud in the cold, clear night. "You hear me? Git away from my animal and git off my property."

Following Walters's line of sight, Rafe muttered a curse. Inside the split-rail fence surrounding the old man's pasture, a bleating crowd of sheep swept back and forth across the uneven foothill terrain, driven by a couple of boys on foot, laughing and yelling...and one equally noisy cowboy holding on to a rope tied to the neck of a llama. Bobby Maxwell.

Walters glanced over as Rafe reached the bottom of the porch steps. "I'm gonna shoot, Deputy. I swear I'm gonna shoot."

Rafe shook his head. "Give me a minute, Mr. Walters. Let me see if I can get them out of there." He walked to the fence, aware of the gun at his back, of Walters's shaky grip and bad eyesight. "Just my luck to get killed for a bunch of sheep and a damn llama." Ducking under the top fence rail, he headed toward the action. "Maxwell, let go of that animal,'' he yelled as soon as he got close enough to be heard. "Now!"

Bobby looked over and waved. "Hey, Deputy, join the roundup. We're gonna bring these here sheep in if it takes us all night long. Lassoed me a llama." He laughed uproariously. "Lassoed me a llama, I did."

"Like hell." Rafe jogged across the pasture at an angle to the llama's path, intending to intercept the animal before it could corner the hysterical sheep again. Whooping at the top of his lungs, Bobby turned the llama away from Rafe and the sheep, dragging it into a trot.

There was no way he could catch up on such uneven terrain. Rafe stopped, hands on his hips, breathing hard, and watched as the llama picked up speed heading downhill. Bobby had lost both control and balance, was barely keeping on his feet. Then the llama twisted its head and turned sharply to the left.

At the same instant, a rifle shot split the night. Instinctively, Rafe ducked.

Bobby hit the ground and started rolling downhill.

Swearing aloud, Rafe straightened and raced after the boy, tripping over rocks, his heart like a fist pumping ice water through his veins. He did not want the next time he saw Thea to be when he drove out to tell her that her little brother had been shot.

The boy lay on his face in the dirt. Not until he was almost on top of him did Rafe realize that Bobby was moving. Laughing, actually, in whistling gasps and snorts. Just as Rafe skidded to a stop, Bobby pounded the ground with a clenched fist and laughed even harder.

Any sympathy or fear Rafe had felt disappeared. He stood for a few seconds, teeth clenched, letting his heartbeat return to normal. Then he stuck out a foot and, without any attempt to be gentle, toed Bobby Maxwell over onto his back.

"Hey!" Bobby stared up at him, still grinning, his face streaked with dust and tears. "Watch who you're kicking."

"I'm watching. Get up."

Dan Aiken and Jerry Heath walked up as Bobby dragged himself off the ground. "I thought for sure the old man had nailed you," Dan said, giving his friend an arm up. "You fell like you'd been shot right between the eyes."

"The damn thing bit me." Bobby examined his jacket sleeve. "See—ripped right through to the skin."

Jerry Heath investigated the tear. "We'd better check for rabies."

Bobby looked up, wide-eyed in the moonlight. "You think I got rabies from the llama?"

"Nah," Jerry said with a shake of his head. "But it might have gotten them from you."

Jerry and Dan laughed, until Bobby put his head down and charged. Suddenly, all three of them were rolling on the ground, punching and gouging and swearing.

Rafe glanced away from the fight to see Mr. Walters at the far end of the pasture, talking to the llama. Even from a distance, the animal looked stressed and exhausted. Bobby Maxwell had struck again.

Out of patience, Rafe bent down to the grappling boys, grabbed the first shirt collar he could reach and hauled backward. Dan pulled away from the fight with a protest, until he looked at Rafe's face. Then he sat on the ground, nursing his swollen nose and muttering to himself.

Separating Jerry and Bobby was harder, but Rafe used his knees, his elbows and his feet to get the two boys apart. Then he jerked Bobby into a standing position, holding him with his hands behind his back. The boy struggled and swore; Rafe jerked his wrists higher and tighter.

At last the fight died away. "Let go, dammit," Bobby said, panting. He added a crude epithet, directed at Rafe.

"My pleasure," Rafe replied, snapping handcuffs around Bobby's wrists. The boy stumbled away, spitting out a string of filthy words. "You're under arrest. You have the right to remain silent." The standard warning sounded ridiculous in the circumstances, but Rafe didn't want to miss a step he could be faulted for later.

"Aw, come on." Dan scrambled to his feet. "He didn't do nothing. We were just having some fun."

"Disturbing the peace. Trespassing. Reckless endangerment. Consumption of alcoholic beverages by a minor. I'm sure I'm missing a few charges, but you get the idea." Rafe took hold of Bobby's biceps and pushed him forward. "Let's go."

Mr. Walters confronted them at the upper end of the pasture. "Hellions, that's what you are. You oughta be horsewhipped. Dolly's about dead from what you did to her."

Rafe punched Bobby in the shoulder. "Apologize."

Jaw set, the boy stared at him, without saying a word. His gaze cut to the old man, who was as shaken as his llama. Bobby's shoulders drooped. "Sorry, Mr. Walters. We didn't mean any harm." He tried out a shamefaced grin.

Walters didn't soften. "We'll just see how many of them ewes lose their lambs. Then we'll know the harm you did. That daddy of yours oughta keep you home. Let you ruin his herd." Like a soldier on parade, the old man rested his rifle on his shoulder, turned and shuffled his way back to the cabin. The door shut with a thud that echoed in the hills around them.

Rafe propelled Bobby across the clearing to his truck, with Dan and Jerry following. The three boys sat silent in the back seat for the drive to town, and didn't protest when Rafe ordered them out and into the sheriff's office.

Under the harsh lights, they looked tired, disreputable and young. Rafe fought down a surge of pity and pulled out an arrest report sheet. Leaving the boys standing, he sat down at the desk and started to write.

"Deputy." Bobby sounded as if he'd sobered up. "Give us a break. All hell's gonna break loose if you arrest us."

Rafe didn't stop writing. "All hell broke loose up at Walters's place tonight. You three need to learn a lesson about respecting other people's property."

"My dad's not gonna let you get away with this. He'll have your head on a plate."

"He's welcome to try."

The sound of pen scratching on paper filled the silence while the level of desperation in the atmosphere increased.

"Let us have one more chance." Rafe looked up as Bobby limped over to stand right in front of the desk. "I promise—no more shenanigans. We'll stay out of trouble for the rest of the year. Right, Dan?"

"You got it."

"Jerry?" The other boy nodded.

"See? We'll keep a low profile, drive like little old ladies." Again he tried out that grin. Somebody most have told him how charming he could be when he smiled. Thea?

Still staring at the boy, Rafe thought about the consequences of letting Bobby off this time. He'd seen it happen all to often in L.A.—kids causing some minor trouble were given a break, excused from responsibility for what they'd done. Next time, the trouble might be more serious, but the kid had learned how to work the system…an escalating situation that turned irresponsible youngsters into real criminals. Like the one who'd killed Rafe's partner and walked away with no penalty at all.

But this wasn't L.A., and harassing a bunch of sheep and a llama didn't qualify as a serious crime. Bobby Maxwell was basically a good kid—Rafe believed that. He just needed some limits.

And there was the question of what prosecuting her brother would do to the relationship Rafe hoped to build with Thea. She was a practical woman, but probably not when it came to jail time for Bobby, assuming Judge LeVay would let things go that far. Just setting up an arrest record for a minor was bad enough. Even without a conviction, tonight's charges—especially the underage drinking— would follow Bobby Maxwell around for a long time. His sister would know that. And she'd resent the man who set the process in motion.

In other words, Rafe realized, if he arrested Bobby, any hope of getting close to Thea was a lost cause. He could stick by the letter of the law. Or he could take the boy at his word and keep his own chances with Thea alive. No real harm had been done. Walters hadn't insisted on pressing charges. Maybe just the honest threat of retribution— probably for the first time in his young life—was enough to set Bobby Maxwell straight.

Rafe put down the pen and got to his feet. "You don't deserve anything better than being locked up tonight so you can face your dad and your sister from behind bars tomorrow morning."

Bobby's face went even whiter, and he swayed a little where he stood.

"But I'm going to accept your word on this. You're saying you'll stay out of trouble?"

"Yessir."

"Keep clear of the bars?"

The boy nodded.

"No buying beer? No reckless driving, no fighting, no harassing livestock or people?"

Bobby straightened his shoulders. "I promise."

"And you're talking for your buddies, too?"

Dan and Jerry nodded vigorously.

"Then I'll cut you loose." He walked around to unlock the handcuffs. "But I'm warning you. One more phone call at two in the morning from a pissed-off rancher because you're bothering his herd, one more free-for-all at the Lone Wolf, one more drag race along Main, one infraction of any kind and I'm hauling your butt in here and making a list of charges so long it'll take you till Christmas to read the whole sheet. And I'll make them all stick, whatever it costs, including my job. Understand?"

The three boys seriously and, he thought, sincerely gave their word. Rafe nodded. "Well, then, get out to my truck, and I'll drive you all home. You can figure out how to retrieve your vehicles when you're sober."

After closing up the office, taking the boys to their homes—a thirty-mile drive each way, then heading back to his house, Rafe wondered if he'd just made a really big mistake.

Could he trust Bobby Maxwell to keep his promise?

Or had he sacrificed his integrity and the dignity of his office, not to mention the safety of the people under his charge, for the sake of an attractive woman and this unreasoning, unruly desire to call her his own?

BOBBY CAME HOME at four o'clock Sunday morning. As he tiptoed past the big leather couch in front of the fireplace, Thea switched on the lamp beside her chair. "We need to talk."

The boy across the room jumped and turned so quickly that his sock-covered feet nearly slipped out from under him. "Why the hell are you hiding here in the dark?" He wiped a hand over his face. "Do you want to give me a heart attack?"

"Would that keep you at home?"

Eyes closed, he shook his head. "Not tonight, Tee. I'm too tired to argue about anything tonight." He really did sound completely drained.

But Thea choked back the urge to soften. "Tough luck. Come over here and sit down."

He sighed and flopped onto his stomach on the couch. "I already know what you're gonna say."

She'd been planning this all evening, but that didn't make it easier. "Are you an alcoholic?"

There was a long stretch of silence. "That's a stupid question." Bobby rolled to face her. "Are you?"

"I don't spend six nights out of every seven drunk."

Again, he didn't respond right away. "What's your point?"

"You're getting famous for how much you drink and the wild stunts you pull."

"That's just talk. You know how they all love to talk about the Maxwells. We can't wipe our noses without somebody making a federal case out of it."

"I got this report from a fairly reliable source."

"Oh, yeah." He nodded. "I heard about your cozy four-hour lunch with our esteemed deputy. He tell you I'm a drunk?"

Thea ignored the flush of embarrassment heating her cheeks and the urge to let her mind revisit the best parts of that lunch with Rafe. *Stick to the point.* "He didn't have to."

"Come on, Tee. Give me a break." Bobby sat up and propped his elbows on his knees, put his face in his hands. "So I drink a little. That doesn't mean anything."

"So you don't need to drink?"

"Nope."

"You could go for a month without a beer? Longer?"

He swallowed hard. "Sure. No problem."

"Then do it."

"Do what?"

She sat forward in her chair. "Spend the next thirty days drinking nothing stronger than Beth's coffee."

"I don't have to prove anything to you."

"Chicken, huh?" She'd finally realized that this was the method to use. Bobby had never refused a challenge in all of his life. "I double-dip-dare you."

"Dammit, I'm not chicken. You'll drink turpentine before I touch—" He fell back against the couch. "Aw, damn."

"What's wrong?"

"Monroe Harper's bachelor party is Monday night— Halloween. You don't expect me to go to that and abstain, do you?"

"Why not?" Give him the least excuse, the whole plan would fail.

"I might as well not go at all."

"You can't have a good time without getting drunk?"

"Sure, but—"

"So prove it."

Bobby stared at her for a minute, his lower lip stuck out in a pout that would have been cute if this weren't such a serious issue. Finally he sighed.

"Okay. I'll show you. I'll spend the next thirty days like a solid citizen, as sober as Preacher Marvin. Satisfied?"

Thea crossed her arms. "I will be when I see it."

He stretched to his feet, yawning. "You're a hard woman, Thea Maxwell. I'll be surprised if there's a man in

Montana strong enough to soften you up." Walking unsteadily, he wandered off to bed.

But Thea stayed awake for quite a while longer, thinking
over that parting shot.

Was Bobby right? Had she become such a prickly pear
that no man would ever make the effort to get past her
shell? And if he did, would there be anything womanly,
anything lovable, left underneath?

RAFE SLEPT UNTIL NOON on Sunday, so he missed seeing
Thea at church, a mistake he blamed on Bobby's im-
promptu rodeo. After freezing his butt off outside at
2:00 a.m., he didn't feel like spending the snapping-cold
afternoon doing anything more energetic than watching a
football game on TV. Maybe a movie.

Then he glanced around his mostly empty, chilly house.
Maybe a movie in Bozeman and a decent dinner.

With Thea?

He called the ranch before he could fall prey to second
thoughts. Hearing her husky voice answer the second ring
was a huge relief. "Hi. It's Rafe. Rafferty." He sounded
like an eighth-grader on his first dating call.

"Oh, hi." After a couple of seconds she said,
"I…um…didn't see you at church this morning."

Did that mean she was looking for him? "I slept through
the alarm. I got a late call last night."

"Bobby?" Worry stressed her tone. "He got home really, really late."

"Well, yeah." Rafe explained about Mr. Walters's
sheep.

She muttered a string of insults aimed at her brother. "I
talked to him about the drinking, but I didn't think about
asking him what he'd been up to. Damn." Her sigh was
easy to hear across the line. "Well, thanks for letting me

know. I'll talk with him and try to get into town as soon as I can to smooth Mr. Walters's feathers. I should be able—''

Suddenly, Rafe realized she had the wrong idea. ''Thea? I didn't call to give you a report on Bobby's latest stunt.''

There was a second of shocked silence. ''You didn't?''

''It's kind of last minute, I guess, but I called to ask if you'd like to ride over to Bozeman this afternoon, have some dinner, catch a movie.''

''Oh.'' This pause stretched even longer, while his pulse jumped and his palms sweated. He started to wonder if she'd hung up on him, when she cleared her throat. ''That would be…fun.''

She didn't sound totally sure, but he decided to take her at her word. ''How about I pick you up at four o'clock?''

''No.'' The word sounded desperate. ''No,'' she said more gently. ''I'll meet you in town. There's no sense in your driving this far in the wrong direction.''

''I don't mind.''

But when Thea Maxwell made a decision, Rafe gathered, that was all there was to be said. They settled on her coming directly to his place and leaving the Land Rover there. ''That's great, then. I'll see you at four o'clock. Thanks, Rafe.''

''My pleasure.''

Thea put down the phone, the deep rumble of Rafe's voice still vibrating along her nerves. A date. She had a date with the deputy sheriff. An attractive, charming man who didn't stand to gain anything by taking out Robert Maxwell's daughter. A man who wanted to see her, strange as it seemed, because he liked her company.

A man her dad had warned her to stay away from.

But she'd said herself, this wasn't *Romeo and Juliet*. She

wouldn't sneak off as if she was ashamed. Or, even worse, afraid.

So she stopped by her dad's study on the way out of the house. He looked up as she knocked, but waited for her to say the first word.

"I'm going into Bozeman to have dinner and see a movie, Dad. I'll probably be pretty late getting back."

He frowned. "We start breeding checks first thing tomorrow morning."

"I know. I'll be up in plenty of time. See you for breakfast." She waved, and turned to go.

"Althea."

"Yes, sir?" She faced him across the length of the room.

"You going to Bozeman by yourself?"

"No, sir. I'm meeting Rafe Rafferty in town. We have a…a date."

Robert Maxwell stood up, tall and formidable behind his desk. "I told you to stay away from him."

"And I told you I would see him if I wanted to. Which I do."

"You're my daughter and you'll do as I say."

"I'm a grown woman and I'll run my life as I please."

"I expect you to follow my rules while you're living under my roof and eating my food."

"Those conditions can be changed." Thea hardly believed she heard herself say it. Was she actually threatening to move out of the only home she'd ever known because of Rafe Rafferty?

Evidently, her dad couldn't believe it, either. If he did, he decided not to push. "You do what you want, then." He sat down again. "But don't come whining to me when he turns out to be a loser."

She almost laughed. When had she ever been encouraged to come to Robert Maxwell for any kind of comfort or consolation? He hadn't been much help when her mom died, and not for anything less important since. Her oldest sister, Jolie, had tried to be a mother figure, but her nature was too quiet, too solitary. She preferred books to people. And Cassie…Cassie had done nothing but get Thea into trouble with her escapades. Many times over.

So Thea just shook her head. "Don't worry, Dad. I won't bother you with my personal problems. Good night."

She did not, of course, hear him say anything in reply.

Beth was in the kitchen, stirring up stew for dinner. "You're eating out? With who?"

"Rafe Rafferty." Thea pulled on her gloves without looking at the housekeeper.

"The deputy." Beth had been the closest to a mom any of them had known since Bobby was four, and she exercised her privileges. "That's who called? He's taking you out?"

"Um…yes."

"He's coming here?"

"I'm meeting him in town."

The housekeeper planted her fists on her rounded hips. "That's not very gentlemanly."

"Better than having Dad greet him with a shotgun, or letting you subject him to the third degree." Thea smiled, to take the sting out of the words.

Beth made a sound between a snort and a sniff. "Somebody should know something about the men you go out with."

"Yeah, and that somebody is me." Putting an arm around Beth's plump shoulders, Thea kissed her cheek. "Don't wait up. I might be late."

"But you will be home?" Her flushed cheeks, her lifted chin, gave the question added meaning.

The idea of spending the whole night with Rafe stopped

Thea in her tracks. She'd thought about kissing him—the generous shape of his lips, his easy smile, made not thinking about it impossible. But she really hadn't gone much farther, even in her imagination. Imagination was, in fact, the closest she'd come to sex with any man so far, not counting some ill-mannered groping from the governor's son.

And now, to have the possibility of such intimacy with Rafe out in the open, under the bright kitchen lights...

She shivered, but not with cold. "Yes, I will be home. Safe and sound, I promise." *I hope.*

Before she could be required to field any more embarrassing questions, or think about the implications—not to mention temptations—of seeing Rafe on a personal basis, Thea ducked her head and retreated into town.

THE WOMAN RAFE FACED across the dinner table was, he decided right away, worth the compromise he'd made with his conscience and his duty. Thea Maxwell in jeans and a jacket was tempting enough, but in a bright red dress of some soft material that skimmed her breasts and her hips, with gold hoops in her ears and a touch of lipstick on her full mouth, she made food a secondary priority, at best.

"You look great tonight," he said when she glanced up from her menu.

Her green-blue eyes widened, and her cheeks flushed. "Th-thanks. I, um, don't get to dress up too often. The cattle just don't appreciate the effort."

"That's why they're called dumb beasts."

Her laugh was rich, full, sexy. "You're really good at this, aren't you?"

"Good at what?"

"Sweet-talking. Getting your way with pretty words and compliments."

He looked at her, not smiling, until her amusement faded. Then he said, "I'm not sweet-talking or trying to get my way. I'm telling the truth. I think you're beautiful."

A waiter approached their table. "Are you ready to order?"

Eyes still wide, Thea raised her menu, hiding her face. Rafe ordered at random. By the time all the details of soup and salad and potato and drink had been taken care of, he and Thea had both recovered, more or less, from his totally unsubtle dose of honesty.

Over steaks, they talked books and movies and sports. Rafe kept the personal comments to a minimum, but every so often, a sudden, intense burst of energy flashed between them…like when he noticed how the deep red of the wine she'd ordered stained her lips. Or when he caught her staring at his hands as he played with his coffee spoon. And there was that brush of her ankle against his. An accident? Three times?

They chose an action film they'd both wanted to see, shared a bucket of popcorn—where their buttery fingers collided more than once—and agreed at the end that the first installment of the series was still the best. On the drive back to Paradise Corners, the silence started out easy enough, filled with music from a classic-country station on the radio. As much as they'd talked, Rafe didn't feel compelled to entertain his passenger. Maybe he was reading Thea wrong, but she seemed as comfortable as he was. At least she didn't rush to fill every second with chatter, unlike a lot of women he'd dated.

The closer they got to town, though, the quieter, tighter, the silence felt. Rafe knew he was thinking about the end of the trip, about how Thea would react if he kissed her. Was she wondering if he would? The radio didn't help—a call-in request program was playing some of country music's sexiest singers performing their sexiest songs.

He didn't need Shania or Faith to help him respond to the music. Having Thea on the seat just a foot away was stimulation enough—catching a whiff of her spicy, exotic perfume, glancing over to see the gleam of her hair and the elegant slope of her nose, the curve of those full lips, the soft swell of her breasts...she was all the woman any man could want. More aroused by simple sight and sound than he'd been in years, Rafe took advice from the current song on the radio and dragged in a deep, deep breath.

When he braked in front of his place and cut the engine, they sat frozen for a second, then both turned to open their respective doors at the same time. Rafe managed to get around the front of the truck before Thea had shut hers.

"You're determined to be independent, aren't you?" He finished the job, reaching past her shoulder to close the panel.

"I couldn't do my job otherwise." Thea stared up at him from within arm's length, closer than she'd been yet this evening. "I told you—"

"You can brand and castrate with the big guys. I heard." He grinned, as a peace offering, and was relieved when she grinned back.

"Just so you remember who you're dealing with here."

"I'm not likely to forget." He took his hand away from the truck door, touched a finger to a sleekly curved lock of her hair. "You might just be the most memorable person I've ever met." Curving his palm along the line of her jaw, he tilted Thea's face up...then set his mouth on hers.

CHAPTER SIX

THE FRIGID NIGHT heated up quickly.

Thea felt Rafe's wonderful lips move against hers and sighed in relief, in pleasure, in encouragement. She'd wondered all evening if this would happen…and now it was happening and it was proving to be the most amazing experience of her whole life.

He was skillful, of course—he'd probably kissed many women before tonight—but not demanding. Or careless. His touch against her mouth was gentle, testing shape and fit and intensity as if this simple kiss really mattered. As if *she* really mattered.

At the hazy thought, she rested her palms against Rafe's chest, feeling the driving rhythm of his heart through her own skin. His hands found their way to her elbows, skimmed up her arms, closed over her shoulders and drew her close against him. Despite her wool dress and their thick coats, she could feel the heat of his body radiating into hers. Her breath shortened, quickened, trembled. Such a big man made her feel small, feminine. He might even be able to make her feel helpless.

For the first time ever, she understood how desirable feeling helpless could be.

Long before she was ready, Rafe pulled back. "You're going to freeze to death," he whispered. "It must be fifteen degrees."

Thea opened her eyes, blinked as she saw the tender light in his. "I don't think so. I feel very...warm."

He grinned, a sexy, man-conquers-woman expression, and she didn't even resent it. "You've got a long drive home. I wish you had let me pick you up."

Without his heat next to her, the cold began to seep in. "My dad isn't your biggest fan. Maybe next time—" She caught herself on the assumption. "I mean..."

Rafe chuckled, put an arm around her shoulders and eased her to the driver's side of the Land Rover. "There will be a next time, if I have anything to say about it." He waited as she unlocked the door and climbed onto the seat. When she turned, he had stepped close, so their faces were level, just a breath apart. "Your dad had better start to adjust."

This kiss wasn't so gentle. Persuasive, yes, with his mouth dominating hers. Seductive, oh, yes, with his tongue tasting the flesh inside her lower lip. Delicious, definitely, as Thea invited an even more complete invasion.

Breathing hard, they broke apart. "You're dangerous." He brushed her hair back from her face. "Get home."

She wanted to lean into his hand like a purring cat. But she caught a glimpse of the clock out of the corner of her eye. After midnight, and she would be in the saddle from seven the next morning until long past dark.

"I'm going." She sighed again, in regret this time. The Land Rover engine cranked immediately, worse luck, and she ran out of reasons to delay. "Thanks. I had a really great time tonight."

He touched a fingertip to her nose. "Me, too. Drive carefully. The law in these parts is really hard on speeders."

Thea grinned at his joke. "Sure it is. G'night." She waited for him to move so she could close the door, but Rafe seemed to have a problem with motivation, too.

Finally he shook his head and backed away. With all excuses gone, Thea put the car in gear and reluctantly headed south toward home. The thirty miles out to Walking Stones seemed like ninety, but she made it into bed before actually falling asleep and enjoyed six hours of sweet, believable dreams.

DROWNING. He was drowning.

Robert opened his eyes to blackness, pushed hard against the mattress and sat up in bed, panting, fighting for breath. In the quiet, air leaked from his throat in ragged gasps—as if he'd run down a coyote on foot, dragging a yearling calf behind him.

Fear cramped his belly. Dear God, he couldn't breathe.

He swung his feet to the floor, stumbled to the window and braced his hands on the sill, pressing his forehead against the cold glass. Almost immediately, his face cooled. His chest relaxed, his heart slowed.

Finally he could get a good deep breath. *Whew.* For a minute there, he'd had the feeling of being locked in a coffin before he was dead.

The bedside clock gave the time as four-thirty. He'd be up in half an hour anyway. Might as well get an early start on a long day's work.

But the hot shower he took closed down his lungs some. Getting into his long johns, his socks and boots and jeans left him breathless. Tired before he'd even left the bedroom, Robert sat down in Helen's green velvet armchair by the window and let his head rest against the high back.

Fifteen years he'd slept alone in this room, but he still felt her presence, imagined her perfume on the sheets. A man never got back to normal once half his heart was gone, and Helen had been the very center of his heart. He'd never been good at saying so, but she'd known. Known, and given him her unwavering love in return.

Then she was taken, leaving him with four children and a business to run. The business he could handle; the kids he couldn't. He still thanked God for Beth Peace, who took them off his hands, saw to their needs, kept them fed and clothed and schooled. Helen had chosen to teach the girls at home. But afterward, the kids all ended up in public school. Maybe that was where the boy's problems had started.

The thought brought him back to Thea's questions. She insisted her brother drank too much. But all youngsters had to test their limits, figure out how much liquor they could handle. He'd done the same at Bobby's age.

As for Thea, she seemed to be testing a different kind of boundary. She'd all but threatened to move out of the house if he kept her from seeing that damn deputy. How could a girl who'd turned down the governor's son see anything in a no-account outsider from California?

But two of his daughters had already abandoned Walking Stones, and Robert had enough self-control to keep from giving the third an excuse. There'd been too much trouble, as it was—Helen would hate to think her children wouldn't stay close to home. She'd be hurt by Bobby's indifference to his heritage, his responsibilities. And she'd always dreamed of having all her grandkids over for Christmas dinner. Cassie's boy Zak was seven, but he'd never been to Walking Stones for Christmas.

With a little warning beep, the alarm clock started its usual buzz. Robert pushed himself out of the chair and crossed the room to hit the button. Outside his window was pitch-black darkness, no sign of sunrise. Good thing—he had at least an hour's worth of figures to tally before he started the day's real work.

At the prospect, he closed his eyes, feeling closer than he'd ever been to crawling back in bed and letting somebody else look after the ranch. How could he be this tired, first thing in the morning?

Anyway, there was nobody else. Herman was a good man, but better at following orders than giving them. Thea was just a woman. And Bobby…

Bobby could be depended on for one sure thing—at some point during the day, he'd screw up. Lose his concentration, give in to a crazy idea or just plain ignore some important part of the job. Most of the time, his mistakes were inconvenient but not dangerous.

The day was coming, though, when all hell would break loose. Even without Thea's warnings, Robert recognized the signs. Bobby had pulled his chain tight as it would go.

Now they just waited to see which link failed first.

BOBBY WISHED he had a hangover. Maybe then he wouldn't feel so damn cold.

But he'd stayed sober all day Sunday, and he was sober now, sitting in a frozen saddle on top of a horse as miserable as he was, staring across the pasture at four hundred cows and heifers. Today's assignment—drive the herd into pens at the breeding barn so they could be checked to see if they were pregnant. Damn, he hated playing cowboy.

A memory of Saturday night's adventure with the llama came into his head, and he winced. Definitely one of his dumber ideas.

He was as drunk as he'd ever been that night, but this time he'd had a good reason. Megan had broken their date. She'd said on the phone that her dad wouldn't let her out of the house, and chances were that was exactly what had happened. Except…Hank Reeves seemed to be showing up a lot these days. Was Megan changing her mind? Did she miss the old boyfriend?

Thea rode up next to him. "Do you want us to let the cows mow you down? Or can you at least move out of the way, if you won't help?"

She sat her pretty palomino quarter horse as if she'd been born there. Which she almost had, he'd heard. Their mother had been out for a ride when the pains started.

Bobby wondered what had happened just before he arrived. Must have been pretty bad. Helen Maxwell hadn't thought he was worth staying around for.

He shook his head, abandoning a line of thought that got him nowhere but mad. "What's the hurry? Sun's not even up yet. We've got all damn day."

"I'd like to get them across Eagle Creek before dark." She settled her black Stetson on her head and gathered her reins. "That'll still leave us a couple of hours of riding before we get to the barn. Unless you want to be out past nine tonight."

"Not much worth getting off early for, is there?"

Thea stared at him closely. "You and Megan have a fight?"

The unfairness of it all burst out of him. "No, but her dad's on one of his binges, won't let her out of the house for anything but her job. I'm stuck here with these stupid cows all day long, so I can't get down to the post office to see her at work. And I can't go drinking—"

"Can't?"

He sighed. "Won't, okay? So what's left to do?"

"Read an article or two in a relevant journal? *Ag News* or *Beef Today,* maybe."

Bobby muttered a rude word under his breath.

Profanity never stopped Thea from making her point. "Help Dad with the books? Clean saddles and stirrups, mend bridles?'' She picked up speed and enthusiasm. ''Sweep barns, shovel stalls, feed, groom and water horses, treat abscesses and cuts and saddle sores, wash brushes and buckets—''

Jaw clenched, he wheeled his horse away. ''Let's just get started,'' he said without looking back. She sure as hell couldn't lecture him over the noise of the damn cattle.

But knowing Thea, Bobby figured she'd give it a try.

As HE DROVE OUT to Walking Stones Wednesday morning, Rafe realized he was taking a risk. He hadn't spoken with Thea since their date on Sunday—a long two days, but he'd made it. There was no reason to make a thirty-mile drive just to say hello. That's what telephones were for.

Sunday during dinner, she'd told him about her schedule this week. Out all day herding, culling, dosing cattle, pursuing the complicated work of breeding prime Angus beef. When she finally got in, all she could do, she said, was shower, sip some soup, and sleep. Rafe didn't want to keep her from relaxing at the end of a long day.

But he did want to see her again, laugh with her a little, maybe make her a little mad, then coax her into smiles again. Her face was lively, her eyes as changeable as the Montana sky. He enjoyed being responsible for Thea's moods, good and bad...especially that dazed look in her eyes, the soft smile on her mouth, after he kissed her.

His nights had been interrupted lately by dreams in which he and Thea stirred up other, wilder, emotions. And by the cold showers that followed. During the day, he tried not to remember much about those fantasies. A grown man ought to be able to stay cool, even about a woman like Thea.

He used the bull's-head knocker when he reached the Maxwells' front door, and waited only a few seconds to be confronted by a plump woman with soft brown hair and bright brown eyes. She looked like somebody's mother—though what did he know about mothers? He hadn't had a real parent since he was six years old. His aunt and uncle had considered him just another responsibility to be tallied on the balance sheet along with the feed bills and mortgage payments.

The smile in the woman's eyes died as she took in his uniform. "Deputy?"

"Rafe Rafferty, ma'am." He took off his hat. "I wondered if I could see Thea this morning."

She pursed her lips. "Why would she be lollygagging around the house? The girl has work to do, which is more than I can say for some people, apparently."

"Yes, ma'am, I'm sure she does. Maybe I could catch up with her where she's working?" He tried out a grin. It had worked with formidable older ladies in the past.

But not this one. She only sniffed. "Thea's too busy to spend time talking. Unless—" Suspicion fired in her eyes. "Are you here on official business? Is something wrong?"

Rafe was tempted to lie and avoid the hassle. Too bad his conscience didn't take many vacations. "No, nothing wrong. I just thought I'd drop by."

Her expression said plainly what she thought of someone who would drive thirty miles out of town to "drop by." She sighed. "They're out at the breeding barn. Take this road back toward the front gate. About three miles on, turn right, toward the mountains. You'll figure it out from there."

"Thanks, ma'am. I'll let you get back to work."

"Do the same for Thea. Her days are long enough as it is." She started to close the door, then opened it up a crack. "And call me Beth. Everybody else does."

Rafe whistled during the whole five-mile drive to the

breeding barn. With the housekeeper on his side, his chances with Thea looked a whole lot better.

He didn't have to wonder where she was working, though he still might have trouble finding her. The gray-and-white barn rose out of the rolling pastureland, a hurricane's eye at the center of a swirl of black-railed fences containing hundreds of cattle. Men edged between the hefty black cows, easing them through gates, into and out of different holding pens, in a rumbling, bawling mob. Rafe spotted a grim-faced Bobby moving through the churning bodies. The boy looked sulky as a mule, but he could do the job. Slowly, gently, he herded cows up an inclined chute and through a door into the barn. Obviously, the herding skill he'd demonstrated with the llama had been gained through hours of practice with Angus cattle.

Shaking his head at Bobby's wildness, Rafe walked through the wider, ground-floor doorway into the barn. There he found Thea on a platform at the top of the chute Bobby was loading, intensely examining the tail end of each cow.

He leaned a shoulder against the stall door nearby, waiting until she noticed him. It didn't take long, and her reaction was everything he'd hoped for. Those green-blue eyes widened, the full lips curved immediately into a smile. She stared at him as if she couldn't look away. Like a fool, Rafe grinned back.

"Hey, Thea, what's up?" a cowboy down the line shouted. "We run out of cows?"

The progress of cattle had stopped when she shifted her attention. Rafe saw Thea flush, glance to her left at the long row of black heads waiting in the chute, and then at her watch.

"Let's take lunch," she called back. "Thirty minutes we'll start up again. Pass the word."

"Yes, ma'am!" The cowboy hopped down from the walkway beside the chute and strode by Rafe, humming. "Thanks, man. I was about to drop dead for lack of food. These Maxwells, they'll keep you working all day, you let 'em."

Rafe gave him an absentminded grin as Thea skipped down the steps from the platform and crossed the wide aisle toward him.

Damn, she made it hard for a man to stay cool.

Slim jeans hugged her legs and hips. Well-worn boots gave her walk a swagger that left him swallowing hard. The sleeves of a plaid shirt were rolled up to her elbows, revealing strong arms and capable hands, tanned from a summer spent working in the sun. A sudden jolt of memory from one of those dreams he'd been having hit him—those hands running over his bare skin.

Rafe straightened and jammed his own hands in his pockets, tried to think about a cold shower in the six seconds it took Thea to reach him.

Her smile warmed the cool barn air. "This is a surprise. Come to arrest somebody?" Her eyebrows drew together as the smile suddenly disappeared. "You haven't, have you? Is something wrong?" She glanced over her shoulder toward the pen where he'd seen Bobby working.

"Nope. Far as I know, Paradise Corners is a quiet and law-abiding place this week." He really wanted to touch her—wind a dark curl around his finger, run his thumb over her palm.

And he might have done that, except for the tall man who stepped up behind Thea.

"Deputy." Boss Maxwell looked him up and down without apparently finding anything to like. "Is there a problem?"

Rafe kept his stance relaxed. "No, sir. I just stopped by to say hello to Thea."

"She's got work to do. Whole operation gets held up when she does."

Thea started to say something, but Rafe put up a hand. "Yes, sir. I don't intend to stay but a few minutes." He didn't waste a smile. "I wouldn't want to keep the cows waiting."

Maxwell stared at him without changing his grim expression. Finally, he gave a snort and turned on his heel. "Ten minutes," he said over his shoulder, then stalked to the other end of the barn and disappeared around a corner.

Rafe looked back at Thea. "You'd better get something to eat, fast."

She beckoned him to follow. "We've got sandwiches and soup. You're welcome to a share."

He'd been hoping for just this chance, so he didn't refuse the invitation. They stood in the grub line together, watching the hands settle in small groups at wooden tables and benches scattered under a stand of pines.

"Cowboys and picnic tables." Shaking his head, Rafe sat across from Thea at a table on the edge of the group. "Whatever happened to the classic crouch around the campfire?"

"It went the way of mule-drawn plows and Indian wars," she said between bites. "We don't miss those, either."

They each got through half a sandwich in silence. "So what are you doing to these poor Angus ladies?"

"Checking for pregnancy. These are the AI cows—" She raised her eyebrows in question.

He nodded. "Artificial insemination. My uncle used it."

"So I'm checking to find out which cows missed. We'll retry with those, check again in a month or so. Depending on their history, we'll sell them off or give them another try next spring."

"Complicated record-keeping."

"You said it. Dad's done the work for years, but he finally had to bring in some help. Becky Freedom works part-time, helping him keep track." She gazed over his shoulder, and Rafe turned around to see her brother at a table not far away. "Bobby would be a big help—he's a math whiz. But..." With a sigh, she crumpled her sandwich paper into a ball. "He's not interested."

"What about you?"

Her laugh was a pleasure to hear. "I keep up my AI training, so I'm the technician in the process. I'd rather work with cows than numbers any day." She pulled a wristwatch out of the pocket of her shirt. "My generous lunch hour is over. I'd better get back to the job."

They walked to the corner of the door into the barn. Thea leaned on the jamb to face him. "It was good to see you. But..." Her cheeks flushed and she avoided his eyes. "Why?"

Rafe put a finger under her chin and lifted her face to his. "Because it was good to see *you*." He rubbed his thumb along her jawbone. "Sunday was a long time ago."

She was getting that dazed expression again. "It was."

"I figure you're too tired most nights for a date."

"Um..." Her tongue peeked out to wet her upper lip.

Rafe swallowed a groan. "But I thought maybe we could grab a few minutes together." He gave in to a crazy impulse, bending to brush her mouth with his. "There. I guess that'll have to last me until the weekend. Saturday night?"

Lips tingling, wanting more, Thea nodded.

Rafe backed away. "I'll call you. Friday. Okay?"

She nodded and lifted a hand to say goodbye. He returned the salute, then turned and walked back toward the parking area, with a swing in his stride that was a pleasure to watch.

Becky Freedom stepped up beside her. "He's something else." Thea could only nod. The other woman grinned. "Lots of girls would kill to have him smile at them like that."

Thea stirred and straightened away from the door frame. "Thanks for the warning. I'll watch my back."

Becky gave her a pat on the shoulder. "I'll let you know if they make any solid plans."

Back on the walkway beside the chute, Thea switched on the ultrasound machine to let it warm up, and got ready for an afternoon that suddenly seemed much brighter than before.

When she turned back to the waiting cows, her dad stood right beside her. Thea lifted her chin. "Things are going pretty good today. I think we'll get this lot done by dark."

Saying nothing, he stared at her, his lips pressed hard together. After a second, she realized he was breathing rapidly, his chest expanding and contracting much faster than normal.

She put a hand on his arm. "Are you okay?"

He nodded once. "What does he want, hanging around you like this?"

Thea closed her eyes. The assumptions behind his question battered her heart and mind. What flaws did her dad see that made it so hard to understand how a man like Rafe could be attracted to her? In what vital ways did she fall short?

She decided she couldn't deal with those issues today. "I don't know, Dad. Hot sex, I imagine. Too bad he doesn't know I'm still a virgin, isn't it?"

Turning back to the ultrasound, she made unnecessary adjustments to the dials, waiting for her dad to leave. It seemed to take a long time before she heard the retreating thud of boot heels, leaving her in peace with her cattle.

SATURDAY, Rafe's long-lost furniture arrived. At Thea's suggestion, they put their plans for dinner in Bozeman on hold and spent the afternoon unpacking boxes.

By midevening, the run-down little house had started to look habitable. Jed greeted the return of his favorite blue plaid couch with a satisfied sigh as he curled into the corner for a nap.

Rafe grinned. "I'm with you, friend. There's nothing like having your own stuff."

Thea came in from the kitchen. "I found the pots and pans—all three of them. Where should they go?"

"I didn't say I cooked a lot." The kitchen cabinets stood open, and he approved the arrangement of his small store of dishes. "Fried baloney sandwiches are about as fancy as I get."

Her eyes lighted up. "Wow, I haven't had fried baloney for years. Do you have any? How about American-cheese slices? And soft white bread with no nutritional value at all?"

He opened the refrigerator. "Ask and you shall receive. Do you want Coke or Sprite?"

"What's best with baloney?"

"Beer, to be honest. Want one?"

"Oh, yes."

They sat at the old oak table he'd salvaged from a demolished L.A. library, eating from paper plates, drinking beer straight from the bottle.

Rafe shook his head. "Nobody can say I don't know how to show a woman a good time. First class all the way."

Thea looked indignant. "I've enjoyed it, thank you very much. I didn't like dinner at the governor's mansion in the least. You shouldn't spoil good beef with mushrooms and pâté.''

"You dated the governor?" Rafe drained his beer, not liking the way his stomach tightened.

"His two-timing son." She stood up and took her plate and bottle to the trash bag, effectively hiding her face from him. That in itself was a clue to how much the admission bothered her.

Rafe followed. "The jerk obviously had no brains and lousy eyesight." Standing just behind her as she stared out the small back-door window, he took hold of her shoulders and pulled her against him. He bent his head and put his mouth near her ear. "I, on the other hand, have eyesight certified by the state of Montana as perfect. And an IQ in the genius range."

She shivered, and relaxed back against him. For a minute she stood quiet in his hold as he kissed a path along her neck and jaw. Then, with a quick turn, she faced him. Her arms went around his neck. Her mouth claimed his.

Thea sensed his restraint from the moment their lips touched. His hold stayed gentle, though she felt him tremble with the effort. His kisses—demanding, devouring—told her what he wanted, and how desperately. Seduced by his nearness, by the idea of being so deeply desired, she offered the man in her arms anything he would take.

Instead, with ever-softening kisses and his shaking hands cupped around her face, he slowed things down into words. "Don't think I'm not tempted," he said raggedly, running his thumb along her cheekbone. "But..."

"But?"

"But two dates and a lunch doesn't constitute a long-term relationship." Smiling, he shook his head. "Anyway, the best things are worth waiting for. That includes you, without a doubt."

Despite her reluctance, he wrapped her in the blanket coat she'd come in, shrugged on his own sheepskin jacket and walked her through swirling snow to the Land Rover, with Jed at their heels. When she climbed into the driver's seat, he moved close enough to put his arms around her waist again. Without a protest or a second thought, Thea dived into another mind-stealing kiss.

"There's snow blowing down my collar," he whispered after a few minutes. "And Jed's gnawing on my leg, ready to go inside."

She pulled away, smiling. "I wouldn't want Jed to get cold out here. You'd better let me go."

"I'll get you for that one." He stepped back and wiped snow out of his eyes. "Are you busy tomorrow?"

"Cassie and Zak are coming over." She'd explained the situation with her sister as they unpacked his books. "I'd ask you to lunch, but Dad's not ready for that yet." Whether he would be at some point in the foreseeable future was a question she didn't address, even in her mind.

"No problem. I don't want to violate your dad's comfort zone. I've got to be in Big Timber every morning this next week for training, so I can't come by for lunch. I'll call you, though. And I'm reserving your Saturday for my own nefarious purposes. Got that?" He gentled the forceful words with the soft stroke of his thumb down her cheek.

"Got it." She started the engine and gave him a smile. "See you Saturday."

BUT RAFE ENDED UP driving out to Walking Stones much sooner than that. On Monday night—Halloween—he was standing on the porch with his hat in his hands when Thea opened the front door. A blast of cold air swept past him into the house.

"Come in out of the wind," she said, and stepped back

to give him room. She shut the door, then turned to face him, eyes bright, smile wide. "This is a surprise. We don't get many trick-or-treaters out here."

Rafe stared at her a minute, trying to figure out how to say what needed to be said. He'd done this before, but none of those other people had been Thea. None of them were the woman he was falling in love with.

Her face paled, tightened. "Rafe? What's wrong?"

He had to be quick. "Bobby's been in an accident. He's on his way to the hospital in Bozeman, with Dan Aiken and Jerry Heath, and the driver of the other truck."

She gripped his wrist below his jacket sleeve. "Is he hurt?" When Rafe didn't say anything, her nails dug in. "He's alive, isn't he? He's hurt, but he's going to be okay. Right?"

There was no way to lie. "I don't know," Rafe said heavily. "I just don't know."

CHAPTER SEVEN

FORTY MILES OF SILENCE to the Bozeman hospital.

Thea sat in the back seat of Rafe's truck with her cold fingers tucked under her thighs. He had turned up the heat, of course. She just couldn't get warm.

In the front, her dad sat staring out the windshield at the highway. His face hadn't changed, and he hadn't said a word since he'd looked up from his desk as she'd stepped into his study and announced, "Bobby's hurt."

The road was dry and clear and empty. Rafe had put his flashers on the roof of the truck, and pushed the speedometer needle beyond eighty. But forever had already passed, and they weren't there yet.

He'd given her the details he knew. Bobby had been driving, had run a stop sign and hit another truck. The other driver had managed to use the two-way radio to call for help. Rafe had arrived at the scene just as the ambulance carrying Bobby pulled away. He didn't know what the injuries were, if any of the boys were conscious. He didn't know whether or not Bobby had been drinking.

But tonight had been the bachelor party Bobby hadn't wanted to miss. Had he kept his promise not to drink?

Oh, God. Thea closed her eyes tight. *Please let them all be okay. We'll get him straightened out somehow. Just let them be okay.*

She felt the truck slow down and opened her eyes. They'd reached the outskirts of Bozeman. Blue-and-white signs pointed to the hospital; thanks to all the outdoor activities available in Montana, trauma treatment was a medical specialty. Whatever their injuries, the boys couldn't be in better hands.

But please, God, don't let them be badly hurt.

Rafe dropped them at the emergency-room door and drove off to park his truck. Her dad went immediately to the admitting desk, while Thea looked around the crowded waiting room. Dan's and Jerry's parents were already there. They looked up quickly as she came through the doorway, saw who it was and looked away again.

She took an empty seat beside Mrs. Aiken. "Have they said anything? Have you talked to a doctor?"

The red-haired woman shook her head. "They said it's serious. That's all."

Thea looked at Mrs. Heath. "They're still alive, though, aren't they?"

"Far as I know—no thanks to that irresponsible brother of yours."

There could be no argument. Bobby had been driving. And Bobby *was* irresponsible. The blame for whatever happened rested squarely on his shoulders.

A nurse stood at the doorway. "Mr. Aiken? We've got some papers you need to sign." The Aikens left, followed a minute later by the Heaths.

After what seemed to be an eternal wait, Rafe came into the room and took the free chair beside Thea. "Dan and Jerry are going into surgery."

She curled up over her thighs and buried her head in her arms. "Does that mean they're hurt the worst? Or that Bobby is…"

His warm hand rested on her back underneath her jacket, rubbing small, comforting circles over her spine. "I think they're all still alive, Thea. They would have told your dad by now, if not. And he would tell you.''

How she wanted to lean into him, to pull his arms around her and draw warmth from his body. A strong urge to hide her face against him possessed her, as if he could make the whole horrible situation go away.

''Althea.'' Her dad stood at the door, grim-faced and pale under his tan. ''Your brother is going to be all right. He's got broken ribs and bruises, glass cuts on his face and hands. But the seat belt and the airbag saved him.''

She dragged in a shaking breath. ''Oh, thank God.'' Rafe pressed his hand firmly against her back, then let his arm fall away from her. She missed the contact immediately, though she understood his caution. ''Can I talk to him?''

''Doctor's still patching him up. He'll let us know.'' Robert Maxwell surveyed the room and sat down in the chair directly opposite the door. Arms crossed over his chest, knees spread wide and feet firmly planted, he was obviously not going anywhere until he chose to.

He wasn't talking, either. But what was there to say? They couldn't discuss the weather or the day's work, with Bobby lying hurt and two boys in surgery. They didn't know enough about the accident to talk about that.

As the minutes crept by, Thea remembered the other driver. ''What about the person in the other truck? What do we know about him…her?''

''Him,'' Rafe said, getting to his feet. ''I'll see what I can find out.'' Losing his presence was like stepping into a cold rain. She hugged her arms around her body, trying to get warm.

''You should send him home,'' her dad said.

For a second she stared at him without understanding. ''Who…you mean Rafe?''

Robert Maxwell nodded. ''He's the law.''

"What has that got to do with anything?"

"He'll be investigating the accident."

For the first time it occurred to her that Bobby would be up against some stiff penalties especially if he'd been drunk. Drinking underage and while driving were serious violations. "Bobby's going to have to face up to some punishment, sure. Maybe this'll finally get him to figure out where he's going with his life."

"We've got worse problems than that on our hands. Yes," he said in answer to the question she couldn't ask. "The other boys are real bad off, the doctor told me."

Thea felt as if her heart had stopped. She couldn't seem to breathe.

"If one of those boys dies, it's going to be all we can do to keep your brother from being tried for murder." Her dad closed his eyes for a second, and she realized what a toll Bobby's troubles had taken on him, how pale he'd become in just a few hours. "This deputy you're so set on getting friendly with will be the one making the arrest, gathering the evidence. And he'll be the one pushing to convict."

Her dad looked at her, his face haggard, his eyes as cold as stone. "Are you willing to let your boyfriend be the man who sends Bobby to prison?"

GOD, HE HURT.

All over, like being pounded with a hammer. What the hell had happened that he felt this bad?

Bobby tried to think, but nothing came up. His brain was jelly. Or maybe peanut butter. Yeah, as thick as cold peanut butter…

When he woke up the next time, his brain worked better, but his body didn't work at all. He tried to put a hand to his face, but a knife slashed at his shoulder with the first move. A deep breath…impossible. Something really heavy sat on his chest. Damn. It wasn't worth the effort.

"Bobby? Bobby, can you open your eyes?"

Why bother?

Something cool fell on his hand. "Come on, Bobby, we need to talk to you. Maybe just one eye?" That would be Tee. She was always making him do something he didn't want to. "I double-dip-dare you to open your eyes."

How many times had she used that line on him when she wanted him to cooperate? Eating peas, taking a bath, getting up for school—everything had been a dare that gained him a double-scoop ice-cream cone if he did what he was told.

What the hell, some ice cream might clear this awful taste in his mouth. He took a deep breath that made him groan, and forced his eyes wide open.

"Good job." The cool clasp on his hand tightened. "We thought you might sleep for another day or two."

Her face was a fuzzy circle with black on top. Somebody stood behind her, too far away to see. "Who's here?"

"Dad's with me. How do you feel?"

"Like crap." This breath hurt a little less. "What happened?" Thea didn't answer, and he thought she'd gone away. "Tee?"

"We hoped you'd tell us. What's the last thing you remember?"

"He doesn't need to think about that right now." The old man sounded as if he had gravel in his throat.

For once Bobby agreed with him. "I…I…" He shook his head, then wished he hadn't. "I don't remember anything." Something lurked out there, beyond the edges of his mind. Something bad. He couldn't reach it.

"He needs to rest." Bobby didn't think he'd ever heard this voice before. "Come back in a couple of hours."

"Sure." Tee bent over, and her face came into focus. She looked really scared. "Dr. Peyton's throwing us out. We'll be back later, though. You get some sleep."

He was too tired to argue. Gratefully, he stopped trying to keep his eyes open.

Thea straightened and let Bobby's hand slip away to lie on the blanket. His tanned face looked gray. The doctors said he would be fine. She wasn't sure she believed them.

"Althea." Her dad waited with the door open. Taking a deep breath and one last look, Thea stepped into the hall.

Rafe waited there, big and solid and comforting. She wanted to walk straight into him, let his arms fold around her, make her warm.

But the cold anger flowing from the man just behind her stopped any move like that.

Rafe drove his hands into the pockets of his jeans and leaned back against the wall. "Did he wake up?"

Thea nodded. "For a couple of seconds."

"Did he say anything about the wreck?"

Before she could answer, her dad stepped forward. "He doesn't remember. Don't think you can go in there badgering him, either. You'll stay out of that room until I say otherwise."

Without seeming to move, Rafe suddenly looked much bigger, much more formidable. His brown eyes, usually so warm, hardened. "I have no intention of talking to Bobby until he's fully awake and on the mend."

Her dad gave a single nod and turned on his heel toward the waiting room.

"But," Rafe went on, "I will be asking questions. This isn't something we can sweep under the rug. Three people were seriously injured tonight."

Robert Maxwell gave no sign that he'd heard, only

walked down the hallway and around the corner, out of sight.

Thea put a hand on Rafe's arm. "Have you talked to the surgeon? Do we know anything about Dan and Jerry? About the man in the other truck?"

His face softened a little as he looked down at her. "Tom Bonner was the other driver. He's got some minor internal injuries. Plus he lost an eye."

Black lines swirled in front of her eyes for a few seconds. She squeezed them shut, then looked up again. "What about the other two?"

"Jerry's still in surgery. Dan..." He cleared his throat and glanced away, as if he wanted to escape. "Dan Aiken has a broken neck. He's in a coma. They won't know the extent of his injuries until he wakes up." Rafe brought his gaze back to hers. "It doesn't look good, Thea. I'm sorry."

She let her hand fall to her side. "Oh, my God. And it's all Bobby's fault."

Rafe wished she hadn't said that. As the investigating officer, he would have to remember a statement by the sister of the suspect, stating her conviction of his guilt.

But he wouldn't be writing up the report tonight. He put his arm around her shoulders. "It's 6:00 a.m. Let's see if there's somewhere in this town open for a cup of coffee, maybe breakfast."

She let him guide her, less because she wanted to leave, he suspected, than because she wasn't really thinking. Robert Maxwell's glare, when Thea told him where they were going didn't help. After a ten-minute walk in the frigid wind they found a run-down diner with its lights on and an Open sign posted. Rafe took Thea's coat off and laid it over the back of a booth, urged her to sit, then sat across the table. When the coffee came she picked up the mug, but set it down without drinking. The breakfast he ordered for her went untouched.

"Thea." He gathered her cold hands between his. "Say something. Doesn't matter what. I'm listening."

She stared at him, her eyes blank. "This is so…so awful," she whispered. "What if Dan can't walk anymore?"

"Everybody'll have to deal with it."

"How? How will Bobby ever be happy again, knowing he caused such a disaster?"

Rafe winced. Maybe he should caution her that there are some things she shouldn't say—to him, anyway. "Let's just concentrate on the here and now. They're all alive and the doctors are doing everything they can to be sure that's the way things stay."

With a little moan, Thea drew her hands out of his, propped her elbows on the table and buried her face in her palms. They sat like that, without saying a word or eating the food on their plates, until the sun rose over Bozeman.

AT THE HOSPITAL once again, they left Robert in the general waiting area and went to find Jerry's mother in the surgical waiting room. She was dabbing at her eyes with a handkerchief.

Thea sat down in the next chair. "How's Jerry, Mrs. Heath? Is the surgery done?" She gripped her hands together until the knuckles bleached white.

Mrs. Heath nodded. "They had to put steel pins in his leg and his arm to keep the bones together. They took out his spleen and part of his liver." The handkerchief came into play again. "But he's alive. And talking."

"You talked to him?" Rafe was glad Thea asked the question before he could. "Did he say what happened?"

"I didn't need him to say what happened." Mrs. Heath got to her feet and walked over to the window overlooking the hospital parking lot. "Everybody in town knew your brother would kill somebody someday, drinking and driving the way he did. We all just hoped it would be himself, and not one of our boys."

Thea gasped as if she'd been slapped. Rafe stepped forward. "Mrs. Heath—"

The older woman looked him in the eye. Overnight she had aged ten years. "I'm expecting you to do your duty, Deputy. That boy had better get what's coming to him, better be put somewhere he can't do this to anybody else's son."

She walked to the doorway, then turned back. "My husband's already gone to talk to the lawyer. We'll be checking up on you, making sure this case gets prosecuted as far as it will go. We're farmers, not millionaires. Somebody's going to pay Jerry's hospital and doctor bills." Her gaze went to Thea's face. "And I think we all know who that will be." Her footsteps in the hallway sounded loud in the silence she left behind.

Suddenly, after a night without tears, Thea put her face in her hands and started to cry.

ROBERT MAXWELL REFUSED to ride home in the deputy's truck. The mayor of Bozeman was a friend of his and had an extra pickup to lend. Leaving Thea at the hospital, Robert drove himself back to Walking Stones.

Beth Peace met him in the kitchen with a cup of coffee. "How is he?"

"He'll be fine." Robert sat and propped his elbows on the table, holding the mug with both hands. He didn't have to worry that the coffee would be too hot. Beth's coffee was always just right. "Busted ribs, bruises and cuts. Less than he deserved, probably."

She settled into the chair across from him. "And the other two?"

He closed his eyes. "The Heath boy will do okay. Nobody knows about Dan Aiken, though. He broke his neck." She gasped, and Robert nodded. "It's gonna be bad. They'll be bringing lawyers in from all over the state. I'd best get in touch with mine."

They sat for as long as his coffee lasted. The sun rose high enough to shine through the window over the sink, warming the room, setting a little halo around Beth's brown hair.

"How are *you?*" Only Beth would ask that question.

He didn't really have an answer. "Same as usual. I've been dealing with Bobby's screwups since he was in grade school. I guess I can deal with this one, too." Brave words, when he wasn't sure of any such thing.

Beth stood when he did and took the mug out of his hands. She stared up at him, a short, plump woman with a sweet, worried face. "It'll be all right, Robert. Somehow it will turn out okay."

He put a hand on her shoulder. "I hope you're right." With a sigh, he straightened his shoulders. "I'll be out at the breeding barn. Call if anybody needs to talk to me."

"When will Thea be home?"

"She said she was staying till Bobby woke up again. I guess the deputy will drive her home sometime." His gut tightened at the thought. Anything Althea said to Rafferty would be used against Bobby. Somehow or other, he'd have to get them split up. "Let me know when she gets here."

"Of course."

Without looking back, he stepped onto the mud porch, grabbed his coat and hat and headed for his truck. The work didn't stop for weather or holidays or car wrecks. A solid day of labor would make the time pass, keep his mind occupied. Concentrating on what had to be done, he wouldn't think about Bobby, wouldn't try to anticipate what lay ahead. There was nothing he could do about the trouble facing them until he knew exactly what it was.

And there was sure as hell nothing he could do about the mistakes he'd made in the past...except to carry the guilt.

WHEN BOBBY OPENED his eyes, Thea leaned over the bed. "There you are. What can I get for you?"

He stared at her for a few seconds with a blank expression. She started to wonder if he recognized her. "Bobby?"

In another moment, his eyes changed. Emptiness gave way to confusion, struggle and fear. Then horror.

Like a window shade, his eyelids lowered. When he opened them again, his expression was completely different—his old devil-may-care attitude had returned. "Hey, Thea. What's a guy got to do to get some food around here?"

"Are you hungry?" She reached for the call button.

"Nah. Not really. What's going on?"

She looked at him closely. "I think you know what's going on. So you tell me."

"Don't have a clue." He tried to shrug, but gasped with pain and stopped.

Thea wasn't fooled. Often when Bobby lied, a muscle twitched at his temple. Just as it was twitching now. "What do you remember?"

"I remember this little hottie dancing on a table at the party." He parodied a lascivious grin. "We were all putting bills into her bikini—mine was a fifty with my name on it."

"Right." She hadn't seen him look at another girl since

getting involved with Megan, so the story didn't bother her. "Then what?"

"No clue."

After she gazed at him in silence for a minute, he shifted uncomfortably. "Okay, I do remember getting in the truck. Jer sat inside, but Dan—man, he was plowed—wanted to sit in the bed. I started driving." He avoided looking at her. "That's all I remember. I swear."

It could be true. "Were you drinking?"

"Nah."

Her heart leaped with hope, which died quickly. "Bobby."

"I swear—" He glanced at her face. "Okay, I had a couple."

"How many?"

"Who knows? Do you keep track of how many drinks you have at a party?"

"If I'm driving, I do." She didn't say anything about his promise. But she had no doubt he remembered.

After a little while he said, "So, what happened to the truck? Is it okay?"

Thea nearly lost her temper right then. She had to walk away, pacing across the room and back a couple of times before she could control her voice. "The truck is totaled."

"Shit."

"Anything else you're worried about?"

He hunched a shoulder, as if to say not really.

"You're unbelievable." Back at the side of the bed, she took his chin in her fingers and forced him to meet her eyes. "You've got two friends in the hospital and all you can worry about is your stupid truck?"

"Jerry and Dan were hurt?"

Did he really not know? "How do you think you got hurt, Bobby?"

"I guess I totaled the truck."

"You don't remember the accident?"

"I—" He pulled his chin out of her grasp. "No. There's something there, but I'm not sure what it is. Noise, lights, somebody yelling." Slowly lifting one hand, he wiped his palm across his forehead. "What happened to Jerry and Dan?"

"They were hurt." She forestalled his next question. "Very badly."

"But they'll be okay, right?" He seemed completely sincere, totally concerned. She didn't know whether to trust him or not. The little muscle in his temple wasn't twitching. Was that positive proof?

Complete frankness might determine whether he was telling the truth or not. "Jerry will be okay, eventually. The man in the other truck lost an eye—"

Thea ignored the foul comment her brother made. "Except for that, he'll be okay."

She paused and Bobby said, "What about Dan? Dan'll be okay, right?"

She hardened her heart against his worry. "Dan's in a coma with a broken neck. They don't know whether he'll make it or not."

Bobby let his head drop back. Tears crept out from beneath his closed eyelids.

"God," he whispered, and it wasn't a prayer. "Dan's gonna die." He pulled in a deep, shaken breath.

"And I killed him."

CHAPTER EIGHT

AT NOON, with Bobby asleep again and Dan's condition unchanged, Thea allowed Rafe to persuade her to go home. November first's weather was cold and bright. After almost twelve hours under the dim lights of the hospital, her eyes watered when hit by the sharp sunlight. The bite of the wind made her shiver.

She climbed into the front seat of Rafe's truck and wiped her cheeks with her coat sleeve. Getting in beside her, he gave her a worried look. "Are you okay?"

Would she ever be really okay again? "It's the sun," she explained. "I think I've already cried my tears out on your shoulder." She summoned up a small smile. "Thanks."

His quiet grin warmed her. "Glad to help."

As they left Bozeman, a thought hit her. "Damn. We didn't call Cassie and Jolie."

"Your sisters?"

She nodded. "They hadn't even crossed my mind till just now. Jolie couldn't help much, all the way from California. But Cassie lives in Billings. She'd want to be told."

"Do you know her number?"

"I should, shouldn't I?" What did that say about the state of their family? "But I don't. She'd be at work anyway. She's an investigator for Child Protective Services."

"There's got to be an office number listed in the directory.'' He reached into the console box between the seats and pulled out a cellular phone. ''So give her a call.''

She stared at him. ''You make things seem so easy.''

He shrugged. ''It's no big deal. Call.''

Thea thought she might get Cassie's voice mail, but her sister picked up on the second ring. ''Cassie Warren. Can I help you?''

''Cassie, it's Thea. I've got some bad news.'' She rushed on, over her sister's quick breath. ''Bobby's been hurt in a truck wreck, along with a couple of his friends.''

The line went dead for a minute.

''Damn.'' When she spoke, Cassie's tone was bitter, weary. ''He was drinking and driving, wasn't he?''

''I think so. He doesn't remember exactly what happened.''

Her sister sighed. ''How badly is he hurt?''

''He'll be okay but...but Dan Aiken is in really bad shape.''

''Is he going to make it?''

''I don't think the doctors know.''

''Oh, God. Bobby could be charged with manslaughter, you realize that? I thought you were going to talk to him about his drinking.''

''I did! He promised me he would stop. But—'' Thea became aware of Rafe, hearing every word she said even if he tried not to. Should she be saying these things? Didn't she trust him enough to be honest about what Bobby had done?

''But he lied,'' Cassie said with scorn. ''I remember how that goes—I used to promise anything to stay out of trouble.''

Thea remembered, too. She'd been the one left to face their dad's anger. ''So, anyway, I thought you should know.''

"I'm not sure when I can get to the hospital. I have to find somebody who can take care of Zak. But I could call Bobby in the meantime. What room did you say he's in?"

With the details conveyed, Cassie said goodbye. Thea turned off the cell phone and looked at Rafe. "Thanks again. She was…she needed to know."

"Sounded to me like she gave you a hard time."

She leaned her head back and closed her burning eyes. "We had a fight about Bobby the last time she was home. I guess she thought I could keep something like this from happening." The tears she wanted to control slipped down her cheeks. "She's probably right. And you were right. I should have made him stop, made him change, a long time before now."

Rafe's palm covered the back of her hand as she held the phone. "You are not his parent. That's who should have dealt with Bobby. And I think your dad knows it."

"Even if he does…" She yawned widely, then yawned again as the night without sleep caught up to her. "I'm sorry. I don't even remember what I was saying." Which wasn't quite true.

But Rafe accepted the dodge. "We've got about half an hour until we reach the ranch. Why don't you take a nap?"

"You didn't get any more sleep than I did."

"No arguments. Put your seat back and close your eyes."

That was all it took. The next thing Thea knew, Rafe was leaning over her from outside, stroking a fingertip lightly down her cheek. "Do you want to wake up and walk into the house, or should I carry you?"

She gazed up at him, thinking that being carried would have definite advantages—his arms around her, his chest under her cheek, his mouth near enough for a kiss…

Scrambling into a sitting position, Thea felt her cheeks

grow hot. "I—I'll walk, thanks. You've done more than enough to take care of me for one day."

He stepped back to let her climb down from the truck. "I don't know about that," he said softly. But before she could think through the implications of that statement, the front door opened and Beth stepped outside.

"You come in here right now before you freeze to death." She shooed Thea inside. "You, too, Deputy. You'll need a cup of coffee before you drive back to town."

Rafe grinned, but shook his head. "I'd like to, but I've got work to do. Maybe next time." He looked at Thea. Her dark hair was tousled, her eyes heavy, with big circles underneath. She'd lost all the color in her face. He thought she was beautiful.

"I'll give you a call later," he promised her. And himself. "Get some rest."

RAFE MADE the long drive back to Paradise Corners alone, except for a lingering trace of Thea's scent in the air. Even that disappeared when he opened the window to let in a cold wind so he could stay awake.

Judge LeVay was waiting for him when he walked into the office.

Rafe went to his desk without a pause. "Maxwell called you?"

"He didn't have a choice. You've got a hell of a mess on your hands."

"There's not much doubt about what happened. The kid was drunk, he ran a stop sign, and now there's hell to pay."

"So what are you planning to do about it?"

"I'm going to talk to Bobby. I'm going to see how Dan Aiken gets along. I'm going to figure out what charges need to be filed and file them. Then it's up to the lawyers." He glanced at LeVay. "And the judges."

LeVay got to his feet. "If you bring any serious charges against his son, Maxwell will call in every favor he's owed to keep that boy out of prison. And then he'll make sure he destroys you."

Rafe stood up behind the desk. "And you'll be helping him?"

The judge suddenly looked old. He wiped a hand over his face. "That depends on whether I decide I'm ready to retire. And move to Arizona, once Maxwell gets me fired as well." He nodded, picked up his hat and left the office.

Dropping back into his chair, Rafe propped his elbows on the desk and put his face in his hands.

LeVay didn't know the half of it. Sure, Maxwell would use whatever leverage he could find to keep Bobby from suffering the consequences of his actions, whether that was what was best for the boy or not. And he'd take revenge on anybody he thought opposed him.

And Thea...Thea was caught in the middle. How would she balance her loyalty to her family, her love for her brother, against the relationship she and Rafe had just started to build? He didn't know much about family ties, not having any of his own, but from what he'd seen he could guess how she would feel. These were the people she'd loved all her life. With her sense of loyalty and responsibility, she would support her family if the situation came to a showdown between the law and Bobby Maxwell.

The law, meaning himself. He could pursue the case, and most likely lose any chance of a relationship with Thea. Or he could let Bobby off, forswearing his duty, disregarding the justice owed to Jerry and Dan, and to Tom Bonner. That would make things easier for Thea.

But he'd already done that, more than once. He'd taken Bobby home after the fight at the bar instead of throwing him into a cell where he belonged. He'd let Bobby get away without consequences after the episode up at Walters's place.

As a result, Dan Aiken might have lost his chance to grow up, get married, make a life. Thea might feel responsible for Bobby's accident, but her part in the whole disaster was small compared to her dad's, Judge LeVay's...and Rafe's.

Had *he* fulfilled his responsibility to the community, those three boys would most likely be waking up in their own beds tomorrow morning, getting ready for another day's work.

Instead, he'd let his own self-interest blind him to what was right. Wanting Thea, he'd put making her happy ahead of every other consideration. If he wasn't careful, he'd do the same thing again. Questioning Bobby was only the first step in the process of seeing this situation through to the end. Thea would hate that, and every other procedure he used to follow the letter of the law. Thea would hate it...and then she'd hate him.

Which was just too damn bad, Rafe thought wearily. Because that was the only choice he could make.

THE RECEPTIONIST at the clinic in California where Jolie worked said she hadn't come in from making rounds at the hospital. Thea left a message for her to call and then sat down to a bowl of vegetable soup and a tuna sandwich, her first food of the day.

Beth was kneading dough for bread. The soft sound of her fists pounding into the flour ball was a reminder of the hours Thea had spent at this table doing homework, or helping Bobby with his. Dan had been part of those hours, too—the two boys had become friends in the sixth grade and Dan had spent a lot of time at the ranch ever since. Bobby never spent much time at the Aiken house—folks around Paradise Corners had rarely invited the Maxwell kids to stay the night, to stay for dinner or to come over for the afternoon. Thea didn't know if it was her dad's money or his ruthless arrogance that had cut them off from regular social relationships. Probably both.

"You talked to Bobby?" Beth set the dough in a bowl and covered it with a towel. "Your dad said he's got busted ribs and such, but was okay otherwise."

Thea stirred her soup. "He seems to be, except he doesn't remember what happened. He says." She put the spoon down, too tired to eat. "But it's pretty easy to figure out."

"What did the deputy have to say?"

"Not much. Dad ordered him to stay away from Bobby, and Rafe said he would until Bobby was feeling better."

"Do you think he'll arrest Bobby?"

"I don't know. I…I don't even know what he *should* do."

The housekeeper turned around to stare at her. "Surely you don't want to see your brother arrested, maybe put in jail. He's only nineteen. Still a boy."

"He's not too young to know what he was doing when he got behind the wheel drunk. There should be some kind of consequences for that decision." She massaged her temples with her fingertips. Her head had started to ache from too little sleep, too many tears and too much worry. "I guess I'd better get out to the breeding barn and get to work."

"You didn't eat anything. And what you should do is go to bed. You're exhausted."

"But we're already one short, with Bobby gone. I'll be okay." Pushing away from the table, she stood up. The kitchen started spinning around her head. Black dots swam in front of her eyes. Thea staggered, catching hold of the back of the chair to keep from falling. "Whew…"

"What did I say?" Beth put an arm around her waist and headed for the bedroom wing. "You'll be no good to them like this. You take off your clothes and climb into bed. I'll call you for dinner."

Thea knew she should protest. Her dad would expect her out at the barn if she was on the property. That was her job.

But her room was warm, her bed smooth, the chance to stop thinking too appealing. Fumbling with buttons and zippers and boots, she fell into bed in just her underwear, and was asleep right away.

BOBBY ASKED about Dan every time somebody came into the room. Nobody would tell him anything. The nurses just looked away, took his temperature and wrote down the numbers on the machines around him, then left. A doctor stopped by late in the afternoon, but all he would say was, "There's been no change."

"What does that mean?" Bobby tried to sit up in bed, but the knifelike pain in his ribs forced him down again.

The doctor looked up from the chart. His face was a blank mask, no expression at all. "Your friend hasn't woken up from his coma. We don't know if he will. And if he does, we don't think he'll be able to move below the neck. Clear enough for you?" Without waiting for an answer, he left, letting the door swing shut behind him.

At least Dan was still alive. Bobby stared at the bumpy tiles on the ceiling and tried to think. He remembered leaving the party. And yeah, he was drunk. So were Dan and Jerry. Dan had been drinking beer and tequila. He'd thrown up a couple of times on the way to the truck, and decided fresh air would make him feel better, so he'd wanted to ride in the back. Didn't matter how cold it was, Dan wanted to be outside.

So Jer and he had given up arguing and climbed into the cab themselves. That was when the shooters he'd had—six? seven? ten?—hit Bobby like a brick wall. That's where his brain stopped now, refusing to go any farther.

The door to the hospital room opened again. Megan peeked around the edge. "Bobby? Can I come in?"

"Sure." He didn't want to be so glad to see her. In a way, this was all her fault. If she hadn't stood him up… "What are you doing here?"

She came to the bed and picked up his hand in both of her soft ones. "I wanted to see if you were all right."

"Your daddy let you do that?" The question sounded meaner than he'd meant it to.

Her eyes widened. Megan wasn't used to him being mad at her. "Racey came to see Dan. She's so upset she needed somebody to drive, and Mama said I could come while Daddy's at work. What's wrong?"

"Besides me lying here with busted ribs, and Jerry's broken leg, and Dan being practically dead?" Bobby looked away from the hurt on her face. "Oh, and you breaking our date?"

She put his hand down on the bed again. "I told you, Daddy wouldn't let me leave the house."

"Yeah, you told me."

After a minute of silence, she said, "You don't believe me?"

The honest surprise in her voice made him squirm. "I heard you were talking to Hank Reeves the other day."

"I see him at the grocery store sometimes, or the post office, when I'm working."

"What a coincidence."

"No, I think he keeps an eye on what I do and tries to

make it seem like a coincidence when he shows up at the same place.''

Bobby looked at her again. ''He's stalking you?''

But she didn't react to his worry. ''He doesn't want to hurt me.'' Her chin lifted. ''But he wants us to go out again.''

''He treated you lousy, Megan. Remember? If he'd been good to you, you wouldn't have started going out with me.''

''That's not what Hank thinks. Hank thinks I started going out with you because you're rich.''

Bobby turned his head toward the window.. ''Did you?''

He wanted her to protest, to swear that she loved him for himself. But when she didn't say anything for a long time, he looked over.

Megan's sweet face was white, her gaze as cold as he'd ever seen it. ''You don't trust me. You think I'm seeing Hank behind your back. You think I lied to you when I said I couldn't keep our date. You don't even believe that I love you.''

''Megan—'' He sat up and put out a hand, ignoring the fire of pain in his ribs and shoulder. She stepped back so he couldn't possibly reach her without getting up.

''That's not fair. I don't know what else I can do to prove how much I love you. I lie to my dad. I sneak out at all hours of the night. I—'' She looked down at the floor. ''I made love with you,'' she said softly. ''If that doesn't mean anything…'' When she shook her head, Bobby saw a bright tear fly off her cheek.

''Megan, honey, come here.''

Instead, she backed up again. ''I guess I'll be going. Racey's got to work tonight, and I need to be back before my dad gets home. I hope you're better soon, Bobby.''

With more tears running down her cheeks, she turned and disappeared behind the door.

Bobby dropped back against the pillow and swore.

BETH CALLED to say that she'd sent Thea to bed instead of out to work. Jaw clenched, Robert did the pregnancy checks, working straight through till dark. Not a hard job, compared to most on a spread like this, but the end of the day found him exhausted. Walking to his truck, he thought he could lie down on the frozen ground and go to sleep. He forced himself on and finally climbed into the driver's seat, breathing harder than the short walk warranted, but thankful to be sitting down for the first time since morning. He thought back and realized he'd been awake since 4:00 a.m. the previous day. That went a long way toward explaining why he was so tired.

When he parked in the driveway behind the house, he sat with his head back for a moment, gathering the energy to get out and walk into the kitchen. Beth would have a cup of coffee waiting; she watched for him to come home, no matter what time it was. She made his life livable. Robert didn't know what he'd do without her. He hoped to hell he never had to find out.

On the mud porch, he sat down to take off his boots. Beth didn't like having barn dirt tracked into her kitchen. Damn, his legs ached. Rubbing his hands over his calves and shins, he could feel the ridges in his skin caused by the seamed leather, and the bump of swelling on his leg above where each boot ended. He'd been wearing these same boots for more than ten years. Hard to believe they were too small all at once. Getting old was a pain in the butt.

With his house shoes on, he stepped inside, and found his coffee on the counter by the door, same as usual. He took a grateful sip. He needed all the energy he could get. There was book work to do tonight before he could get some sleep.

"Thanks for the caffeine," he said to Beth.

She turned from the stove with a smile on her face. "You're welcome. Dinner will be about fifteen minutes. Can I get you some cheese and crackers while you wait? Or some of those peanuts I fried up last week?"

Robert shook his head. "Just the coffee's fine." He sat down in his chair at the table. "Thea still asleep?"

Beth shook her head as she stirred her gravy. "Deputy Rafferty brought her home a little after twelve. She slept all afternoon, but I woke her up a little while ago to shower before dinner."

"Damn deputy."

She glanced at his way. "You don't like him dating Thea?"

"I don't like him anywhere around here at all. Bobby's in enough trouble without having the law practically living in the house." Robert set down his mug and rubbed his hands over his eyes. He couldn't remember ever being this tired before. Not after missing just one night's sleep. "I called the hospital. Bobby's doing okay. He'll be sent home in a day or two."

"And Dan?"

"No change." Robert picked up his coffee again, to have something to do. He felt bad about that boy, damn bad. Dan had worked with them in the summers, when he wasn't needed on his own family's small spread—he had an interest in ranching that Bobby completely lacked. Always asking questions, making suggestions, rethinking decisions…he'd been a trial to deal with, but at least he was involved. Bobby did the work he was told to do, but his mind and heart belonged somewhere else.

And only the good Lord knew where. If the boy was passionate about anything, dedicated to a place or a job or a way of life, Robert hadn't heard about it. The only thing Bobby appeared to be interested in was having a good time.

A soft footstep sounded in the hallway behind him, and Thea came into the kitchen. Her hand touched his shoulder briefly as she passed. "Hi, Dad. How'd things go today?"

He took a sip of coffee. "Would have been better with more people to do the work. Most folks can't afford to take a day off to sleep."

Thea stopped with her hand raised as she reached to get a glass out of the cupboard. She considered protesting the reprimand. Since she was sixteen, she'd worked right alongside him, taking vacation time only if he did. One extra day off didn't make her a slacker.

But saying so wouldn't have any effect on her dad. "I'm sure that's true. I should have been out there."

"I don't like having to depend on outsiders to get the work done. That's what family is for."

Beth turned away from the roast she was carving, a frown on her face aimed at the man across the room. Thea caught the housekeeper's eye and shook her head. No sense making this a full-fledged argument. With a sigh, Beth went back to her slicing, Thea ran water into the glass and took a long drink, then faced her dad. "So, how's the pregnancy rate? Still up around eighty percent?"

They talked cattle for a few minutes, until the phone rang. Thea moved to the wall phone. "Walking Stones Ranch."

"Thea, it's Jolie." Her oldest sister's voice was quiet, authoritative. "What's happened?"

Once again, Thea explained. "I know there's nothing you can do from California, but I thought we should tell you."

"I'm glad you called. You said the boys were taken to the hospital in Bozeman? Have Dan's parents called in a specialist? There are several good people in the Bozeman area."

"I don't know what they've considered. They're not exactly talking to me, or Dad. But I doubt they've got the money for super-specialized doctors. Mr. Aiken still works a second job as a night guard at the bank."

"Given that the whole situation is Bobby's fault, I would think Dad would be willing to pay whatever it takes to aid Dan's recovery."

"You'll have to talk to him about that." Her sister's grasp of facts, her ability to take charge always flustered Thea. She felt slow and a little incompetent when Jolie was around. "Here he is." Handing the phone to her dad, she moved back to the counter to get her glass of water and stared out the window over the sink as she listened to his half of the conversation.

"I'm fine." Hearing his neutral tone, Thea doubted Jolie would think he was glad to talk with his oldest daughter for the first time in months. "Bobby'll be home in a day or two."

He cleared his throat. "I expect I'll be able to help them out some. Have to find out what the problems are, and that means waiting for the boy to wake up."

Jolie must have voiced an opinion.

"I don't see that at all." His voice tightened with irritation. "Those boys had a choice. They could have gone home with somebody else. They bear some responsibility for what happened." Another tense silence as he listened. "Considering that you're fifteen hundred miles away, I don't think you've got any business telling me how to handle this situation and what I do or don't owe the people around here. You want to get involved with what's going on, then come home.'' Banging the phone into its cradle, he stalked out of the kitchen.

Beth hurried to the doorway. "Dinner's ready, Robert."

"I'll eat in my office," he growled, then slammed the door at the end of the hall.

"The Brady Bunch we aren't," Thea commented.

"Some days, I could strangle that man." The housekeeper started to fill his plate. "If I didn't know that his gruffness hides a lot of pain, I swear, I'd just leave. Let him take care of himself."

"But who would take care of me?" Thea asked the question with a laugh, not expecting a serious answer, hoping to tease Beth out of her uncharacteristic impatience.

But the other woman regarded her with a serious expression. "I think I know the answer to that." She set the dinner plate on a tray, filled a mug with fresh coffee and added a piece of blueberry pie. "I'm just not sure whether you're smart enough to figure it out, let alone brave enough to take the chance." Hoisting the tray on one hip, Beth left the kitchen without another word.

A NURSE CAME IN about 3:00 a.m. to check his temperature. They'd disconnected the rest of the machines around dinnertime, so she left in just a few minutes, without saying a word. Alone again, Bobby lay in bed in the dark, waiting for sleep that didn't come.

Finally, he stopped waiting. He rolled to his left side, the one that didn't hurt so much, pushed himself up on one arm and swung his legs off the bed. The world dipped and swayed around him, and he thought he might be sick. But after a minute the dizziness eased. Still braced on his left arm, he slid his feet to the floor and stood up.

Pain speared through him, but not as bad as he'd expected. The first step hurt, the second a little less. By the time he got to the bathroom, he was feeling almost normal, except for the ache in his ribs and his head and his back. And except for the agony in his soul.

Instead of heading back to bed, he detoured toward the door to the hall, pulled it open with his left hand and sort of revolved his body through the opening. The nurse's desk was far down to the right. A quick survey of room numbers told him that Dan's room was in the opposite direction. Letting the door shut softly behind him, Bobby hobbled down the hallway to the left.

He didn't think about the possibility of finding anybody else in the room with Dan until he opened the door and saw them all there—Mr. and Mrs. Aiken in chairs on either side of the bed, Jessica and Kelly, Dan's sisters, and Nick, his little brother. The kids, all younger than Dan, were asleep on a couch against the wall. Mr. Aiken was asleep, too, with his head in his arms resting beside Danny's legs on the opposite side of the bed.

But Mrs. Aiken was wide awake. She turned toward the door as Bobby stepped into the room. Her eyes went round as she recognized him. "What are you doing here?" she whispered.

Bobby took a step forward. "I wanted to see him."

She got to her feet and stood in front of the bed like a guard dog. "Haven't you done enough damage?"

She'd never liked him very much. Bobby tried to be gentle and quiet. "I won't hurt him. I just needed—"

"*You* needed. It's always about you." Mrs. Aiken walked toward him. Bobby backed up unsteadily. "You dragged my son around like a toy—played with him when you felt like it, ignored him when you had something better to do. Now you *need* to see him? Make sure he's still breathing? Find out whether or not you're gonna be charged with murder?" Her voice had risen. Mr. Aiken stirred, then looked up. "Paula? What's..." Now he, too, stood. "What the hell's he doing in here?"

Bobby gave up. "I'm sorry. I'm going." Fumbling behind him with his left hand, he found the door handle and pulled. The move twisted his ribs, and tears of pain stung his eyes. He got the door open with his shoulder and half stepped, half fell back into the hallway. Then he lurched back toward his room.

"You stay outta here," Mr. Aiken yelled after him. "Don't you ever come near my son again!"

Bobby fell onto his bed, sobbing at the pain. His body, his mind, his...heart...was one big burning ache. Whatever punishment waited for him, Bobby figured it didn't matter much.

He'd already arrived in hell.

CHAPTER NINE

WHEN THE CADILLAC pulled up to the front of the hospital, the nurse opened the passenger door, then moved to help Bobby out of the wheelchair. But he brushed off her hand, getting up and into the car by himself. The old biddy still won the contest—she closed the door before he could.

Turning out of the hospital grounds into traffic, his dad threw him an irritated glance. "What happened to your manners?"

Bobby shrugged. What was the point of talking about it?

He got a cuff on the shoulder for that. Not hard, and it wouldn't have hurt—normally. This time, he bit his lip to keep from making a sound of pain.

"Answer me when I ask you a question."

His lowered defenses broke down completely. "What am I supposed to say? Was I supposed to thank her for treating me like a criminal while I was in there and like a baby on the way out? She only talked to me if there was a question she couldn't take care of any other way."

"You're surprised that people are treating you bad?"

Regretting he'd ever opened his mouth, Bobby turned to stare out the window.

But his dad wasn't finished. "You've been pushing the limit for months now. Something like this was bound to happen, and you can't blame anybody for being upset."

"Fine. I won't blame anybody." He didn't have to. The

culprit—a two-dollar word for murderer—was right inside of him.

They rode through the outskirts of Bozeman without talking. "I've heard from three different lawyers," his dad said once they'd reached the interstate. "They're getting ready to file big claims with the insurance company."

Like money would make any difference if Dan died. "I guess that's what insurance is for."

Robert Maxwell hit the steering wheel with the heel of his hand. "You don't give a rat's ass about any of this, do you? Doesn't bother you how much money you cost me, how much you mess up your life and your friends' lives. What *does* matter to you, boy? What do you care about?"

Bobby thought about Megan. About spending warm, sunny days with her in a house by the ocean. About a job that didn't involve cows or horses. Or dirt or wind or rain.

"Nothing," he told his dad. Nothing he'd ever have, anyway.

To THEA'S SURPRISE, her dad took Thursday off to bring Bobby home from the hospital, and Cassie made an effort to be there when they arrived at the house shortly after two o'clock. They were all sitting around the fireplace making uncomfortable small talk, cups of tea and coffee—for Zak, hot chocolate—in their hands, when Beth answered the doorbell.

She stood silent for a moment, hiding the visitor behind one open panel of the door. Then, shaking her head, she stepped aside. Holding his hat in his hands, Rafe came into the house.

Before Thea could find her voice, her dad got to his feet. "What do you want?"

"Good afternoon, Mr. Maxwell. Thea." She thought his eyes warmed a little when he looked at her, but she wasn't sure. He nodded to Cassie and Zak, then took on her father again. "I need to ask Bobby some questions."

Robert Maxwell moved to stand between Bobby, lying on the couch, and Rafe. "He's not answering questions today. The boy just got home, for God's sake."

Rafe nodded. "That's lucky for him. Two boys and a twenty-year-old father-to-be haven't been so fortunate. I've given your son as much time as I can spare. I need some answers."

Thea glanced at Bobby, saw him close his eyes and press his lips together. Did he think he could make himself invisible somehow and avoid this scene?

She set her mug on the hearth and stood up. "Dad, surely Rafe can ask a few questions for his report without hurting Bobby. It's probably more stressful to fight than just to cooperate and get things over with."

Robert fixed her with a withering stare. "I want a lawyer present before anybody in this family says one more word to the deputy, here."

"Come on, Dad." Cassie was wiping up a chocolate spill on the hardwood floor. "The surest way to draw attention is to act suspicious. Why don't you just let the man ask his questions and be on his way?" She gave Rafe a smile. "He doesn't look like he's planning a lynching this afternoon, anyway."

Thea felt a fire in her stomach that she recognized as jealousy. Cassie, with her red hair and creamy skin, her athletic build and flirtatious ways, had always attracted boys like honeybees to a flower. Thea had watched from afar, never understanding the technique. She'd had her share of male attention, but not the kind Cassie usually received.

The kind she was getting now, from Rafe—the sexy grin, the warmth in his brown eyes, unmistakable this time.

"This is lousy weather for a lynching," he said, as if they'd been friends for years. "I'd settle for a cup of coffee and a few simple answers."

"I'll supply the coffee." Cassie got to her feet with the grace she'd always been able to command. "Come on, Zak. Let's see if Beth's got a batch of cookies finished." The little boy looked for a second as if he would refuse, and Cassie's smile wavered. He glanced at Rafe, at his grand-dad, then stood up without protest and followed his mother out of the room. The hesitation surprised Thea. Zak was usually obedient and quiet—too much so for anybody to believe he was really happy.

But Cassie's words had a softening effect on their dad. "You can ask what you want," he said grudgingly, and backed into his chair across the fireplace from Thea. "But I'll tell him what he can and can't answer."

Rafe nodded. "That'll work, for the time being anyway." He sat in the chair near the couch without being invited. "So, Bobby. What were you doing before about ten on Monday night?"

Bobby put an arm over his face. "I don't remember."

"How about Monday afternoon?"

"I don't remember."

"What's the last thing you do remember before waking up in the hospital?"

The boy on the couch started to shrug but winced, instead, and said nothing.

"Bobby, cooperate." Embarrassed beyond tolerance, Thea could hardly look at Rafe. "I can tell him what I know about where you were that night, but he'd rather hear it from you, I think."

"You can just keep what you know to yourself, young lady." Her dad used a tone she hadn't heard for years, as if she were a misbehaving eight-year-old.

"Excuse me, Mr. Maxwell." Rafe's voice was low and hard. "Thea is absolutely right. I can question her, and you, and every member of the household, if I need to." Somehow, the words carried more threat than their simple meaning suggested. "I would like to hear what Bobby has to say. If he won't tell me what happened, though, I have no choice but to use other sources." He looked at Bobby again. "I should tell you that I've already talked to Jerry Heath and I have his version of Monday night's events. You'd be wise to give me yours as quickly and as accurately as possible."

Bobby moved his arm and opened his eyes. "What'd he say?"

Rafe shook his head. "That's not the way this goes. What happened Monday night?"

"We went to a party, damn you. We left the party in my truck. Dan wanted to ride in the back. Jer and I argued with him, but he wouldn't come inside. That's all I remember."

"Were you drinking alcohol at the party?"

"Don't answer that." Robert Maxwell got to his feet again. "You've asked your questions, Deputy. Now get out."

"Not without his coffee." Cassie brought Rafe a mug. "And Beth sent out some cookies." Just like that, the tension eased. The finesse with which she defused the argument resulted from years of practice at getting out of any real trouble for the stunts she pulled as a teenager. Thea had never understood that skill, either.

"I know about Beth's cookies." The grin Rafe sent toward Thea recalled the night they'd met. "They're not something I can refuse."

Cassie controlled the conversation for the next few minutes. She was bright and dynamic, and she'd seen enough of the world outside Paradise Corners to be interesting to a man like Rafe. Thea listened and realized the narrowness of her own experience, bounded mostly by ranch work and the fences of Walking Stones. She'd chosen her life, and she loved it. But suddenly she caught a glimpse of what she'd given up by staying home.

"I appreciate the coffee." Rafe got to his feet. "And your cooperation." He said that without any sarcasm. Thea felt her cheeks heat up. "I'll be getting back to you as the investigation progresses."

"Don't do us any favors," her dad said.

For the first time, anger flashed in Rafe's face. "I already have, Mr. Maxwell." He caught Thea's eye. "Can I talk to you a minute?"

Thea was aware of Cassie's surprise as she followed Rafe out onto the porch. Then she forgot everything as she pulled the door shut behind her and he turned to look at her with that special light in his eyes.

"Can I see you alone? Soon?"

Her knees wobbled at the urgency in his voice, the warmth of his palm along her cheek. "I don't know. It's complicated."

"And going to get more so. If you wait until the situation straightens out..." He shook his head.

She shocked herself by asking, "Tonight?"

His ready grin was her reward. "That would be great. I'd pick you up, but...maybe you'd rather come to town?"

"Cassie and Zak won't be staying for dinner. I'll leave after they do."

"Sounds good. I'll have something for us to eat at my place." Regardless of who might be watching, he leaned close and brushed his mouth over hers. "Later."

"Mmm."

She watched him drive away into the graying afternoon. The sky had been spitting snow all day, and a decent accumulation was predicted for that night. Good thing she'd already put the snow tires on the Land Rover.

When she went inside, the great room was empty except for Cassie. "Zak's driving Beth crazy helping to make cookies. Dad got Bobby to bed and then marched off to his office." She dropped into a chair and stretched out her long legs. "Why in the world did a man as gorgeous as Rafe Rafferty come to Montana?"

"The fishing?" Thea picked up her cold coffee, trying to be detached.

"I didn't realize you and he were involved until he asked you to talk to him outside. To continue the metaphor, that's quite a catch you've made."

"I haven't made any kind of catch." Thea turned to the fire in an attempt to cover the heat in her cheeks. "We've been out a couple of times, that's all."

"Not as far as he's concerned." Cassie watched her over the top of her coffee mug. "What's this investigation going to do to your relationship?"

"Good question. I don't have an answer."

"Bobby's not going to get away with a slap on the wrist this time. I don't think your Rafe is the kind to ignore what's right in favor of what's easy."

"I wouldn't ask him to."

Her sister laughed without humor. "Then you're a better woman than I am. I'm furious with Bobby, and my heart aches for Dan's family. But I don't want my little brother in jail. And that's where Rafe is duty-bound to put him."

"Maybe not."

"You know better than that."

She did. But she didn't have to like it.

WHEN BOBBY WOKE UP, he couldn't tell for a minute where he was. The room was dark and cool, like the hospital, but the medicine smell was missing. He turned his head, saw the illuminated, digital numbers of his alarm clock and recognized his own bedroom. Oh, yeah—his dad had brought him home. Was that this afternoon, or yesterday?

Had Dan woken up yet? Was he still alive?

The door opened, letting in a wedge of light. "Bobby?" Cassie stepped across the threshold. "You awake?"

Talking to anybody was better than being alone with his thoughts. "Kinda. Turn on a light."

"I wanted to talk to you before I went back to Billings." She switched on a lamp, then leaned an elbow on the dresser. "How does it feel to be home?"

"About as lousy as it felt to be in the hospital, but the food's probably better."

She didn't say anything for a minute, then cleared her throat. "Thea called to check on Dan. No change." He didn't have a smart response to that piece of information. But Cassie didn't seem to expect one. "You've gotten yourself in a real mess this time."

"Thanks for the news. I hadn't noticed."

"I recognize the bluff, you know." Her hazel eyes, just like their dad's, seemed to see right through him. "You're scared spitless. And you deserve to be."

"Did you come in here to cheer me up?"

"I came in to let you know you'd better be doing some serious thinking."

"About what?"

"About how you're going to be arrested and charged with drunk driving and underage drinking, maybe even criminal-assault charges."

He shrugged the less painful shoulder. "It hasn't happened yet."

She raised her eyebrows. "You're going to let Dad take

care of this for you, too? Are you ever planning to grow up and manage your own life?''

''Like you did such a great job with yours you can give advice?'' She meant well, but the last thing he needed was advice from the world's expert in causing trouble. He could remember lying in bed nights listening to her fight with the old man over where she'd been and what she'd done.

''I'm familiar with the mistakes, Bobby, and the self-delusion. I'd like to help you avoid some of the traps I fell into.'' Cassie straightened up, rearranged some of the junk on top of the chest of drawers. ''Dad's hard to work with, but he's even harder to work against. If I'd listened to some of what he had to say when I was your age, I could have saved myself some grief. Then again, I might not have had Zak.'' Her red hair caught the light as she shook her head. ''That would have been a shame.''

''He's a cute little guy.''

''You won't get an argument from me.'' Leaning over the bed rail, she patted him on the leg. ''Take care of yourself. I'll keep in touch. If I can do anything, let me know.''

''Sure.'' That was about as close to ''I love you'' as he and Cassie had ever come. The nearly twelve years between them had always seemed like too big a gap to cross. ''Tell Zak I'll take him sledding if there's snow next time he's out here.''

''I'll do that.'' Her footsteps retreated toward the main part of the house.

Left alone, Bobby's thoughts flew back to Dan, and to Megan. How had he managed to screw up his life—and theirs—so totally? What was the first mistake? Had there been a point where he could have made a different decision, and changed everything?

As surely as his brain wouldn't show him what happened after he drove away from the party on Halloween night, he couldn't identify that one vital point where he could have made a difference.

Which led him to the inescapable conclusion that his whole life had been nothing but one failure right after the other.

ROBERT STEPPED into the kitchen to get a refill on his coffee and found Zak at the table, squirting orange icing onto cookies shaped liked turkeys. The tang of ginger in the air identified Beth's spice thins, a November tradition since the girls were tiny. He thought he could probably set the clock and the calendar by the schedule of Beth's baking, cleaning and gardening chores. At least something—*someone*—in his life remained dependable.

Zak glanced up from his work and stared, mouth open, as if seeing his granddad in the kitchen was a big surprise. He forgot to ease up on the icing tube, though, and a big blob of orange goo piled up on the cookie. The boy glanced down, saw what had happened and dropped the tube. His lower lip started to quiver, and his hazel eyes filled with tears.

"Now don't get all blubbery." Robert sat down at the table. "Cookies are easy enough to fix." He picked up a knife, scraped the blob of icing off Zak's cookie and handed it back. "See? This time watch what you're doing."

Tongue stuck firmly in the corner of his mouth, Zak returned to his decorating work. When he finished—with a result that didn't look much different from the unintentional blob—he set that turkey on a platter of finished products and picked up another one. Robert went to the counter for coffee, headed for the hallway and his office…then turned to sit down again in the chair next to Zak. Something about watching the little boy focus on such a simple job brought him a sense of peace he hadn't known in days. Maybe not even in years.

Could be it was time to get to know the boy better. "Your mother says you're liking your school."

Zak shrugged. "It's okay."

"You get good grades?"

"Sometimes." The answer wasn't sullen or disrespectful. Just…indifferent.

"What is your best subject?"

The boy started another cookie. After a while he said, "Reading, I guess."

Robert quelled his dismay. "What do you read?"

Another shrug. "King Arthur. Knights and stuff."

Not much use to a cattle rancher. "You ever read about horses?"

"Knights rode big ones called destriers." For the first time, Zak looked him in the eye. "The horses wore armor just like the knights. And they learned to fight—the horse would rear up, to scare the soldiers on the ground. They pawed the air, maybe even hit some guys and knocked them down. There was this really neat move where the horse jumped all the way off the ground and kicked out with all four legs—that really made all the foot soldiers back off." He took a deep breath. "That would be so cool, to train a horse to do stuff like that."

Robert found himself smiling. "Schooling a horse is a tough job. But worth the effort. I've done my share over the years. But we could work on that colt you saw, when he's a little older."

"Really?" The boy was grinning ear to ear.

"Really."

The brisk click of boot heels in the hallway announced Althea's arrival. She stopped when she saw him sitting at the table, her jaw hanging a little loose. "What's going on?"

He took a sip of coffee and swallowed it, along with the irritation at being interrupted. "Spice cookies."

"Um, yeah, I was helping Zak a while ago. But...what are *you* doing?"

"Just watching." As if he'd never sat and watched Thea and her sisters and Bobby ice the turkeys. He had...hadn't he?

"Okay." She shook her head, as if to clear it. "That's great."

When she pulled on her heavy coat, Robert realized she planned to go out. "Where are you headed in the middle of a snowstorm?"

She turned away from him to finish doing up her buttons. "Into town."

He knew the answer, but he asked the question anyway. "For what?"

The glance she threw over her shoulder challenged him. "Rafe asked me to dinner. I thought it sounded like fun."

His temper snapped. "Fun's all that matters to you, when your brother's entire future is on the line?"

"My having dinner with Rafe doesn't relate in any way to the trouble Bobby's in."

"You say anything even a little damaging, that deputy'll use it against us. You'll be convicting your own family."

She closed her eyes and blew out a breath. "The family isn't on trial, Dad. Neither is Bobby, for that matter. Not yet, anyway."

"We will be. You watch. The whole county will take this opportunity to take shots at the Maxwell name."

"Maybe we shouldn't have given them such a good target, then." With a flick of her keys, she headed toward the back door. "I don't know how late I'll be. Don't wait up."

"Althea Marie Maxwell, you—"

She slammed the door over his shout. He swore and dropped back into his chair, then turned to find little Zak staring at him with an expression close to terror on his face.

Wearily, Robert shook his head. "I'm sorry, son. Nobody's mad at you. Get back to your cookie icing." He put out a hand and touched Zak's arm. The little boy jumped, but didn't run away.

Picking up his mug, Robert took a long drink, aware of his pulse pounding and a tightness in his chest that was more than just rage. What had gone wrong with his life these last weeks?

And how the hell was he ever going to make things right again, when his daughters defied him, his son ignored him and his own body betrayed him?

THE SNOW WAS FALLING steadily when Rafe opened the door to Thea's knock. "Come in out of the cold."

She stepped past him into the living room, brushing heavy snowflakes from her dark hair. "I'm dripping on your floor. Sorry about that." Facing him, she grinned. "If you'll hand me a mop, I'll clean up."

With color in her cheeks and lips from the cold and a sparkle in her eyes that he claimed for himself, she looked more beautiful, more alive, than he'd ever seen her. Rafe's first impulse was to grab hold, to draw all that life into his arms and make crazy love with her until they both were too exhausted to move.

But he wasn't sure enough of her reaction for even a hello kiss. She'd handled a lot of trouble in the last few days, with more to come. "I think the linoleum will survive a few drips," he said, instead. "Let me take your coat."

Underneath she wore a soft purple sweater that begged to be touched. Keeping himself on a tight leash, Rafe hung her parka on hooks he'd put up for the purpose, then turned back to find Thea closer than he'd realized, within easy reach. Before he thought about it, he stroked his thumb across her cheekbone, along the side of her throat, and across her collarbone under that soft, soft sweater.

"I don't mean to pester you." He brought his other hand up to cup her shoulder. "But you're practically irresistible."

She smiled and moved a little closer. "You're not pestering. I want—" Her flushed cheeks got even brighter. She bit her lips and glanced away.

"You want?" He lifted her chin, but couldn't force her to raise her lashes to look at him. So he simply bent to put his mouth on hers.

At the touch of Rafe's lips, Thea sighed and took the step that brought their bodies into contact. Warmth rushed through her, and the core of ice deep inside began to melt. She smoothed her hands up his chest and over his shoulders, then combed her fingers through his hair, hungry for every sensation. All during the long, slow drive from the ranch to town, she'd hoped for this, imagined herself in Rafe's arms. There was no point to holding back.

She felt the room spin around her, then realized that he'd tightened his arms and turned them both so her back was against the wall. Smiling against his mouth, she took advantage of the support to pull him closer, his thighs pressing into hers, his chest hard against her aching breasts. His palms stroked along her ribs, his tongue played with hers, and the pleasure of wanting Rafe, being wanted by him, nearly overwhelmed her. In another minute she would forget her own name.

But that minute never came. Suddenly he was drawing back, gently brushing her hair away from her face, his fingers shaking, his breathing as rushed as hers.

"Shh." He ran his knuckles along the side of her face. His thumb snagged on her lower lip and she heard his breath catch. Watching his eyes, she saw him fight the urge to pick up where they'd left off. Thea closed her eyes and hoped.

Instead, Rafe put his hands on her shoulders, pressed a soft kiss to her forehead, then stepped back. "I didn't intend to seduce you before dinner. I thought my spaghetti sauce would make my case first."

She drew a deep breath. "I'll admit I'm a pushover for a good spaghetti sauce." But then, she'd been a pushover for Rafe from the very beginning. He probably knew that, which made it all the more amazing that he hadn't taken advantage of what she so obviously was offering. "What's your secret ingredient?"

"Bloodhound supervision." He led the way toward the kitchen. "Jed keeps a close eye on the process. He likes the leftovers."

Thea played with the dog while Rafe put the finishing touches on dinner, but she insisted on helping him clean up afterward. With the sleeves of her sweater pushed up to her elbows, she washed and rinsed the dishes then handed them over to be dried and put away. Just the slightest brush of Rafe's fingers against hers accelerated her heart rate. By the time they got to the last of the pots, she was nearly breathless with anticipation.

Jed led them back into the living room, climbed onto the couch and stretched out, taking up nearly two-thirds of the seat.

Thea laughed. "Well, he's pretty sure about where he belongs, isn't he?"

Rafe put a couple of logs on the fire and stirred the flames. "He owns the place. I get to stay around because I can open the dog-food bag." When he straightened up, he saw Thea at the window, staring out into a whirlwind of snow. He walked up behind her, close but not quite touching. "A bad night for driving."

To his satisfaction, she leaned back against him. "I've driven in worse. I've got great snow tires and four-wheel drive. But it will be a slow trip."

He folded his arms around her. "Did your dad give you a hard time about coming here tonight?"

Thea shrugged. "He wasn't happy."

But she had come anyway. If he brought up the situation with Bobby, they would spend the rest of their evening together trying to resolve the unresolvable.

There would be time in the days ahead for conflict. Tonight could be theirs alone.

"Jed's got the couch," he said quietly against the curve of her ear. "All I can offer you is a blanket in front of the fire, if you'd like to stay a while."

Sighing, Thea tilted her head, giving him the curve of her neck and shoulder to nuzzle and kiss. "That sounds just right."

They lay together on that blanket in front of the fire, talking, kissing, talking…and then more than kissing, as need swept through them. Her sweater came off, and her bra…and then Rafe's hands were on her skin and she thought she would melt from the pleasure. She pulled his shirt out of his jeans to run her hands over his back, his broad, muscled shoulders. Then his shirt, too, was gone. The hair on his chest curled against her breasts, and his mouth pressed hard, hot kisses along her throat.

Thea heard the rasp of a zipper, felt the sudden looseness of her jeans, and then the heat of Rafe's palm against her hipbone, the small of her back, the curve of her rear. With a sigh of pleasure, she pressed into him, asking silently for more.

But Rafe pulled back a little, slipped his hand outside her jeans. "Thea," he whispered, "have you ever been with someone else? Like this?"

Looking into his deep brown eyes, seeing everything she'd ever wanted right there in his soul, she didn't even try to pretend. "No. I never knew anybody like you before."

He smiled but closed his eyes as if something hurt. "We need to slow down."

"Next time," she said, urging him closer.

But he shook his head. "No, wait. Think a minute."

For the minute he suggested, she stared at him, caught between surprise and chagrin and outright anger. Why had he gotten her so...so worked up if he didn't intend to follow through? Did he not want her after all? Had she failed some kind of test she hadn't known about?

"Listen to me," he ordered when she tried to pull away, and weighted her down with his lower body. "You don't want to make this decision on the spur of the moment. It's too important."

Thea continued to struggle. "Don't tell me what I do or don't want to do." She glared up at him. "And it's not spur of the moment. I came prepared!"

A grin spread over his face, and he bent and kissed her. "That's the nicest thing anybody has ever said to me."

She finally stopped moving. "Would you make up your mind?"

"I made up my mind the first time I saw you."

That idea stopped her breath. "But?"

"But I want you to be sure."

"What do I have to do to convince you?" She punched his shoulder, but he didn't flinch. "How much proof do you need? I practically ripped your clothes off. And my own. And—and..." Reason finally caught up with her. She sputtered to a halt and closed her eyes. "I guess you're right. We should both think about this some more. Things are…complicated."

"Exactly." Easing back, he helped her sit up, then turned to put on his shirt while she reclaimed her own clothes. Given the choice between lying down to zip her jeans or standing, Thea opted for dignity and got to her feet.

Rafe came up after her, brushed her hair back and cupped her face in his hands. "I want you." He whispered the words against her lips. "But I don't want there to be any regrets."

Tears burned her eyes as she nodded. "Me neither."

Then, with a sigh, she put on her coat and started the long, snowy drive home. At the entrance to the ranch, she called Rafe on the cell phone to tell him she'd made it. "Get some sleep," he said. His rough voice created shivers up and down her spine.

She eased the Land Rover to a slippery stop beside the garage and glanced at the dashboard clock: 4:00 a.m. Friday morning. Most of the windows in the house were dark, except for the kitchen and the master bedroom. The kitchen light stayed on all night, every night, but she wondered why her dad was still awake. He always got up early. But not usually this early.

She sank six inches into new snow with each step she took toward the back door. Leaving her boots and wet socks on the mud porch, she eased quietly into the kitchen, ran a drink of water, and then sipped slowly, staring out the window at the moon-silvered landscape.

Not too many people would believe that she'd left Rafe's house tonight as much a virgin as she was when she arrived. She hardly believed it herself. Especially since he'd given her the choice.

Rafe's patience, his willingness to wait, his insistence that she be sure…she'd never dated a man like this. If he wasn't careful, she might actually begin to believe that she was important to him, that what she wanted mattered.

Such an amazing idea, that her choices, her needs, her desires came first with Rafe. The kind of relationship she'd never thought possible.

Setting her glass in the sink, she left the kitchen and headed left down the hallway, toward the great room and her own bedroom beyond.

But something—a sound she wasn't even sure she'd heard—turned her around and sent her in the other direction, toward her dad's room. She knocked softly, in case he'd simply fallen asleep with the light on. "Dad? Are you awake?"

There was the sound again, a kind of strangled groan from behind the door. Hands shaking, Thea turned the knob and stepped inside.

In the low light, she could see her dad in bed, lying on his back, clawing at the sheet. His face was a mask of terror.

"Dad? My God, what's wrong?" At his side, she reached for his wrist, thinking to check his pulse, but his desperate moves defeated her. "What's happening?"

"Can't—" He choked, and his hand grabbed at her sweater. "Can't breathe."

CHAPTER TEN

"I FORBID YOU to mention anything about this to your sisters or anyone else."

Lying back in an armchair, his face white with fatigue and stress, Robert Maxwell didn't look strong enough to be giving any kind of orders at all.

Thea stared at him in frustration. "Then I'm calling a doctor."

"No, you're not." He straightened up in his chair. "I don't have any problem that a doctor needs to deal with."

"Except that you're having trouble breathing."

"One episode doesn't mean I'm sick. I'm just getting old."

"This is the first time it's happened?" He didn't answer. "I didn't think so. You can't just ignore something so serious, Dad."

"I'll decide what's serious and what's not." On his feet again, he'd obviously decided to take back control. "I appreciate your help. Now it's time for both of us to get to bed."

She stood her ground, refusing to leave. Her dad simply waited, with a force of will she'd recognized all her life as the key to his power and success. He'd won many a negotiation, broken many an opponent's resolution, just by refusing to concede.

And she gave in, as so many had before her. "I don't

argue with sick people," she said in protest as she turned to leave. "I'll see you at breakfast."

As she put her hand on the doorknob, he cleared his throat. "You just got home?"

"A little while ago."

"That deputy let you drive all this way in the snow alone?"

"He trusts me to take care of myself."

"Or else he's just using you to make his case against your brother."

The cruelty of the suggestion left her speechless for a few seconds. She wanted to exit without another word. But the pain drove her to retaliate.

"If that's all I'm useful for—as a weapon to use against you—then at least I got a good roll in the hay out of it."

"Althea—"

Before he could stop her, Thea shut the door and bolted across the house to her own room. Locked in, she threw herself on the bed and covered her head with a pillow so she wouldn't have to hear her dad's knock, his attempts to "discuss" the issue. Not apologize—Robert Maxwell never apologized. And anyway, she didn't want an apology.

But she would give her soul for a decent measure of respect.

DESPITE THE SNOW, the deputy county attorney showed up right on time for his appointment with Rafe.

"Deputy Rafferty? I'm Ernest Gardiner." A round-faced guy barely out of college, he shook Rafe's hand, sat down in the chair across the desk and took a file folder out of his leather satchel. "What can you tell me about this Maxwell case?"

"Would you like some coffee first?" Having waited up

to be sure Thea got home safely, Rafe was depending on caffeine to keep him functioning this morning.

"No, thanks. You go ahead. What's the status of your investigation?"

"I'm still conducting interviews. The forensics unit did get to survey the scene before the snow hit. You have their report?"

Gardiner pushed up his wire-rimmed glasses with one finger, then flipped through his file. "Yeah. Skid marks, debris pattern and range...a high-speed collision, for sure. One kid got thrown out of the truck bed, right? Is he still alive?"

"I talked to the hospital a few minutes ago. He might be coming out of the coma."

"That would be useful. How about the other passenger? What does he say?"

"Not much. He says he doesn't remember the accident."

"The third victim, Tom Bonner...you've interviewed him?"

"He didn't see the truck coming. He stopped at the sign, pulled out into the intersection, and the next thing he remembers is waking up in the hospital."

"Missing an eye. Mmm." The attorney ticked off a couple of points on one of his pages. "That leaves us with the driver. Bobby Maxwell."

"Yes." Rafe swallowed a gulp of coffee, fortifying himself for the tightrope walk ahead.

"I'm not finding a record of previous arrests. This is his first offense?"

"The so-called record is misleading. He's been in trouble before, but nothing was allowed to stick."

Gardiner glanced up over the tops of his glasses. "If there's no record, we can't make any legal assumptions about previous violations."

"Maxwell's stunts are no secret." In his mind's eye, Thea's hurt gaze reproached for that comment. Rafe blinked and focused on the attorney's smooth face.

"Still, it's the record the court will rely on. Did the hospital get a blood-alcohol level when he was admitted?"

"Point twelve." Damn Bobby Maxwell, anyway.

"Quite legally drunk. But since this is his first DUI—"

"This is not his first DUI." He set his mug down, splashing coffee on the desk top.

"There are no other charges on the record, Deputy."

And whose fault was that? "The entire population of this county can testify that they've seen Bobby Maxwell drive under the influence."

"The only relevant observations would be for the night in question. So if this is his first offense, we can only hope for a misdemeanor charge at best. Unless, of course, the Aiken boy dies."

Rafe stared at the man across the desk. "Maxwell owns you, too, doesn't he?"

"I don't understand the question." But Gardiner's pale, pudgy cheeks turned red. "I work for the county."

"And Robert Maxwell is paying you to shrink this case to misdemeanor status with no real penalties. Right?"

"I—"

"It's not going to work. I'm as sorry for Bobby Maxwell as anybody, but I'm not letting his dad or the county attorney's office or the governor himself interfere with the prosecution of this case."

Gardiner got to his feet and stuffed his papers into his briefcase. "You're up against the big guns in this state, Rafferty. If you push too hard, you'll be out of a job."

"I stand to lose a lot more than just a job." Rafe went to the door and pulled it open. "But I intend to see that justice is served."

"Who are you, anyway?" Gardiner sneered at him as he scooted out into the cold. "Dudley Do-Right?"

He probably did sound like good old Dudley, Rafe reflected as he walked back to his desk. Law enforcement was an equivocal process these days. Police and prosecutors walked a tightrope of legal regulations. A single missed step could bring the whole case down. Then there were the small crooks you let slide in order to hook the bigger ones, and the charges you knew in your gut were solid but couldn't be proved well enough to convince a jury.

The worst were the cases like his last one in L.A., where a slick attorney had managed to twist all the evidence and make the accused appear to be the victim. Rafe had worked like a dog for the better part of a year, pulling together tiny pieces of evidence, a consistent motive, a clear record of payoffs.

And in the end, that high-priced lawyer had gotten his racketeering, cop-killing client off free and clear, leaving Rafe standing in the courtroom staring at his dead partner's wife without any excuse or any hope of justice.

He'd thought Montana would be different. Too many episodes of *Bonanza* as a kid, he supposed. Though he'd never been there, a great big state with a small population had seemed like the perfect antidote to the crowds and corruption in L.A.

And practically the first thing I do when I settle here is get involved with the most powerful rancher in the state, his out-of-control son and his totally distracting daughter. Hardly a recipe for peaceful nights and trouble-free days.

Not being involved wasn't an option anymore. He and Thea had been so close last night...and had come so close to making the kind of commitment that lasted for a lifetime. She would have given him anything he wanted. And Rafe wanted it all.

But he'd never been one to pile up debts. He'd lived with his aunt and uncle for twelve years, and worked hard every single day he was there so he could walk away without obligations when the time came. He paid his credit cards off every month, saved up and paid cash for his car.

He didn't want Thea to owe him anything, either. Whatever they meant to each other should be clear of obligations and ambiguities. They would be together because they wanted to be, not because they'd rushed into a relationship before the time was right.

As he flipped through his copy of the report on Bobby's accident, though, Rafe found himself seriously doubting that the time for him and Thea would ever be right. If he took on Robert Maxwell and lost, he wouldn't be able to stay in Paradise Corners—or anywhere in the state, for that matter. How could he ask Thea to leave her home, her family, the land she loved?

If he did his job the right way, Bobby would pay heavily for his irresponsibility. Robert Maxwell wouldn't take defeat easily and he'd do everything he could to sway Thea to his side. Either way, Rafe thought, his hopes to make a life with Thea were doomed. That realization made waiting to make love to her a wise choice.

But it made the rest of his life look like a long, empty waste of time.

THEA CALLED the hospital Friday afternoon and then went to Bobby's bedroom. "They think Dan might be waking up."

"Yeah? He's talking and stuff?" He sat up in bed, with the first enthusiasm he'd shown for anything since the accident.

She hated to disappoint him, but false hope was worse than none. "I don't think he's come that far. The nurse said the doctors are getting responses to stimuli. His pupils are reacting to light, that sort of thing.''

''Oh.'' Bobby eased back against the pillows and put his arm over his eyes. Though he wasn't technically confined to bed, he hadn't left his room except for meals.

''What are you thinking?'' Thea sat lightly on the corner of the mattress. ''You haven't said much.''

''I'm planning a vacation in Hawaii.'' He dropped his arm and stared at her, fury and pain in his gaze. ''What the hell do you expect? I'm thinking what a total screwup I am.''

She couldn't argue with his logic. ''Drinking gets you in trouble every time, Bobby. You know that.''

''I don't need a lecture.''

''No, because you don't listen. So you get to learn the hard way.''

He picked at a loose thread on the bedspread, avoiding her eyes. ''Your boyfriend thinks he's gonna put me in jail, doesn't he?''

Suddenly there was a gulf between them. He'd put her on the opposing side with Rafe. ''He's going to treat this case the same as he would if he didn't know anyone involved. But it's not his decision what the consequences are. That will be up to a judge and maybe a jury.''

Bobby shrugged, as if he didn't care. ''No problem, then. Dad has the judges in this state in his pocket.''

Thea choked on her outrage. ''How can you be so worried about Dan but not expect to take responsibility for what you've done to him?''

''Dan wouldn't want to put me in prison.''

''I'm assuming you didn't want to put him in the hospital. There's only one answer to both those statements— too bad.''

The expression on his handsome face turned mulish.

"Why don't you go share the doom and gloom with Deputy Dull? The two of you are about as cheerful as a broken tooth."

She stood up and went to the door, intending to leave, but stopped on the threshold and looked back over her shoulder. "You know, I care about you because you're my brother and because I think you're basically a good person. You've always been the baby in the family, the kid brother we all wanted to see enjoying himself.

"But if you don't get rid of this chip on your shoulder, ditch the selfish, resentful attitude and develop a little humility, there won't be anybody left who gives a damn one way or the other what happens to you. Think about it."

Bobby winced as Thea slammed the bedroom door. He'd had to make her mad to get her to leave him alone. The trouble with being the youngest was that he never really got a chance to be by himself. Somebody always wanted to know where he was, what he was doing and why he wasn't doing what they'd told him to do the last time they'd looked for him.

Dammit, he needed time to think. Or a drink.

Make that many drinks.

No...what he really needed was to talk to Megan. She listened, and she didn't give him a hard time about what he *should* say or think or do.

Grunting at the pain, he rolled onto his good side and pulled the telephone onto the bed. Their dad had never allowed televisions in the kids' rooms, but at least they each had a private phone line. He punched in the autodial code for Megan's house and waited, breathing fast.

Her little sister answered. "Meggie's busy."

"Tell her it's Bobby, Lisa."

"She don't want to talk to you. I heard her tell Racey."

Bobby groaned. "You tell Megan she has to say that to me or I'll call every five minutes until she does."

"Hey, Meggie," the little girl yelled. "Bobby says you hafta talk to him or he'll call—"

He heard the phone change hands. "Go away," Megan told her sister. "Or I'll tell Mama you wet the bed last night." The argument that followed left Bobby on the verge of screaming, but finally Megan came to the phone without interference. "Bobby?"

"Hey, honey. Listen, before I say another word, I'm really sorry about the other night. I was out of my head, I think. I know you don't care about Reeves. Sometimes I just can't believe I'm lucky enough to have you all to myself."

She was quiet for so long he thought the apology hadn't worked. But finally she sighed. "It's been a really terrible week," she said softly. "I knew you didn't mean what you said."

He felt weak with relief. "That's my girl. Your dad'll be out of the house tonight, right?" Mr. Wheeler considered Friday his personal starting gate for getting drunk and staying that way all weekend.

"Um…as far as I know."

"Can I see you?"

"Where? Your dad would have a fit if I showed up at your house."

"So we'll go somewhere else."

"Are you driving, Bobby?"

"Hell." He'd forgotten for a minute that he'd totaled the truck. And even if Rafferty hadn't confiscated his driver's license, even if the doctors hadn't ordered him not to drive, asking to use one of the ranch-owned trucks at this point would be like asking for a chance to live his own life. Not an option.

His dad probably wouldn't even let him leave the house. He tried to think, but desperation kept getting in the way. "Racey could come get me. I'll meet her down by the front gate."

"How will you get there?"

"I'll figure out something. And then she could bring me to where you were."

"And where is that?" She sounded almost impatient, for Megan.

"Uh, how about that motel on the far side of Big Timber? The Lovelace Inn, right? We could meet you there about eight o'clock."

"That's not a very nice place, Bobby."

"We don't have to live there, Megan. We just need to…talk. Please. I really need to see you again."

Her sigh of surrender was sweet. "I'll be there at eight."

"Look for Racey's car. I'll station her outside the room I'm in. See you in a little while. I love you, Megan."

"I love you, too, Bobby. Be careful."

He hung up the phone, grinning. The hard part—convincing Megan to come—was done. Now all he had to do was get out of the house without being caught. After sixteen years of practice—he'd run away from home for the first time when he was three, so he'd been told—that particular trick would be a piece of cake!

RAFE CALLED just as dinner ended Friday night. Thea heard his hello and turned her back to the rest of the kitchen. "There are a lot of…people…in the room," she told him. "I need to call you later."

"Anytime. I'll be home all night." He sounded tired. She wanted to ask why, but she could feel her dad's eyes on her back. She hung up quickly, instead, and went back to help clear the table. "I hear we've got chocolate cake for dessert."

"A woman who bakes a chocolate cake on a snowy day deserves sainthood," Herman commented, with a wink at his sister. Bobby, staring into the beans he was pushing around his plate, hadn't given notice that he heard any part of the conversation. Thea could tell by the quirk of her dad's grim mouth that he'd heard, but he wasn't in the mood for jokes.

A glance at the housekeeper revealed that Beth, too, had caught the lack of response to Herman's teasing. Her gaze rested longest on Robert, as if waiting for him to make a tardy comment.

"I'm going for the ultimate snowy-day treat," Thea added a little desperately. "Chocolate-swirl ice cream, hot-fudge sauce and nuts on top of my cake. Anybody want to join me?"

Awkwardly, Bobby got out of his chair. "I'm really...tired. Think I'm going to put some music on in my room, just call it a night. Thanks for dinner, Beth." His smile was the sweet one that usually won folks over, but he limped out of the kitchen before he saw if it worked this time.

Robert Maxwell stood and brought his plate to the counter. "Think I'll pass on dessert tonight. Just keep the coffee warm. Thanks." He left as quickly as Bobby. They heard the door to his office shut firmly.

Beth sighed. "I think I'll have ice cream and fudge sauce, too, Thea."

"We'll make that three." Herman got up to help them, then they all sat down at the table again. But the jolliness that should have accompanied such a decadent dessert never materialized.

They all knew the reason, of course, which Thea explained to Rafe when she called him later from her bedroom. "He got more phone calls this afternoon, from an attorney for the Heaths and a different one for the Aikens. After only four days, the lawsuits are on the way."

"I know."

"I guess you do." She rubbed her eyes with the fingers of one hand. "Both lawyers mentioned that they'd talked to the *officials* involved in the investigation." From down the hall, Bobby's rock-edged country music rattled the floorboards with a hard, loud bass line.

Rafe was silent for a minute. "Your dad's done some investigating of his own. He's already got the county attorney's office primed to dismiss the case."

"You can't blame him for protecting his son." They were both speaking quietly, in friendly tones, but there wasn't much doubt they were about an inch away from an argument.

"It would be best for everybody if your dad could let the process take its course and then see what happens. Dan's waking up a little, and the charges might be considerably lighter than the worst-case scenario."

"I heard about Dan, and I'm really glad, you know that." It was Thea's turn to sigh. "But if you think I can convince my dad to do anything against his will, you've got a mistaken impression of his stubbornness and my powers of persuasion."

"Actually, I think I have a pretty accurate idea on both of those issues." His voice was warm again, a verbal version of that sexy grin she loved. "You could persuade me to do just about anything. Speaking of which…"

Some devil drove her to reply, "Except drop the case against Bobby."

He drew a deep breath. "Are you tied down with work all day tomorrow?"

"It depends on the weather. If it warms up as much as they're saying it will, I'll need to get out into the pastures, check the herds."

"On horseback?"

"Probably, if it's not too windy."

"Want some company?"

The thought of Rafe coming along on her daily chores had never crossed her mind. "You want to spend a day in the saddle, cold and probably wet, looking at cows?"

"I'll let you look at the cows. I'll look at the scenery…and you."

"Well…well, okay, sure." The compliment just about floored her. "Dad's going to a meeting, and I imagine I'll head out about eight in the morning."

"Sounds good. I'll show up at the horse barn with enough time to saddle up."

"If you change your mind—"

"I won't." She could hear his grin again. "Sleep tight."

"G'night." Thea put the phone down and rolled over, pulling a pillow over her ear to block out Bobby's music.

Rafe Rafferty in the saddle. A whole day out in the country with just him. No one eyeing them with curiosity, wondering what they were saying. A chance to share the work she loved with the man she…

Tomorrow was going to be a very interesting day.

BOBBY HAD SKIED across Walking Stones land before, but never with broken ribs. Just getting his boots fastened took more bending than he could stand, so he didn't try. The gentle slopes between the house and the entrance to the ranch didn't pose a challenge to someone who'd been skiing almost as long as he'd been walking. He could have mapped out the terrain in his sleep.

But Racey kept him waiting in the cold for almost half

an hour before her headlights finally glanced off the snow piled up around the stone columns flanking the entrance to the ranch.

Bobby slammed into her smoke-filled truck and immediately flipped the heat to high. "Where the hell have you been? I thought I was going to freeze to death out there."

Holding a cigarette between her teeth, she didn't glance his way as she backed around to head toward the highway. "There's been some snow, 'case you haven't noticed. They don't plow out our way as quick as they do Maxwell roads."

"Okay, okay. Don't get so pissed off. What's wrong with you, anyway?"

Still without looking at him, she didn't say a word. They were almost to Big Timber before Racey made a comment. "Dan's woken up some."

"That's what I hear." In the silence that followed, he realized she expected him to ask questions. And Bobby realized he didn't want to know anything else. Because whatever he heard wasn't going to be good. Until Dan was walking and talking and riding and cutting up just like he had when they'd played football Sunday afternoon, and then Monday night as they'd headed out to Monroe's party, nothing would ever be really right again.

When he didn't respond, Racey shut up completely. They rode through town in an atmosphere almost as frigid as the air outside.

He checked in at the motel, then got back into the truck with a room key. "Number twenty. At the far end."

Dragging hard on yet another cigarette, she pulled into the parking space in front of the room and stared through the windshield as he eased himself out and turned around.

"I told Megan you'd be out here so she'd know which room I'm in. She should show up in a few minutes."

Racey jerked around to face him. "I'm not sitting in the parking lot waiting for you to finish your grope session. I'm going to a movie."

At the hate-filled tone of her voice, Bobby felt his stomach drop. "What's the problem, Racey? You're treating me like—like—"

"Like a murderer, maybe?"

He was suddenly cold inside, as if his guts had frozen. "I didn't murder…anybody."

"We don't know that yet, do we?" She tilted her face and he could see tears running down her cheeks.

"Dan's getting better."

"No, he's just waking up some. He's still got tubes going in and out everywhere and a broken neck, still letting a machine breathe for him. He could die whether he wakes up or not."

Here he stood, in the wide open spaces of Montana, feeling cornered. Bobby fought for air. "What's this got to do with you waiting until Megan comes?"

"You think people are just gonna keep taking care of you, keep doing things for you, because of that handsome face? Or maybe because your name's Maxwell and your old man owns most of Montana?" A smoke cloud billowed between them. "Take a reality check, why don't you? People are fed up with you and your stunts. Fed up with your old man and his God complex. Run your truck into a ditch, I'm not sure there's anybody in the county who'd stop to pull you out. Except maybe the new deputy, because he's got the hots for your sister."

She hadn't said anything he didn't know. "So why'd you come get me? Why'd you bring me down here? Why didn't you just tell me to go to hell on the phone and save us both the trouble?"

Racey took a deep breath. "Because we've been friends,

I guess. Because I like Megan and I know she loves you. Because…'' Her hands tightened around the steering wheel. ''Because I thought maybe you'd be different now. I expected…''

He waited for her to go on. When she didn't, his temper took hold. ''Well? Expected what?''

''That you'd be sorry, you son of a bitch.'' She slammed the truck into Reverse. ''That hurting Dan and Jerry and that other poor man might have put a dent in your attitude. That you'd finally admit you're human like the rest of us, and you make mistakes—really, really bad ones—that you have to pay for.''

She threw her cigarette out into the snow. ''But that's not what I see. All I see is the same stupid pride, the same belief that you're above the rest of us. You get away with half killing people, and nobody's supposed to feel any different about you? You'd better be nice to your old man, Maxwell. I think he's about the only friend you've got left.''

Bobby barely managed to jump out of the way of the open truck door as Racey backed around. Spraying snow into his face, she skidded out of the motel parking lot without looking back. The passenger-side door was still open when she rounded the corner and disappeared into the night.

Numb from the neck up, Bobby stumbled under the awning over the motel walkway, unlocked number twenty and stepped inside. The setting was as bad as Megan had feared. The air in the room was cold and damp, the bed covered in a brown flowered spread that looked dirty even from across the stained carpet.

Well, they wouldn't stay. He could spare the thirty bucks he'd paid. When Megan got here, they'd go find a place to eat, somewhere warm and quiet. Just holding her hand would make him feel better. Seeing her smile, watching her eyes shine for him…that was what he needed. Megan could ease some of the pain that Racey had caused him.

But Megan never arrived.

CHAPTER ELEVEN

THEA WATCHED as Bobby climbed awkwardly into the
Land Rover. "I cannot believe I'm in the parking lot of the
Lovelace Inn at midnight, fetching you home. What is go-
ing on in your head?"

He shut the door and leaned his head back against the
seat. "I wanted to see Megan."

"So you sneak out of the house like a little kid running
away to the circus?"

"I didn't want to deal with the hassle I'd get if I told
people I was leaving."

"That's certainly a mature way to handle the situation—
don't let anyone know where you are at all."

"Okay, okay. It was stupid."

His lack of fight worried her more than a full-scale outburst would have. "Megan didn't come?" Bobby shook
his head.

"Did you call her?"

"Her dad answered. He usually goes out on Friday
nights. I guess he changed his mind or something. Maybe
he found out Megan was leaving and stayed home just to
be the bastard he is."

"Did you talk to her?"

"I hung up when her dad answered."

"Adults 'R' Us. Why didn't you ask to talk to her?"

"Because he would have yelled at me, and then beat her

up, okay? He doesn't want Megan having anything to do with me.''

"I'm sorry...I didn't know it was that bad.''

Bobby didn't answer. Backing the Land Rover around, Thea searched her brain for some kind of older-sister wisdom, but came up short. "Dad went to bed before you called,'' she said, hoping to offer a little comfort. "He doesn't have to know you were out of the house.''

"Thanks.'' They rode through the dark streets of Big Timber without talking, and had almost reached the town limits when Bobby straightened up. "I want to go to the hospital.''

Fear sliced through her. "Are you feeling bad?''

He shook his head. "I need to see Dan.''

"Bobby, it's forty miles to Bozeman, and it's already after midnight. Visiting hours ended a long time ago.''

"Nobody'll catch me. The nurses don't care what's going on down the hall, as long as no alarms go off.'' He glanced her way, and she saw the suffering in his eyes. "Please.''

Shaking her head, she headed toward Bozeman. Once there, discovered Bobby was right. None of the nurses noticed them slip through the stairway entrance at the far end of the hallway and into Dan's room. At that point, nurses became the last thing on Thea's mind.

The boy lying absolutely still on the bed looked thin and small, totally unlike his usual rowdy self. His face was as pale as his whtie-blond hair. Not moving, barely breathing, he looked like a ghost against the green pillowcase.

But his eyes were open.

Beside her, she heard Bobby swallow. Then he stepped up to the bed. "Well, look at this. They've got you tied down good and tight. Must be some champion calf ropers in this hospital.''

Dan's blue eyes flickered, almost seemed to smile.

"I've been hanging around waiting for you to wake up. You always were a lazy SOB." After a long silence, Bobby shook his head. "Looks like I screwed up again. We're in pretty deep shit this time, buddy."

The boy on the bed blinked. Bobby touched Dan's still hand with one finger. "I...I didn't mean to hurt you." He looked away from his friend's face, so only Thea saw the wrinkling of Dan's forehead.

"I wish it was me lying there," Bobby said, barely above a whisper. "But, hey, we're gonna get through this, right?" His voice returned to its normal cocky tone, with only a vestige of strain in it. "You'll be out of here before deer season ends. I want to hit that spot above the Walking Stones again. I'm betting there's a good rack or two hanging around up there by now."

Dan's gaze brightened...then faded. Though his eyes stayed open, he didn't seem to be there anymore. Bobby bent over the bed. "Hey, Dan?"

One of the monitors began to whine. Three seconds later, a nurse pushed open the door. "What are you doing in here?" She glanced at Thea, then glared at Bobby. "Haven't you done enough to this poor boy? Get out." Bobby hesitated, and she pushed at his shoulder. "Go on, get out."

He was gone so fast, Thea didn't catch up until he reached the Land Rover, and then only because the doors were locked. She unlocked the truck, they both climbed in, and without a word headed for home.

When they reached the house, Bobby walked straight through to his bedroom. Thea stopped in the kitchen and called the hospital. Dan's condition remained critical, someone told her. But he was still alive.

She stopped at Bobby's door on the way to her own

room. "He's okay," she said through the closed panel. "Whatever happened, he's not worse." No answer. "You didn't hurt him tonight, Bobby. He was glad to see you."

Still no answer. Thea sighed and gave up. Lying in bed in the dark, she tried to sort through the confusion and pain of the situation, to make some sense out of the mess Bobby's life—and, by extension, the whole family's—had become.

But though the questions kept her awake until after three, she never did come up with the answers.

THEA WASN'T AT HER BEST when she got to the horse barn the next morning at seven. Her palomino gelding, Sundance, wasn't feeling much better. He shied as she tried to brush him.

"I know it's cold," Thea told him. "And it's windier than you'd like. But the job's out there and we're the ones to do it. At least we'll have company today."

"I'm glad you're looking forward to that part," Rafe said from behind her.

Thea jumped and turned. "I didn't hear you come in." The man had no right to look so wide awake while it was still dark outside. Or so capable, in well-worn jeans and boots and his big sheepskin coat. She remembered the softness of the hide against her cheek, and felt herself blush. "There's a thermos of coffee on the bench by the door. Help yourself while I get your horse ready."

"Why don't *you* have the coffee while *I* get my horse ready?" He opened the door of Sundance's stall for her and shut it again. "You look like you need a shot of caffeine. Late night?"

"Very. Bobby decided—" She suddenly wondered if last night's stunt was something she should share with the deputy. Rafe Rafferty, she thought she trusted. But the man behind the badge?

"Bobby decided…?"

"To play his music loud enough for the entire county to hear." A glance at Rafe's face told her he knew that wasn't what she'd started to say. His eyes conveyed how her lack of candor hurt him.

But he didn't make an issue of it. "Kids forget that some people need sleep. So which of these fine animals do I get to spend the day with?" Some of the warmth had left his face, and his voice was cool.

Betting that he rode well, she gave him the frisky pinto named Cisco. The way he handled the horse as he brushed and saddled him justified her confidence. In a few minutes they were mounted and heading out across the snowy pasture, with Jed padding along beside Cisco as if he'd like nothing better than a day chasing down cattle.

At the top of a rise, Thea pulled up and drew in a deep breath, watching a pink dawn break over the plains. "Why would you want to live anyplace else?"

"Good question." Rafe leaned an elbow on his saddle horn. "I'm wondering why I ever did."

"You didn't like California?" They'd never talked about how he had come to take a job in Paradise Corners.

"I liked the beach, yeah, and the sunshine."

"So why did you leave?"

His face was solemn. "My…partner got killed. And I couldn't get the guy who arranged it convicted. I wanted to live in a simpler place than L.A., where the rules hold, where the good guys win and the bad guys pay."

Instead, he'd come to the place where Robert Maxwell would do whatever was necessary to keep the law from being applied justly.

That admission would be disloyal to her dad, so Thea

pressed Sundance into motion again without further comment. "I guess we should go find some of those cows."

By noon they'd checked on the herds nearest the barns, all the while talking about whatever subject came up—as long as it wasn't Bobby. Rafe proved to be as able as any cowboy she'd worked with, sensitive to the mood of the cattle, clever with his horse. And Jed's manners were exceptional. He showed no inclination to chivy the cows. Thea only wished she'd brought a lunch with her so they wouldn't have to go back to the house.

But she carefully timed their arrival so that her dad had already eaten before she and Rafe came in, a deception that made her not all that different from Bobby. Why should they have to hide their…friends…from the family? What was the real problem here?

"I'll be up in the foothills all afternoon," she said, stirring cheese into her bowl of thick potato soup. "The riding gets pretty rough."

Across the table, Rafe lifted one eyebrow. "Are you asking if I can take it?"

"Um, why don't we say I'm just worried about Jed?" They'd left the bloodhound out on the mud porch with a bowl of leftover stew and rice.

"Jed'll do just fine." Rafe took another piece of garlic bread. "And I promise not to slow you down too much."

She couldn't help appreciating a man who would laugh at himself. Her dad and Bobby had such an aversion to looking foolish. When she said, teasing, "See that you don't," Rafe only grinned.

They spent the early part of the afternoon apart, searching out huddles of cows in shallow ravines, under stands of trees, behind boulders. Jed proved a real help when it came to finding and running down the stragglers. After one particularly energetic chase, Thea pulled up beside Rafe, breathing hard. "Can I keep Jed? He'll be a real bonus at calving season, helping me locate all the babies."

Again Rafe shook his head. "Sorry," he said. "We're a package deal." His eyes smiled at her, but there was a serious note in his voice that left her even more breathless than the ride.

Around three they reached the edge of the Maxwell property, tucked up against the base of the Crazy Mountains. Thea took off her hat and ruffled her hair with one hand. "This is actually land my granddad sold the government to establish a national forest, and they let us rent it back."

"Nice of them." Rafe resisted the impulse to shiver. He'd never spent such a long, cold day in the saddle. What a man did for love...

"The name of the ranch comes from an Indian site about a mile from here. We could go up there, if you're interested. Or—" her smile was apologetic "—we can head back to the barn. It's been a long day, and the light will start going fast."

Not much of choice there—an extra hour with her or a reputation as a wimp. He pulled his gloves tighter and straightened his back. "Let's check out the Indian site."

There was no trail to speak of and the horses moved slowly, climbing steep, rocky slopes, stepping through snow-covered underbrush. But the effort was rewarded when Thea led the way through a last barrier of cedars. "Here we are."

Rafe sat speechless for a minute. "Amazing," was all he finally came up with. The clearing they'd come to sat on the edge of a cliff that dropped sharply away for probably five hundred feet to the gentler foothills below. The view across the countryside was Montana at its very best. Rolling plains stretched east and west, with another mountain range just barely visible as a set of jagged white teeth to the south.

"The Absarokas," Thea said, following his stare. "The sky has to be really clear to see them. We're lucky this afternoon."

No argument there, he thought, watching the satisfaction in her eyes, the soft sunglow on her cheeks. "So what's the source of the ranch name?"

"The legend says that the Indians would camp below, in the foothills, every spring and every fall. They had a ceremony they performed at the base of the cliff—dances and chants, a feast, sometimes riding contests. Then the chief and the elders would climb up here during the night, pretty much the way we came but without horses, so they would arrive at dawn, just as the sun rose. All these stones..." She waved her arm, indicating boulders lying scattered over the clearing, some skull-size, some the size of small cars. "All these stones would be arranged in some kind of pattern, a sort of map, that told the chief where to take his people for the season, which hunting grounds would be good for the summer, where the buffalo would run, or where they would find the best shelter during winter and the most likely source of food."

"You mean the stones moved?"

Thea nodded. "The legend says that they were never exactly the same from spring to fall to spring again. And so the Indians called them the Walking Stones." She swung off her horse, tied the reins to a spindly pine and crossed the clearing. "I've been here at dawn in all seasons. It's a truly sacred place."

Rafe dismounted and tied Cisco nearby. The stones were even larger close up, deeply embedded in the soil. "A man—a dozen men—couldn't move something like this without heavy machinery." He braced a boot against one of the biggest boulders. "That's quite a legend your family got themselves."

"Great-great-great-Granddad Maxwell knew a good thing when he saw it." She grinned. "He traded guns for the land in the 1860s, but let the Indians retain the right to use this place for their ceremony, and even to winter on the ranch." Her grin faded. "When the reservations were set up, of course, not many of them came back year after year, and the tradition died away. A couple of our hands claim kinship with the tribe. I think they still climb up here occasionally."

She had leaned back against the straight, branchless trunk of a lodgepole pine and taken off her hat. The gray coat she wore covered her from neck to gloves and boots, and with her short hair she might have been a cowboy from another time...if you ignored the full, feminine mouth, the vulnerable, long-lashed gaze.

Which Rafe did not intend to do. "I'm honored that you brought me up here." He joined her at the pine tree. "I've only seen one part of Montana I liked better."

Her eyebrows lifted in disbelief. "And that would be...?"

He set his fingers under her chin. "You."

This kiss was like all the others—incendiary. When it ended, Rafe wouldn't have been surprised to look down and find the snow around their feet melted away. But he was too busy simply looking into Thea's face.

"You're beautiful," he said, brushing her hair back. "Come home with me tonight."

The request was impulsive, and he knew the answer even before regret clouded her eyes. "I can't. Not with...all that's going on."

Rafe nodded. "I know. Wishful thinking, that's all. You make me forget my good intentions." A glance over his shoulder showed him the deepening shadows. "We'd better get back."

They led the horses down the steepest parts of the descent, not talking much except to warn each other of a slippery spot or loose rocks. On easier ground, they stopped to share the last of the coffee Thea had brought along after lunch, then turned to their horses again for the ride to the barn. While Thea mounted Sundance, Rafe stopped to check his saddle. He put his foot in the stirrup just as a sharp crack sounded above his head.

A rifle shot.

Cisco reared and bolted. Jed put back his head and howled. Rafe crashed to the ground on his back, swearing. He rolled to his stomach and propped himself up on his elbows, wildly scanning the surrounding field. He didn't see a shooter. And he couldn't find Thea.

Another shot broke the silence. Panting, Rafe lay for a few seconds, figuring the odds. He had no cover, no horse. If the marksman wanted him, there wasn't much hope of hiding or waiting him out. And if Thea was the target...

On his feet, Rafe ran flat out for the next rise with Jed at his side, praying he'd be able to see her horse in the growing dusk, prepared every second for a bullet slamming into his back.

But he made the top of the hill without getting shot. Below him, about half a mile away, he saw the two horses. Closer was a dark hump on the ground.

Dear God. Thea.

Running again, he chanted the same prayer over and over in his head. Just one word. *Please. Please. Please.*

She lay huddled in a small hollow, her head invisible, knees drawn close to her chest. Rafe dropped to his knees just behind her. "Thea?" There was no sound to her name, only his rasping breath. He put his hands gently on her back. "Thea?"

She shuddered, moved a little. Jed sniffed at her shoulders, then sat back on his haunches and whined.

Rafe ran his hands along her spine, gently, and the arm and leg he could touch. No obvious broken bones or blood. His heart started to slow down. "Can you talk to me? Can you roll over?"

After a minute that seemed to last forever, Thea groaned and straightened out. Then she rolled to her back and lay flat, eyes closed, breathing in gasps.

Checking out her other arm and leg, unbuttoning her coat to look for evidence of a wound, Rafe finally got his own fear under control. The horse must have thrown her. But she hadn't been shot. He fastened up her coat, then knelt by her side, waiting, stroking his shaking fingers lightly over her hair, her cheek.

At last she opened her eyes. "Where's Sundance? Is he okay?"

"I'll get the horse in a minute. Are *you* okay? Can you sit up?"

"Sure." With his help, she did so. In another minute, she tried to stand, but fell against him with a gasp. "I think I wrenched my knee."

"Sit down." Rafe lowered her to the ground again. "I'll go get the horses. You stay put. Jed'll keep you company."

She looked up at him and tried to smile, but her face was white. "I'm not going anywhere."

When he returned, leading only one horse, she sat with an arm around the dog, the other elbow propped on her thigh with her head in her hand. But she lifted her head at the sound of his footsteps crunching the snow. "Where's Sundance?"

"I tied him to a bush where he was. He's lamed his right foreleg. But I found your hat."

"Damn, I knew it." A puff of snow erupted as she hit the ground with the flat of her hand. "He stumbled in this stupid hole when I fell off. Can you tell how bad it is?"

Chuckling, Rafe helped her to her feet. "I was actually more worried about getting back to you and getting you home. We'll check him out when we reach the barn. Think Cisco can carry us both?"

He could, and did, which should have been a lovely experience, Thea thought, riding through the early evening as the moon rose. She sat in front of Rafe on the saddle, with his arms loosely around her as he held the reins for both horses. Every so often, he pressed a kiss against her ear, or her temple, or the side of her neck. She almost forgot about her aching knee.

But she couldn't forget those rifle shots. Who would be hunting on Walking Stones land? Her dad allowed a few of his friends in during the season. And he and Bobby and Herman, of course, went out when they had the time. But Bobby wasn't in any shape for a hunting trip, even if he was in the mood. And her dad had planned to meet with his lawyers today.

The trip home took three times as long as it should have, with one horse overburdened and one severely lamed. From a distance, Thea saw the number of trucks parked near the horse barn and a flurry of activity as animals were pulled out of the corrals and pastures and saddled. The posse was just about ready to head out when she and Rafe rode into the barnyard.

Her dad jerked his head around. "Althea? Where the hell have you been?" His eyes narrowed as he recognized Rafe. "What's going on?"

Rafe slid out of the saddle and helped her down. He

would have held on to her, but she shook her head and stepped out on her own, though her knee nearly buckled from the pain. "Rafe rode out with me today. Somebody fired a couple of shots as we were heading in, and the horses bolted. I got thrown, and Sundance is lame. That's all there is to it."

"Fired a couple of shots?"

"Hunting, I guess." Except that she'd practically felt the bullet whiz by her face. "Bobby didn't go out, did he?"

Her dad glanced sharply at Rafe. "Boy's not that stupid. He's in no condition to go hunting."

"I guess somebody was trespassing, then." Willing her knee to work, Thea walked to Sundance and ran a hand down his neck. "Let's get you inside, son. See what you did to that leg."

Rafe wouldn't let her have the reins. "I'll take him in. You should get somebody to drive you home and take care of your knee."

She shook her head. "He's my horse. I want to see for myself."

"Thea—"

"The girl's right, Deputy. Her first responsibility is to the animal in her care." Her dad's voice really did cut like a whip, Thea realized. Funny, she hadn't heard that before.

Rafe straightened up, as if to argue. She distracted him by taking Sundance's reins. "Let's get inside. The horses need their feed."

Every lurch in Sundance's stride as she led him to his stall made her feel worse. If she hadn't been worried about Rafe, wondering if he'd been shot, she would have had her mind on her riding. She would have kept her horse under control. She would have seen that damn hole ahead of time and Sundance wouldn't be hurt.

Rafe led Cisco into the stall across the aisle. His anger

filled the chilly air of the barn. Every time she limped out with a piece of Sundance's tack, she felt his gaze on her. But the horse came first.

Finally, she brought a bucket into the stall with her and turned it upside down for a place to sit while she examined Sundance's leg.

"Well?" Rafe watched her from the other side of the stall door.

"I'm not sure. Maybe just strained. Some swelling and tenderness, but I've seen worse. I think I'll get the vet out to look at him tomorrow. Sundance is too good a friend to take chances with."

She patted the horse on the shoulder and tried to stand. But her bad knee screamed. Her head swam and those little black dots floated in front of her eyes again. Staggering, she backed into the wall of the stall and slid to the floor, kicking the bucket over. Sundance startled at the clang.

"Thea!" Rafe was inside with her, picking her up, carrying her out. "Damn your dad. I knew you should have gone home." He took her all the way to his truck and deposited her gently on the front seat. Jed hopped nimbly into the back seat as Rafe came around to the driver's side. "I'm taking you to the doctor."

"No, you are not." Nice as it was to be taken care of, enough was enough. "All I need is a hot soak and some pain medication. Definitely not a drive all the way to Bozeman and a long wait in the emergency room. Just take me to the house, Rafe." His eyes were furious as he stared at her. She put her hand on his arm. "Please?"

He blew out a long breath and jerked the truck into gear. Thea eased her head back and closed her eyes. The warmth of the heater made her sleepy and achy after a day in the cold.

Before she could doze, they stopped in the front driveway. Rafe came around and opened her door. He reached in to pick her up.

It was so tempting to let him carry her in. Almost as tempting as his invitation to come home with him tonight. Her brain fought a hard battle with her heart—and won.

"I can walk, Rafe. Just step back and let me slide down." He did as she asked, and Thea managed to get out of the truck without disgracing herself a second time. "See?" Then she looked at the steps up to the porch. "Um, want to give me a hand here?"

She used him as a crutch to get up the steps and across the porch, then leaned against the door frame and looked up at him in the lamplight. He was tired, and worried, and angry. And he had a thirty-mile drive home.

"I would invite you in for dinner," Thea said, laying a hand along his cheek. "But none of us needs more fireworks tonight. You and Jed should get yourselves home, get warm and fed. I'll be fine."

Rafe shook his head. "Leaving you here like this is against every instinct I have. But I don't have a choice." He looked at her, a spark of humor in his eyes. "Do I?"

"Nope."

"That's what I thought." He leaned forward and pressed a sweet, deep kiss on her mouth. Then, with a flash of that sexy grin, he left her on the porch. Suddenly tired beyond belief, Thea fumbled the front door open and limped inside.

Her dad waited by the fireplace, his usual cup of coffee in hand. "Get that horse seen to?"

She shrugged out of her duster. "I'll call Doctor Garrett in a little while, get him to come out tomorrow afternoon. I think it's just strained, but I'd like an X ray."

"What did you have that deputy out here for?"

On her way to the kitchen, she stopped unsteadily but didn't turn around. "He asked if he could ride with me. I wanted to see him, so I said yes. We checked the herds, then I took him up to the Walking Stones. It was a very nice day.''

''You're going to help him put your brother in jail?''

''No.'' She took a deep, patient breath. ''I'm going to hang up my coat and take off my boots, beg a sandwich from Beth and take a long hot bath. Any other schemes I have for ruining the Maxwell reputation will have to wait until tomorrow.''

''I don't like your tone.''

Thinking carefully, she turned on her good leg. ''I don't like yours, either. I don't like being called a girl in front of the hands, and in front of a man I'm dating. I don't like being questioned like a criminal, when I've spent my whole life trying to follow your every order straight down the line. I may be just a woman, but I'm good at the job. And I deserve respect for that, if for nothing else.''

Fighting tears, Thea started once again for the kitchen and the refuge of Beth's concern, since she couldn't have Rafe's. ''Good night, Dad. Sleep well.''

In response, she heard his mug shatter against the stone hearth.

CHAPTER TWELVE

RAFE RAFFERTY CALLED Sunday night. "Mr. Maxwell? I wanted to give you a report on those shots fired at Thea and myself. I spent some time up on the hillside this afternoon. I didn't find anything useful for identifying the gunman."

Robert snorted. "I didn't expect you to."

"But I did find a fresh whitetail carcass, decapitated, untagged. Were you aware there were hunters on your property yesterday?"

"No."

"Do you allow other people access to your property?"

"Friends, sometimes. But my son and my manager and me are the only ones hunting my land this year." Not that it was anybody's business but their own.

"Well, you'll need to keep your eyes open. Report any other poached animals to the game warden, or to me."

"Is that all you wanted to say?" Keeping his voice level required a fierce effort of will.

"No, as a matter of fact." Robert drew a deep breath to argue, but the damn deputy went on without stopping. "I'd like Bobby to come in tomorrow morning for questioning. About ten, if that's convenient."

The pencil he'd been working with snapped in two under the pressure of his fingers. "Nothing convenient about any of this damn nonsense. What do you need to know that's not already obvious? I got better things to do than drive into town just to talk to you.''

''I can arrest him,'' Rafferty said after a pause, ''or he can come in on his own for questioning.''

Robert heard the deputy's words with a rage that nearly choked him. ''Have you talked to LeVay about this?''

''I don't have to. Bobby was involved in a motor vehicle accident that resulted in serious injuries. That circumstance alone demands an interview.''

An image flashed through Robert's mind—a buck he and Bobby had been stalking a year or two ago backed up against the wall at the end of a ravine with no way out, and death staring him in the face.

This wasn't death, but the thought of his boy going to prison—hell, facing any kind of serious charge at all—made him want to hit something. Or someone.

''We'll be there,'' he told Rafferty, and hung up the phone. He called his lawyers and ordered them to show up at the diner at 8:00 a.m. sharp. Then he went looking for his son.

Loud music led him to the bedroom where Bobby had been hiding out since he came home from the hospital. Robert knocked, but opened the door without waiting to be invited in.

The boy lay on his bed, arms over his eyes. He sat up fast, wincing, when Robert stepped across the threshold. ''What's wrong?''

He hadn't been in Bobby's room in at least a couple of years, but a glance around showed him few changes to what he remembered. Dark blue walls, red, white and blue striped curtains and bedspread. A few books on a shelf, a desk and computer equipment, turned off, pictures of ball teams from ten years ago on the wall. The only personal items were the clothes piled in an armchair, spilling onto the floor and some clutter on top of the dresser. Clean the room, and you'd never know anybody lived here.

"Dad?"

Robert brought his attention back to the matter at hand. "The deputy wants you in his office tomorrow morning to answer questions."

Bobby swore, but Robert didn't reprimand him. Some situations in a man's life called for profanity. "I got in touch with the lawyers. We're not going into this without protection."

"For all the good it'll do." The boy swung his feet to the floor and propped his elbows on his knees. "Rafferty will make sure I take the fall for this one."

"You're saying you weren't drunk that night?" Dear God, how he wanted to hear Bobby say that. The tightness in his chest might finally ease if he knew his son hadn't caused the wreck.

Hanging his head, Bobby took a deep breath. "I was drunk, all right."

Robert felt his throat close.

"But I wasn't driving crazy." He lifted his head and met Robert's stare with an indignant gaze. "And it's not my fault Dan rode in the truck bed. Jerry'll tell you—we tried to talk him out of it. He's hurt so bad because *he* was drunk. If he'd been in the cab with us, he probably wouldn't have more than a scratch or two."

"You ran a stop sign."

"I didn't see the damn stop sign. It's dark as hell out there and I must've looked away to change the radio or something. Next thing I know—bang."

Wishing he could believe that story, Robert studied his son. Bobby had a talent for lying. Spoiled by three sisters and Beth Peace, he'd learned how to wheedle his way out of just about any punishment. When Helen died, they'd all been too lenient with a little boy who'd lost his mother.

Robert himself didn't remember much about the couple of years after the funeral. He'd worked all day and late into the night, driving his body into exhaustion so he could sleep in their bed alone. Next thing he knew, Bobby was six or seven, a real Dennis the Menace, with all the females in the house wrapped around his finger.

He'd done his best to correct the mischief, demanding that the boy pull his share of the workload on the ranch, that he play on a sports team every season and that he make decent grades in school—which would have been easier if some of the teachers hadn't penalized him just because they hated the Maxwell name.

But the damage had been done. Bobby had continued in his willful ways, and this was where he'd ended up.

Shaking his head, Robert turned toward the door. ''Well, this deputy will do his best to trip you up. You better have the details clear in your mind before you talk to him.''

''What happens if…if he arrests me?'' The question was that of a little boy, scared of the dark and the monster under the bed.

Robert had never known how to deal with those fears. ''Then we'll get us a smart lawyer who can handle himself in court,'' he said without looking back. ''Don't worry.''

Bobby watched his dad close the door, then flopped back against his pillow, regardless of the pain in his ribs.

Don't worry. Oh, sure. Boss Maxwell thought he could fix anything with enough money and enough leverage and enough sheer meanness.

But even if by some miracle the nightmare of the crash went away—if Dan got up and walked out of the hospital tomorrow, if the guy in the other truck and Jerry's family decided to forget everything—there were still problems that money and power couldn't solve.

Like why Megan hadn't come to Big Timber. Why she wouldn't talk to him on the phone, whether he called her at home when her folks weren't there, or at work, or at Racey's house. Hell, Racey wouldn't talk to him, either. And most of the guys he used to hang out with were suddenly "busy" these days.

Dammit, he hadn't meant to hurt anybody. Didn't they know that?

He should have left town last summer, after graduation. Before he got serious about Megan, before they...before they screwed. If she didn't want to talk to him, if he didn't mean any more to her than that, then that's all they'd done. Screwed.

The old man had given him two options—stay in town and work those damn cattle, or get ready to go to college. More school, after twelve years of being carped at by know-it-all teachers and picked at when he got home because his grades weren't good enough? Some option.

If he could even have taken a real break—gone somewhere like California, Florida, somewhere warm with water and rain—maybe he could have faced college. A degree would give him a chance to leave as surely as anything else.

He'd realized soon enough that even running away wouldn't be simple. The old man held the note on the truck. The now-totaled truck. The old man cosigned Bobby's bank account and his credit cards. He knew he would've found the account closed and the cards canceled before he'd been gone two days.

He could have gotten a job, earned the money...except that he'd still have been stuck doing something he didn't like, still in Montana. And getting stuck had a way of becoming a permanent condition. Like living at home.

So he'd stayed around, met Megan...and here he was. Facing arrest for drunk driving at the least. If Dan didn't make it...

He shook his head. Dan had to make it.

I am not a killer.

He hoped.

WHEN HER DAD CAME to breakfast in a suit and tie, Thea knew this wouldn't be an ordinary day.

"Heading to town?" she asked casually, as if the answer didn't matter.

He nodded to her and accepted a mug of coffee from Beth with a slight smile.

"What's going on?" Had he decided to go to the doctor? The idea both scared and pleased her. Something might be really wrong. But at least they'd know and could deal with it.

Before she got an answer, Bobby walked in. He, too, had dressed for town, not work. His skin was pale, his eyes dark and shadowed. The fear in her stomach clamped down like a vise. "Where are you going this morning? What's happening?"

"Your friendly deputy wants to have a chat," Bobby said, pouring a tall glass of juice. "Guess he's ready to make his move."

Thea looked at her dad. "Why didn't you tell me?"

He stared at her, obviously puzzled. "Why would I?"

"Because I'm going with you." Favoring her stiff knee, she took her plate to the sink. "I'll be dressed by the time you've finished breakfast."

She was almost out of the room when he said, "You're not going."

Turning, Thea held on to her temper. "Why wouldn't I?"

"There's work here. Somebody's got to do it."

"Herman knows what's to be done." Her glance caught the manager's nod of agreement.

"You're not going," her dad said again.

Herman set down his coffee cup. "Seems to me she has a right to be there, if Bobby don't mind."

"The more the merrier," Bobby said wearily.

But Robert Maxwell flashed Herman a sharp, furious look. "None of your business."

"After more'n thirty years, I'd say most anything goes on in this family is my business." Stretching to his feet, Herman headed for the door, with a pat on Beth's shoulder as he passed. "Time to get started on the day."

"You don't deserve him," Thea told her dad after the back door closed. "There was no need to be rude."

He just stared at her a minute, hard-eyed, his mouth a thin line, then returned to the breakfast Beth had set in front of him.

"I'll get changed." Again she turned to go.

"Don't bother."

She whirled back, regardless of the pain in her knee, mouth open, temper out of control.

But she didn't get a chance to let loose the waiting tirade. Beth stood at the table with her hand on Robert Maxwell's shoulder. "Thea should go with you," she said quietly. "She's worried about her little brother, as she should be. And maybe if she's there the deputy will back off a little. He likes Thea and he won't want to make her mad at him."

The man at the table gazed straight ahead for a long time without saying anything. Then he shook his head. "I guess you can go," he told Thea over his shoulder. "Fifteen minutes, we're leaving."

Even with a bum leg, she made sure she was waiting for him out by the Cadillac in ten.

THE PARADE FILING into Rafe's office at ten o'clock held some surprises. He should have expected LeVay to show up. Two lawyers wasn't surprising for a man like Maxwell.

But he hadn't expected Thea. And he hadn't expected Bobby Maxwell to look so...beaten.

He didn't think a hello kiss would earn him any points with either Thea or her dad, so he stayed behind his desk. "Good morning. Pull up as many chairs as you need."

The invitation left them one chair short, thanks to the bareness of the office furnishings. Somehow, in a roomful of "gentlemen," Thea was the one left standing—on one leg, no less.

Rafe rolled his chair out from behind the desk. "Here you go." She started to shake her head, but he just grinned at her. "Please sit down, Ms. Maxwell." With an exasperated glance, she did as he said.

Leaning a hip on the corner of the desk, he braced himself for the ordeal ahead. "I'd like this meeting to be as informal and friendly as possible, to get the facts straight on what happened that night. I've got statements from Jerry Heath and Tom Bonner. Now I need one from you." Eyeing Bobby, he picked up his notepad, then clicked on the cassette player. "This'll be more accurate if I record the session. Okay?"

Bobby glanced at the lawyers, who nodded. "Okay."

"Great." He recorded identities and the date, then turned the microphone toward Bobby. "Where you were the night of October 31?"

"At a bachelor party for Monroe Harper."

Rafe wrote it down. "Can you tell me the address? How

many people were there? Just guys? Anybody over the age of twenty-five?''

One of the lawyers sat forward. ''What difference does that make?''

''Helps me get a picture of what was going on.'' He waited for another comment, but the lawyer was quiet. ''What did you do at this party? Movies? Poker? Video games? Pool?''

Bobby looked down at his hands. His cheeks reddened. ''There were a couple of strippers.''

On Rafe's right, Thea stirred in her chair. ''How long did they stay?'' he asked. ''Do you know their names? Were they local? Who hired them?''

Bobby wasn't sure.

''Was there food?'' Rafe wrote down the menu—steak, potatoes, chips and dip. And then he reached the first real question. ''What were you drinking?''

''Beer, mostly.''

''What else?''

The young man hunched a shoulder. ''I can't remember.''

''It's not that hard. What did you drink?''

''Beer, I said.''

''What did Jerry Heath drink?''

With a sudden snarl, Bobby flared up. ''How the hell should I know? I'm not his baby-sitter.''

''I'd expect you to notice, that's all. How about Dan Aiken?''

''Tequila shooters. Beer. I don't know what else.''

Nodding, Rafe wrote it down. ''Did you have tequila?'' Bobby didn't say anything and Rafe looked up. ''Well?''

''Yeah, a couple.''

''Does that mean two?''

''Two or three.''

"How many beers?"

"I didn't count, damn you."

"A six-pack? A case?"

Bobby just shook his head.

"Okay. So you had some drinks and some food. What time did you leave?"

"About ten, maybe."

"Kind of early to end the party, wasn't it? Why'd you leave?"

"Dan wasn't feeling too good. He came in my truck, so I had to take him home."

"You walked outside—the temperature was about fifteen that night. Were you cold?"

"Cold as sh—" Bobby glanced at Thea. "Yeah. I was cold."

"So you three piled into the truck and turned the heat up high?"

"You sure as hell know that's not what happened." One of the lawyers put a hand on his arm, and Bobby backed down. "Dan got sick a couple of times, and decided to ride in the truck bed. We argued with him, but…" He shrugged.

Rafe picked up the pace of the questioning. "How long have you known Monroe Harper?"

"God, I don't know—since sixth or seventh grade."

"You're pretty good friends?"

"Yeah."

"You see him a lot?"

Bobby brushed his hair out of his eyes. "What's a lot? We get together once in a while."

"How many times have you been to his house?"

"I don't have a clue."

"How long have you been driving by yourself?"

"I got my license on my fifteenth birthday."

"What were the roads like? Snow, ice, clear?"

"Uh...clear." But he obviously didn't really remember.

"So you headed away from the party, toward where?"

"Dan's house."

"How fast were you driving?"

He shrugged. "Don't know."

"Did you pass any other vehicles?"

"Don't remember."

"What do you remember, after leaving the party?"

"Nothing." He gripped his hands together, released them. "I don't remember anything."

"You don't remember tearing down the highway at more than ninety-five miles an hour?"

Thea gasped, then put her hand over her eyes.

Bobby stared for a few seconds with his mouth hanging open. "No."

"That's what the skid marks say your speed was. You don't remember the stop sign?"

He shook his head.

"So you've been driving for four years, must've made at least a few trips out to Monroe Harper's place, yet you didn't remember the stop sign at the end of the road?"

"I don't remember every frigging stop sign in the county."

"Obviously not. Do you remember headlights in your eyes? Do you remember Jerry Heath yelling at you to stop? Do you remember Dan's scream as he flew out of the truck bed and landed in the ditch on his head?"

The lawyers were on their feet. "That's enough, Deputy."

"This is over." Robert Maxwell stepped forward, murder in his face.

But over the men's protests, Rafe heard Thea's voice. "Stop it, Rafe. Why are you doing this?" She stood in front of her chair, anger and horror and, yes, guilt on her face. Thea knew the answer to her own question. She just couldn't bring herself to face the consequences of what had happened, or the steps he was now required to follow.

He started to say he was sorry, but Robert Maxwell grabbed him by the shoulders of his shirt and jerked him to his feet. They met eye to furious eye. "You are not railroading my son into jail," he said between clenched teeth. "I'll see you dead first."

"It might come to that." Rafe clamped his hands onto the older man's wrists and tightened his grip until the fingers clutching his shirt relaxed. Then he pushed Maxwell back a stride. "But that's the only thing that will stop me from being sure justice is done on this case."

"You're free to go," he told Bobby. "For now. Don't leave the county for any reason. I'll put out an A.P.B. before you have enough time to use up a tank of gas."

With a final enraged glance, Bobby dragged himself out of the chair and stalked out. The lawyers followed, threatening complaints and lawsuits and spouting legalese.

With his hand on the doorknob, Robert Maxwell turned back. "I mean it," he said, and slammed the door behind him.

Rafe looked at Thea. "I'm sorry."

She shook her head, avoiding his eyes. "Did you have to be so hard on him?"

"Cops in L.A. would consider what I just did the kid-glove treatment."

"Well, this isn't L.A. and Bobby isn't a...a gang leader or a drug lord." She ran a hand through her hair as she paced around the room. "What happens now?"

"I file a report with the sheriff."

"Are you going to arrest Bobby?"

"I'm going to charge him with driving while impaired

and reckless endangerment. He'll have to appear in court to answer those charges. And maybe more.''

From the other side of the office, she gazed at him. ''There's no other way?''

Rafe shook his head. ''You know there isn't.'' He crossed the floor to put his hands on her shoulders. ''Bobby needs to take responsibility for his actions. He'll never grow up if he doesn't.''

She stiffened and pulled out of his hold. ''He might never grow up anyway if you send him to prison.''

The rejection stung. ''How did this become my fault? I didn't force him to drive that night, drunk or otherwise. In fact, I did just about everything I could think of to keep this from happening. It would be nice if somebody in your family recognized that fact.''

''It would be nice if you recognized what it feels like to see your little brother facing this kind of problem. When you've taken care of somebody all his life, you tend to be protective.''

Her sarcasm, the implication that he didn't understand family caring and concern, kindled his temper. ''Too bad my background is deficient when it comes to families— that's going to be a real handicap in this case. I tend to think in terms of upholding the law and seeing justice done, instead of coddling spoiled brats.''

''That's it.'' She grabbed her coat off the chair and shrugged into it on the way to the door. Just like her father, she slammed it hard behind her on the way out.

Rafe swore, loud and long. It was either swear or punch a hole in the wall.

THEA CAME IN from work on Thursday night feeling as if she'd been dragged behind a horse all day, instead of sitting in the saddle. Sundance's leg was improving with rest, but not well enough to work on, so she'd ridden High Five, a bad-tempered roan gelding who fought every command she gave. The weather had warmed up a little—into the high thirties—so the snow was soft and slippery underfoot, which did nothing for High Five's mood.

Even worse, while bringing in a few stragglers from the high country, she'd come across another illegal kill—a bighorn sheep, left to rot with only the head taken. Heavy snows sometimes drove them down from the higher elevations. And this one had met up with the wrong stranger.

Dinner was quiet. Bobby didn't speak much these days. He disappeared between meals, sometimes to his room, sometimes outside. Her dad looked twice as tired as Thea felt, his face lined, his eyes heavy. She didn't have anything to say, either, so Herman and Beth Peace made the only conversation, but even that wasn't much. As soon as they'd finished eating, everyone went their separate ways.

In her room, Thea sat on the bed and stared at the phone. Rafe would want to know about the poached bighorn. But after the way he treated Bobby on Monday, and the things he had said...

She sighed and dialed his number. Sometimes you just had to do the hard things first and think about them later.

"Hello?" The man had no right to own such a deep, stirring voice.

Thea cleared her throat. "Hi."

There was a pause. "Hi. How are you?"

"Okay." Why was this so hard? "Um, I wanted to tell you that I found a slaughtered bighorn up in the mountains today."

This silence was even longer. "That's too bad," Rafe said finally, his tone cool. "No sign of the hunter?"

"Not that I could see. But it's just like all the others. The head was gone."

"Somebody's got a great trophy wall. Assuming, of course, that these are all done by the same person."

"We don't usually see this much poaching in three years, let alone four weeks. I can't believe it's just a string of unconnected people from out of state, killing and then leaving."

"Yeah."

Another minute went by with no words. Thea stirred, shifted the phone to her other ear. "I...I wanted to say I'm sorry about getting so upset on Monday. You were doing your job. I do understand that."

"Thanks. I know it's hard to see your brother go through this. Nobody wants to face this kind of trouble."

"No."

From that very first night, when he'd brought Bobby home, they'd always found something to talk about. They knew each other better now, had nearly made love...and yet she couldn't find a subject to bring up about that wouldn't take them straight back into the battle. Rafe didn't offer any openings.

Thea felt her heart crack. This man-woman thing had been so different with Rafe. She'd hoped for so much.

But that was her problem and hers alone. "Well, I just wanted you to know. I hope this person gives himself away at some point, so you can catch him. I'll let you go now."

"Thea?"

She waited, holding her breath, for his voice to return, warm and sexy, the way she loved. If he would just take one step...

"Have a good night," Rafe said in a totally impersonal tone. "And thanks for reporting the kill."

"Sure. Anytime. Goodbye."

"'Bye."

The phone went dead, and she clicked it off. Without thinking at all, Thea dragged off her clothes and stepped into a hot shower. That way, she couldn't distinguish her tears from the water pouring over her head.

CHAPTER THIRTEEN

FOR THE FIRST TIME in five years, all four Maxwell children were home for Thanksgiving. Jolie flew into Bozeman from Los Angeles, rented a car and drove through a snowstorm to arrive Wednesday afternoon. Cassie and Zak came the opposite direction from Billings in the same storm. Beth baked pies all of Thursday morning, then started on a holiday dinner of epic proportions.

Thea looked around the dinner table that evening with mixed feelings. On the one hand, she was glad to have the whole family in one place. But the atmosphere wasn't particularly cheerful. They'd come together for the wrong reasons.

Ten days ago, Rafe had arrested Bobby for drunk driving and a host of other crimes. Judge LeVay had released Bobby without bond, but the charges were there, hanging over their heads like a broken branch about to fall.

She hadn't seen Rafe since the afternoon he'd come to get Bobby. He'd glanced at her once, a look of wary apology, but hadn't spoken to her directly. Or since. He hadn't called her, and after the disaster of their last conversation, she hadn't called him.

Thank God they hadn't had sex. How much worse would she feel if they'd shared that ultimate intimacy?

Then again, how could she possibly feel any worse?

Shaking her head to clear Rafe from her mind, she forked

up some of Beth's sweet-potato casserole and studied her family around the table.

Jolie, sitting on their dad's right and across from Thea, was as quiet as ever and a little formidable, with an innate air of authority that years of practicing medicine had reinforced.

"Low-income families have trouble maintaining a stable family structure," she was saying to Cassie. "When there is only one parent who must work at two jobs, or two parents, both working, the children are left on their own. Without extended family to look after them, these youngsters have no guidance, no roots to draw from."

"But the extended family can, in fact, be the problem," Cassie countered, "when the kids are left with uncles or aunts who aren't responsible or who don't have any emotional investment in keeping them safe. And if they are actively abusive, you've compounded the problem."

"So what is the solution?" Thea helped Zak spoon gravy over his mashed potatoes.

"A mother ought to stay home with her children," Robert Maxwell said. "A man ought to be able to support his family by his own efforts."

Dead silence fell in the dining room as Jolie and Cassie and Thea stared, slack-jawed, at their dad.

"You really believe that?" Cassie's voice shook. "You think women shouldn't work outside the home?"

"You're the ones saying how bad it is for the kids when the parents work. Pass the turkey, Herman."

Wordlessly, the manager handed the platter to Jolie, who passed it on. "Why shouldn't a dad stay home if he wants to," she asked calmly, "and let the mother support the family?"

Her father gave a snort. "Men weren't created to take care of babies and little children."

At the opposite end of the table, Bobby slouched in his chair. He hadn't touched his food. "Some of them don't do so hot with older kids, either."

Thea held her breath as Robert Maxwell looked at Bobby through narrowed eyes. "What's your point?"

"Hell, I don't know." Bobby ran both hands through his thick, dark hair. "Except that there oughta be somebody who'll consider what the kid wants out of life. Somebody to give a kid the chance to expand, to try new things. Not just lock down on him, leave him no room to breathe."

All of them except little Zak sat paralyzed for a moment. Beth stood up, finally. "Let me get another pan of rolls out of the oven."

"So, Dad, what's new in your work this year?" Jolie's soft voice held a note of determination. "What size herd are you running these days?"

He answered with his usual matter-of-fact attitude, leaving the rest of the table to recover. On Zak's other side, Cassie looked down at her plate and pushed her stuffing around, muttering softly.

"Don't be too hard on Dad," Thea told her sister quietly, over the little boy's head. "The situation with Bobby has been really tough. And he isn't feeling good."

"None of us are feeling good," Cassie said. "Little brother made sure of that."

A lull in the talk around the table allowed everyone to hear her comment. Bobby sat up slowly, his face red, his eyes blazing.

"Screw you." He pushed away from the table; his chair crashed to the floor as he jerked to his feet. "Screw all of you."

They listened in silence as his boot heels pounded a retreat against the hardwood floors. The slam of his bedroom door rattled the windows.

Thea blew out the breath she'd been holding. "Happy Thanksgiving. God bless us, everyone." No one laughed, or even smiled.

Bobby didn't reappear. The rest of the family finished dinner quietly and left the table, with Herman heading out to the barn and Robert Maxwell to his office. Jolie cornered Thea by the fireplace later that night, after the dishes were done. "How long has Dad looked so run-down?"

"You mean tired?" Thea considered. "For some time now. But that's not surprising, is it? He probably doesn't sleep well, with Bobby in trouble like this. And if he wakes up very often like he did that one night, then he should be exhausted."

Her sister's gaze sharpened. "Wakes up how?"

The fear she wanted to ignore expanded in Thea's stomach. "He couldn't breathe. He was lying on his back in bed, choking. I helped him up, and after a couple of minutes on his feet he got his breath back. It was scary."

"Has this happened before?"

"I've never seen it. But when I asked him that, he wouldn't answer, which probably means yes. And he ordered me not to tell anybody."

Jolie shook her head. "From what you've said, he may have a serious problem. He needs to see a doctor as soon as possible."

Thea laughed. "Right. I'll just rope him and drag him into town behind me."

"No, not in Paradise Corners. This isn't a case for a visiting physician's assistant or a nurse practitioner. You need an appointment in Bozeman with an internal medicine specialist."

The familiar feeling of incompetence stirred in Thea at Jolie's take-charge attitude. "I don't know any of those."

"I'll make some calls, see who I can recommend. And

I'll talk to Dad the first chance I get. He's got to know this is not a symptom he can ignore.''

Her cool assumption that Robert Maxwell would listen irritated Thea. ''He hasn't become any less stubborn since you left home, you know. It's not as if I didn't try to get him to a doctor.''

''Coming from another doctor, perhaps the warning will have more impact.'' Jolie smiled, and patted Thea on the shoulder. ''Don't worry about it. I'll make sure he understands.''

''Oh, right,'' Thea muttered as her oldest sister walked away. ''Just waltz back in and take over. How did we ever get along all these years without you?''

ROBERT FOUND his three daughters seated around the fireplace late Thanksgiving night. He would have thought they'd be talking, catching up on their lives. But Jolie sat on one end of the couch with her head buried in what looked like a medical book. Cassie held down the other end while she flipped through a magazine. Althea slouched in her usual chair by the hearth, staring into the fire, doing nothing at all.

At the sound of his step, they all turned their heads. Jolie closed her book. ''Hi, Dad. Beth is bringing in coffee and pie. Come join us.''

He was tired to the bone, and Bobby's outburst had left him with the feeling he'd been on the losing end of a fist-fight. But his daughters had made the effort to come home, and it was his duty to make them welcome.

So he sat down in the chair near Althea and nodded to Cassie. ''Where's the boy?''

''I put Zak to bed in the guest room.'' She laid her magazine on the coffee table and pushed back her red hair. ''He likes spending the night. But we'll have to leave pretty early tomorrow. I need to put in a couple of hours of work in the afternoon."

Robert frowned. "Where's he go while you're at work?"

"On easy days like tomorrow, he comes with me and plays nearby." Cassie's chin was up, her attitude feisty, as usual. "Most of the time, I work while he's in school, of course. And he's enrolled in a great after-school program."

"Young one like that ought to be with family, doing homework and chores." Robert knew she didn't want to hear that, but truth couldn't be avoided.

"I don't have family close enough."

"You shouldn't have to work. A decent husband would support you and the boy. Or you could come home where you belong. You'd be here for him all the time."

Cassie got to her feet with a grace that reminded him of her mother. "I don't have a husband—"

"Good riddance. If you'd listened to me at the beginning—"

She chopped at the air with her hand. "And I can support my son and myself on my own. We don't need to live here. In fact, I wouldn't live here if—"

"I don't think this argument is going anywhere. Let's change the subject." Jolie had inherited her mother's quiet authority, her peace-making ways. "I want to talk to you, Dad. I think you're looking tired these days."

"I look like I have every day for the five years since you were home last."

Her lips pressed together. "You're having some trouble sleeping at night, I understand. Do you wake up often having trouble breathing?"

He stared at Althea, who met him eye to eye and shrugged a shoulder. "I ordered you to keep that to yourself."

"So this has happened more than once?" Jolie insisted.

"That's nobody's business but mine."

"Look, Dad, we're concerned about your health." She leaned forward, resting her elbows on her knees and clasping her hands. "What other symptoms are you having? Fatigue? Shortness of breath? Do you have some swelling in your feet and legs?"

"No." His boots seemed to shrink at the lie.

"Do you find yourself breathing hard when you're going up steps or walking a long distance?"

"No. I told you, I don't have a problem. And I'll thank you to stay out of my business." Robert stood up just as Beth entered from the dining room with a tray of coffee cups and slices of pumpkin, pecan and mincemeat pie.

"Dessert," she announced, smiling, and set the tray on the ottoman in front of the fire. "Robert, what will you have?"

"Nothing." He saw her startled look and tried to control his temper. "Thanks. I'm not hungry. And I've got some work to do."

Beth gazed around the room, no doubt reading the tension in their faces. Her smile died, to be replaced by worry. "Surely you'll have some coffee?"

Before he could answer, Jolie piped up. "It might be good if you cut down on your caffeine intake, Dad. And your smoking. At least until—"

Choking back an oath, Robert stepped to the tray and picked up a mug of coffee. "Later," he said, and left them there, staring. In his study, he set the coffee down with a slosh and went to stand at the window behind the desk. His breathing was harsh in the silence, too fast. He felt as if lead weights dragged at his arms and legs. Turning his chair around, he dropped onto the leather seat and tipped his head back.

Not much doubt there was something wrong, if Jolie

could predict problems she hadn't seen, like his swollen feet, how fast he got out of breath these days. Could be something serious.

If it was…well, a man had to face up to his own mortality at some point. His time on this earth was set, and not a whit of worrying on his part would change it.

But if he died, what would happen to the land he'd tended all these years? What would happen to his son? With Bobby in prison, who would care for Walking Stones?

Althea's face flashed in front of his eyes. Yes, she did the work, but she was a woman. She would be married one day, with children to care for. Cassie was a good example of what happened when a woman tried to work and be a mother. She couldn't do either job as well as it should be done. And Althea's children would not be Maxwells. They would have a different last name. Rafferty?

Robert clenched his fists. He couldn't afford to get sick now. Whatever was wrong would just have to wait until he got Bobby's future settled, until the boy came to realize his heritage and his responsibility to the land.

Then there would be time for illness, even death.

THE FOUR WOMEN STARED at each other in silence for a long moment after Robert left the family room.

Finally, Beth sighed. "What was all that about?"

Jolie leaned back on the couch. "I was asking about his health. He got angry."

"Only after he as much as told me that I'm a lousy mother and he'd like to take my son away." Cassie walked to one of the front windows, looking out into the darkness, her back stiff and straight. "I should just wake Zak up right now and go home."

Thea sat up out of her slouch. "Don't do that. He won't be back out tonight. Just have some pie and relax."

"Like anybody can relax around here these days." But she walked back to pick up a plate and mug. "Why were you asking about his health, anyway, Jolie? Has he been sick?"

"I think he looks…" Jolie cast a glance at Beth's worried face. "I think he looks as if a checkup would be a good idea."

"In what way?" Beth said, twisting her hands.

"Pale and tired, breathing a little too hard after small exertions. I noticed when he and Zak came in from the barn this afternoon he seemed quite out of breath. And Thea told me he's been waking up at night unable to breathe. That's a pretty significant symptom."

"Of what?" Cassie set down her mug and plate again.

"Any number of things," Jolie said a little impatiently. "I can't make a definitive diagnosis on something like this without tests. So there's no point in pursuing the subject further."

"Then why did you bring it up?" Cassie took another turn around the room. "You could have talked to him in private and done just as much good."

"I thought we all should be aware of a potential problem, and since I'll be leaving on Sunday and you will be here to help Thea—"

"Oh, right. You're just taking off again, leaving us to deal with everything."

Jolie held out her hands. "I have responsibilities in Los Angeles. I have to go back."

"You have responsibilities here, too." Cassie pointed a finger at her older sister. "But you dumped them to go to college—even left early, to take summer courses. Summer internships and study sessions, part-time jobs—you made sure you wouldn't have to come back and deal with anything at home. So I suppose we shouldn't expect anything of you now.''

"Come on, Cassie.'' Thea couldn't tolerate such an obvious distortion of the facts. "You cleared out, just like Jolie did. Don't make it sound like you stuck around being the dutiful daughter. High school ended and you took off. When you were here, the stunts you pulled kept the place in an uproar.''

"I needed some space, for heaven's sake. At least I grew up.'' She brushed back her red hair. "You're still here, Thea, staying a little girl, hoping one day he'll notice you and treat you like an adult. Don't hold your breath.''

"There's no need to attack Thea.'' Jolie had switched to her big sister voice, the one she'd used in their childhood to get her way. "She holds an important place here at the ranch, just as Beth does. We should be grateful to them both for keeping things together as well as they have.''

"Keeping things together?'' Cassie mocked. "With Bobby under arrest for assault, maybe even murder? How is that keeping anything at all together?''

"Bobby is not only my responsibility,'' Thea said, standing up. "Both of you could have—*should* have—talked to him.''

"That presupposes we were told about the situation to begin with,'' Jolie retorted. "Instead, I have to wait until something truly dire happens to be made aware of my family's problems.''

They were well into the wrangle now. After another minute of argument, Beth threw her hands in the air and left the room. The pots and pans banging in the kitchen were sure signs of her reaction to the entire scene.

The fight didn't end, it simply stopped—with Cassie storming off to the guest room she shared with Zak, Jolie burying herself again in a medical journal, and Thea in her

own bedroom fuming. Her mood wasn't helped by the realization that she wanted to call Rafe and share the whole
hopeless situation with him.

Knowing that he would have given her both the comfort
she sought and the levelheaded advice she needed made
her loneliness and desolation all the more intense.

She really should have gotten herself a dog.

RAFE SPENT the Thanksgiving weekend in the mountains
with Jed. Mona Rangel had asked him to join her at her
daughter and son-in-law's dinner in Bozeman, but he'd de-
clined. A family celebration would have been more unfa-
miliar and uncomfortable to him than spending the day
alone. Jed was as much family as he'd ever needed, anyway.

Since Thea had stopped speaking to him, Rafe had begun
to wonder if Jed might be the only relative he'd ever have.

Hard days of walking and cold nights sleeping outdoors
kept thoughts like that at bay. Starting at first light, they
followed the perimeter of the national forest closest to Paradise Corners, zigzagging back and forth across the actual
boundary. Rafe examined the snowy ground closely, looking for tracks, animal or human, and any signs of hunting
activity. The first poached animals had shown up a few
miles north and west of town. But when Rafe studied a
dated map of the reported kills—six in all—he discovered
that most had occurred close to or on Maxwell property.
As Thea had pointed out, the pattern seemed too obvious
to be an accident or the actions of an out-of-state visitor
passing through.

So someone in the area was poaching and, for some reason, drawing attention to the Walking Stones Ranch. Con-
veying a message? Or just making trouble?

By Saturday afternoon, he and Jed ended up, as he had
intended, at the Walking Stones themselves. Rafe stood

gazing over the vast view of the ranch for a long time. He could see a plume of smoke rising in the distance from the fireplace at the ranch house. Of course, Thea was probably still out working, doing the job she loved, the job for which her dad gave her no respect. Things would be different, Rafe thought, if she shared a spread with *him*. She could run the place, and he'd give her nothing but praise for her stamina and talent. If they were married, he'd make sure she started out every day knowing how special she was.

But they weren't married, weren't even close, and might never be. Dan Aiken's condition hadn't improved much. Jerry Heath had gone home, but his parents' attorney was pursuing their suit with enthusiasm. Financially and legally, the outlook for Bobby's future remained cloudy. And as long as that was the case, Rafe's future with Thea stood no chance at all.

He turned from the view to examine the clearing. Behind one of the big boulders, Jed was pawing at the icy snow, trying to get through to the ground below. Rafe walked over to see what he'd found.

A plastic trash bag had been buried beneath the surface snow but above ground level. Rafe pulled the bag free, went to a level rock and tipped the contents out. Chip bags, a dozen beer cans, sandwich wrappers. The weekly newspaper for Paradise Corners, the *Standard,* dated the Monday after Bobby's accident, with the article reporting the crash torn out.

Whoever had left the trash had some sort of connection to Bobby Maxwell. Or was it Bobby himself? Surely busted ribs and a body covered with bruises would have prevented him from getting up this high into the mountains, even on horseback.

And anyway, why come sit in the cold, unless…he wanted a drink and couldn't get one at home?

At the bottom of the sack, Rafe found two real pieces of

evidence. A squishy little packet proved to be latex gloves, turned inside out. When he carefully pulled the gloves apart, he found them coated with a brown crust. It didn't take much imagination to believe that the crust was dried blood.

Human or animal? Only a lab test could tell for sure, but from the coated nature of the gloves, Rafe was betting these had been used to cover the hands of a hunter prepared to field-dress a deer. Or maybe just cut off its head.

The other item was even more telling—a wrinkled credit card receipt for two cases of beer from the convenience store in Paradise Corners.

With Bobby Maxwell's name in the imprint and his signature on the line.

ROBERT MAXWELL DROVE his four children and his grandson to church on Sunday morning. Zak went to children's church and the adults occupied their family pew in a state of armed neutrality, very careful of what they said to each other, avoiding any possibly contentious topic, as they had for the last three days. Bobby had appeared only rarely during that time, with absolutely nothing to say when he did.

Longing for a respite from the family warfare, Thea looked for Rafe but didn't find him. Disappointment settled in her chest like a heavy cold. The source of conflict between them—Bobby's arrest—hadn't changed, but somehow she'd thought just seeing him would make her feel a little better.

After the service, Cassie went to fetch her son while the rest of the family started back to the car, without speaking to each other or the people around them. None of the townsfolk said anything aloud, but the empty space around the Maxwell family widened every week. The minister still shook their hands. Everyone else pretended they didn't exist.

Just as they reached the parking lot, Cassie raced down the sidewalk. "Have you seen Zak?"

Thea shook her head. "He's not in the children's class-room?"

Cassie shook her head. "One of the other boys was teasing him—something about his Uncle Bobby. The teacher wouldn't say exactly what. Zak pushed the kid out of his chair and ran from the room. They've looked for him, and were just coming to get me." She pushed back her red hair. "Dear God, he could be anywhere by now!"

The parking lot had emptied quickly, leaving them virtually alone on the church property. "Cassie, you stay on the front steps in case he shows up," Robert Maxwell ordered. "Bobby, you take the east side of the church, Jolie the north. Althea will go south and I'll go west. We'll find him."

Thankful that she'd worn her knee-high dress boots, Thea combed the snowy cemetery, calling Zak every few minutes, hearing the rest of the family do the same. Their voices faded as they each drew farther from the church building without finding the little boy. Heart pounding, Thea reached the far side of the graveyard and stood listening, staring into the hills beyond the church grounds, wondering what they would do if Zak had wandered so far.

She heard a sudden shout to her right. When it was repeated, she stepped over the low wall separating the grounds from wilderness and headed toward the sound of her dad's voice.

She found his tracks first, leading down a slope and along the edge of a steeper ravine. Zak's footprints were here, as well. At least they knew where he'd gone. Now all they had to do was get him back safe...

"Althea!" The call stopped her just as she found the

path of smoothed snow leading down into the ravine. "Althea, we're coming up."

Her dad appeared through the saplings and low brush growing from the side of the gorge. Held tight against the older man's body as he climbed, Zak had his arms wrapped securely around his granddad's neck. He only began to struggle when Cassie was in sight, and ran, sobbing, into his mother's arms as soon as they reached the safety of the churchyard.

Thea cupped her hands around her mouth to call the others. "Bobby? Jolie? We found him. Come back."

Their responses hailed from a fair distance, but they'd heard. She turned to congratulate her dad, and found him leaning against a tree, fighting for breath.

"Dad?" She put her hand on his back as he curled sideways into the trunk. His face was gray, his eyes closed, and his breathing more of a choking gasp. "Oh my God. What can I do?"

He shook his head and bent over to put his hands on his knees, still struggling to drag air into his lungs.

"Jolie!" Thea screamed. "Quick!"

Just as her sister appeared at the corner of the church, Robert drew one effective breath. By the time Jolie and Bobby reached them, the horrible attack was over. Robert straightened, but still leaned back against the tree with his eyes closed. Thea explained where he'd found Zak and how he'd brought him back. Jolie nodded several times at the description of the symptoms Robert had suffered. Then, without a word, she walked over to Cassie and Zak.

After a brief argument with her father, Thea drove home. Cassie and Zak and Jolie went into the guest room to patch up the little boy's scrapes. Robert went to his study and shut the door firmly. Thea was left in the kitchen with Bobby and Beth.

"He's sick," Beth said, her usually smooth forehead wrinkled. "We have to get him to a doctor."

"There's one in the house," Bobby pointed out, "and he won't let her near him."

"He'd better see someone, and fast." Jolie came into the kitchen, took down a glass and went to the refrigerator. "What I saw today leads me to believe Dad may be suffering from congestive heart failure. He needs treatment right away."

Thea gripped her hands together. "What's that?"

Jolie turned around as she poured milk into the glass. "The heart muscle weakens, pumps less efficiently, so the blood doesn't move as well through the body. Often this shows up in the lungs, where fluid will leak from the blood vessels into the lung space, essentially filling them up with water."

"That...that sounds like drowning."

"Pretty much." She looked from Thea to Bobby to Beth. "There are treatments. CHF isn't curable, but it can be managed for a long time. By a specialist. That's why he needs to see one. As soon as possible." She put the milk away, went to the doorway, then turned. "I'd stay to help, but the clinic in L.A. is short-staffed as it is. I have to fly back tonight. But I'll talk to Dad before I leave, and I'll do whatever I can by telephone. Maybe...maybe I can get back here to help you in a few weeks. I know it's not fair to make you handle everything, Thea. But you have to take him to one of the doctors on the list I gave you. Tomorrow wouldn't be too soon."

Bobby stirred. "Or what happens?"

She stared at him. "Or else you're going to be the Robert Maxwell running this ranch."

CHAPTER FOURTEEN

JOLIE RETURNED to California, Cassie and a scratched-up Zak went home to Billings, and Robert Maxwell adamantly refused to see a doctor. Rafe Rafferty, of course, did not call or come out to the ranch.

"Everything's back to normal," Thea told herself grimly as she stood in hip-deep snow with a couple of the ranch hands on the Thursday after Thanksgiving, working to haul three wayward heifers up the steep slope of the ravine.

Normal, except that the house was as silent as a tomb, with Zak's little-boy noises missing and Beth's usual good humor subdued. Herman had given up trying to tease his sister out of her somber mood or joke his boss out of a stonier silence than any of them could remember since Helen Maxwell's death.

And normal except for the fact that Bobby got thinner every day, the circles under his eyes turning as dark as bruises. He rarely spoke, hardly ate. Judging by the footfalls Thea could hear pacing his room at all hours of the night, he didn't sleep, either.

She decided to take him in hand, and showed up at his bedroom door Thursday evening with two cups of hot chocolate. "Bobby, open the door. My hands are full."

After a long moment, he did as she asked. Thea didn't waste time commenting on his messy hair and clothes, the complete disaster he'd made of his room. Or the beer she could smell in the air. She shouldered her way past him, handing off a mug as she did so, then swiped a pile of clothes off the armchair and made herself comfortable.

"Shut the door," she told him. "And your mouth."

"Thea, I don't want company."

"Tough. You can try to throw me out bodily, but I'm not betting you'll be successful."

He sighed, kicked the door shut and leaned back against it. "What the hell do you want?"

"I want to know why you're holed up like a wounded bear in its den."

"In case you've forgotten, I'm not allowed to leave the county. I have major arrest charges hanging over my head. And a best friend in the hospital."

"None of those situations will be improved by the way you're acting."

Bobby set the mug on the chest of drawers, then reconsidered and took a sip. "I may be insensitive and oblivious, but I know when I'm in deep shit. And this is it."

"Insensitive and oblivious? Who told you that?"

His gaze avoided her face. "Nobody told me. Nobody's talking to me."

Thea suddenly made the connection she'd missed. "Bobby, when did you last see Megan?"

He didn't move a muscle, which told her quite a bit. "A few weeks ago. I don't remember. Doesn't matter."

"Since that night in Bozeman?"

After a long silence, he said, "No."

"Because of her dad? Did he find out about you two seeing each other?"

"I don't think so." The words came out slowly, as if some kind of extra force was required to make them heard.

"Have you talked to her friends?"

"Yeah."

"And what did they say?"

"That I'm oblivious and insensitive, dammit!" The mug of hot chocolate crashed into the opposite wall. "That Megan's sick of sneaking around and sick of not being good enough and sick of me. Satisfied?" He turned on her, eyes wild and wounded.

"At least you're talking to me now." But her voice shook more than she would have liked. "She's scared, Bobby. You have to see that."

"Like I'm not? Why…?" He shook his head. "Never mind."

"Why what?"

"Why can't we be scared together? Why wouldn't that be better for both of us?"

His voice cracked, and Thea realized that his heart was truly broken. She went to stand behind him as he stared at the wall with his arms braced as if he was holding it up— or it, him. "It can be that way, I guess. But Maxwells don't seem to have much luck when it comes to love." Rubbing a circle across his back with her palm, she offered what comfort she could.

Finally, Bobby drew a deep breath. "You're not seeing Rafferty these days?"

Since he'd been honest, she would be, too. "No."

"I guess you don't feel much better than I do."

"Not too much. I'm older, though, so I do know the pain fades. Being alone gets easier."

"Yeah?" He gave a ghost of a laugh. "I'll look forward to that."

"It'll happen. I promise." *I hope,* she told herself silently. "Meanwhile, you'd better get that wall and the floor and the bed cleaned up. Beth's going to have a fit if she sees hot chocolate everywhere."

"I will." She'd reached the door when he spoke again. "Tee? You think Dad's really sick?"

"Jolie says so, and she's the doctor."

"What are we going to do?"

It was her turn to sigh. "I don't know, Bobby. I really don't know."

THEA JUST HAPPENED to answer the phone Saturday evening at dinnertime. Her heart jumped when Rafe said her name. And fell a thousand feet with his next words.

She hung up with a shaking hand and turned blindly toward the kitchen table where dinner had just been set down. "Dan's taken a turn for the worse," she told them. "Pneumonia and a blood infection. He…they're not sure he'll make it."

Beth gasped. Her dad and Herman just stared. Bobby had skipped dinner. Again. Someone would have to tell him….

"I'm going into Bozeman, to the hospital." Thea headed for the back door. "I'll call when I know something."

"Be careful," Beth called after her.

Robert Maxwell didn't say anything at all.

Rafe met her at the hospital entrance. "He's hanging on," he said in answer to her anxious stare. "That's all they'll tell me."

They rode the elevator without saying anything else. Thea glanced at the man beside her. He was still tall, strong, gorgeous. Subdued, though, and thinner than she remembered. Had these horrible weeks taken a toll on Rafe, too?

The waiting room for the intensive care unit was crowded with Dan's family and friends. Their quiet conversations stopped as Thea stepped through the doorway. What felt like fifty pairs of eyes stared at her with hostility and outrage and sadness.

"Sorry," she whispered, backing out again and straight

into Rafe's solid support. "I can't go in there," she muttered as much to herself as to him.

"We'll find someplace else." His hand closed around her upper arm, gentle but firm, and urged her farther down the hall. At a window they found two folding chairs probably set up by other people who'd had to wait. Thea sank onto one with a sigh, put her elbows on the narrow windowsill and gazed out into the dark.

Rafe turned his chair around and straddled it with his arms resting along the back. He let himself watch Thea, savoring the details of seeing her again after three weeks. Her dark hair shone, but her eyes were tired. She looked pale—her tan might have faded some during the short, cloudy days, but he thought the stress of the situation was a more likely cause. And maybe, just maybe, she'd been missing *him?* Could he hope for that?

She turned away from the window and caught him staring. What he was thinking probably showed on his face. Her eyes widened, and suddenly there was light in her face again, a smile on her wonderful mouth. He couldn't help grinning, himself. For the first time since their afternoon at the Walking Stones, his world felt right.

But then they both remembered why they were here, and the connection broke.

"What happened?" Thea pressed her fingers against her eyes for a second. "When I called yesterday, the nurses said Dan's condition was unchanged."

"His temperature went up suddenly last night." Nothing like always being the bearer of bad news. Just once, Rafe would have liked to give Thea something happy to think about. "They ran tests, found the pneumonia and the blood infection. He's been on heavy antibiotics since then, but the fight isn't over yet."

"He hasn't ever come completely out of the coma, has he?"

Rafe shook his head.

"The longer it lasts…" She blew out a breath. "I wish there was something I could say to his mother. Something she would believe."

Since he'd had the same problem himself, he couldn't offer any advice. "Just being here shows her that you care."

"She probably thinks I'm just worried about the stupid lawsuit. Or what happens to Bob—"

With that comment, the atmosphere between them grew cooler. Rafe realized he'd again become the man who would arrest her brother for murder if Dan died.

He couldn't stand the change. "I'll go see what I can find out," he said, getting to his feet. Leaving Thea alone in the hallway behind him was easier than staying to face the huge wall now separating them once again.

WHEN THEA CALLED about 2:00 a.m., Bobby picked up the phone. "What's going on? How is he?" She didn't say anything for a long time. His stomach cramped. "Tee? Tell me something."

"It's not good, Bobby." Her voice sounded as if she had a sore throat. "The medicines aren't taking hold. The doctor has just started him on a different one, the strongest antibiotic they've got. We won't know if it works for a few hours yet."

After that, there wasn't much to say. Sweating and shivering at the same time, Bobby hung up the phone and sat staring at the floor between his feet.

Dan would die. Rafe Rafferty would see to it that he paid the highest possible penalty for Dan's death, and Bobby doubted even his dad could change that outcome.

He might spend ten, fifteen years in prison, and come home an old man. To what? Megan wouldn't speak to him *now*. She sure as hell wouldn't wait for a convicted murderer. The only job he'd be able to get at that point would be on his dad's ranch. Which wasn't all that much different than prison itself.

Bobby knew he would carry the weight of killing his best friend with him for the rest of his life, behind bars or not. Going to prison for murder wouldn't make any difference once Dan was...dead.

The walls of his room closed in, and he fought to get a decent breath. No way could he stay here. No way could he just sit and wait for Dan to die, wait for Rafferty to come take him to jail...

He didn't leave a note behind, didn't take anything with him but twenty bucks, a change of clothes and the keys to one of the ranch's trademark blue trucks. In the parking lot of the hospital in Bozeman, he sat for an hour wondering if he could sneak in to see Dan, or if he was too late.

Finally, he decided to take the chance, and got as far as the stairway door onto the intensive care floor. Through the window, he could see the nurses' station and Mr. Aiken talking to a doctor, holding Mrs. Aiken in his arms as she cried. Beyond them, he saw Thea turn to Rafe Rafferty and rest her cheek on his chest. Rafferty's arms went around her, tight, and he kissed the top of her head.

Choking on his own tears, Bobby took off.

"I CAN'T BELIEVE IT." Thea looked up at Rafe, comforted by the strong circle of his arms around her, encouraged by his smile. "An hour ago the doctors had all but given up. And now the fever's broken, and they think he's going to pull through."

"Pretty close to a miracle, in my opinion." He brushed

her hair back from her face, wiped her wet cheeks with his thumbs. "But Dan definitely deserves one. And so do you."

Her cheeks got hot and she looked away from his eyes to her hands pressed against his chest. "I'm just so thankful—"

Someone tapped her on the shoulder. "Althea?"

She turned out of Rafe's hold to discover that Dan's mother had come over. "Mrs. Aiken, I'm so glad that he's getting better. I don't mean to intrude by being here, but we're all worried. Especially Bobby."

The older woman's mouth tightened. "'Better' is a strange word to use when we still don't know if he'll ever wake up again. Or walk or talk." Her eyes, blue like her son's, filled with tears that didn't fall. "I wanted to thank you for your concern, and ask you and your family and the deputy here—" she glanced at Rafe "—not to come back. Our lawyer says it's a bad idea, you hanging around when there are legal issues to deal with."

"Mrs. Aiken—"

Having said her piece, Dan's mother turned and went back to her family.

Eventually Thea started to breathe again, though tremors of cold ran through her. She turned toward the empty hallway. "I've got to get out of here…"

"Thea, wait." Rafe caught hold of her shoulders and brought her around to face him. "You don't have to leave. They can't throw you out of a public hospital without a good reason."

She couldn't look at him. For the first time in her life, she understood the depth of the hatred people felt toward her family. It made her ashamed. "They don't want me here. That's reason enough."

He wouldn't let her go. "Dan is your friend, and your brother's. That's reason to stay."

"I—"

"Oh, dear God!"

The cry from Dan's mother drew Thea down the hall at a run. Surely he hadn't...they'd said he was improving...

The Aiken family was celebrating—hugging and laughing and crying all at once—while the doctor tried to talk to Mr. and Mrs. Aiken. Thea came close enough to hear his words.

"...questions about the year, about his family, and he knew the answers without hesitation. He seems to be unimpaired, mentally, at least, though weak, of course. His speech is clear. We'll wait until he's stronger to discover the extent of his physical limitations."

"Can we talk to him? Oh, please..." Mrs. Aiken clasped her hands around the doctor's arm. "Please let me talk to my boy."

"For just a moment." Smiling, he ushered Dan's parents into their son's room.

"He's awake." Thea breathed a prayer of thanksgiving. "Oh, Rafe, he's awake!"

Rafe grinned. "And you're dead on your feet. Me, too, for that matter. Now that you know Dan's doing better, why don't we head for home?"

In the parking lot, though, they were faced with the need to get two vehicles back to Paradise Corners.

"I suppose we have to drive separately," Rafe said. "Doesn't make sense to leave one here and then come back and get it."

The disappointment in his tone echoed Thea's sentiments. "No, it doesn't." She opened the door to the Land Rover and climbed inside. "So I guess I'll say good-night.

Thanks for calling. I'm glad I was here to get the great news about Dan.''

Rafe moved into the shelter of the open car door. "I'd hoped we could share a cup of coffee, maybe talk a little bit." He stroked his cold knuckles down her cheek. "But it's crazy for you to drive past the ranch to go into town, then turn around again to go home."

Their faces were at the same level. Thea stared into those dark brown eyes, mesmerized by their warmth, by the conviction they conveyed that this man needed her. Wanted her, no matter the differences between them.

Just as she wanted him. "That would be crazy," she agreed breathlessly. And smiled. "But not out of the question."

His grin was everything she'd hoped—wickedly sexy, relieved and just plain happy. "I'll call Jed, tell him to put the coffee on."

RAFE'S INTENTIONS were good. He wanted a chance to talk with Thea, to watch her face, find out what had happened during the weeks they'd been apart. Dan Aiken's progress restored the possibility of a future Rafe believed he and Thea could share. If Bobby wasn't charged with murder, surely they would be able to fight their way past any and all obstacles the law—and Robert Maxwell—put in their path.

Then she came into his house, smelling of cold air and snow and that unique fragrance that was all her own. She laughed, smiled, brushed snowflakes out of her hair and shrugged out of her oversize coat to reveal a long-sleeved white T-shirt and worn, faded jeans. Not the clothes a man usually fantasized about, but on Thea's curves, the reality of cotton and denim proved much more seductive than fancy silk lingerie.

The first kiss got complicated right away, as her warm, immediate response drove ideas of coffee to the back of Rafe's brain. Holding her tight against him, tasting her sweet mouth, feeling her hands roam his back and hips and comb through his hair, he lost track of everything but the need for more of this woman he loved.

The door to his bedroom was only a few steps along the hallway. He lifted Thea against him and walked into his room, then lowered her feet back to the floor, letting his fingers slip under her shirt onto smooth, warm skin. Her ribs lifted on a sharp breath and he felt as if he held her life between his hands. When he cupped her breasts, her heart pounded against his palms. With a fierce cry Thea took the last step, falling backward onto the bed, pulling him with her.

Her shirt was off in seconds, his only moments later. They laughed without the breath to do so, helping each other drag boot tops out from under narrow-legged jeans. Then the jeans themselves hit the floor.

Rafe hesitated, struck by the sight of Thea's dark hair against his pillow, her breasts bared to his gaze and the sweet, feminine practicality of the last wisp of pink cotton remaining between them.

"Thea..." He whispered her name and she drew him close for another sanity-stealing kiss. "Thea, this is your first time. Are you sure? We can stop—"

She opened her eyes, dark and dazed with need. "Oh, yes. I'm very sure." Her chest rose and fell on a deep breath. "Whatever happens tomorrow, I want this with you tonight."

"God help me," Rafe prayed, and let go of his remaining doubts.

He was careful—careful to protect her, careful to go slowly at first, giving her body and her mind a chance to adjust. His reward was her desire, her growing passion, her desperate search for satisfaction—his as well as her own. At the end they were completely joined, completely swept away.

Completely at peace.

RAFE WOKE to daylight and the aroma of coffee. He opened his eyes and found Thea, wearing her T-shirt and not much else, sitting on the side of the bed with a mug in each hand. "Jed made a fresh pot," she said with a grin. "He figured we wouldn't want to bother with last night's brew."

"Smart dog." He took a mug and placed his other hand on her bare knee, conveniently nearby. "Are you okay?"

"Mmm." She covered his fingers with her palm. "Very okay. A little stiff, but that might be because High Five dumped me yesterday afternoon when I asked him for a gallop."

"I'll be glad to take the credit," Rafe assured her. "What time is it?"

"Just after seven." Thea glanced out the window, where daylight had started creeping across the snowy hills. "I'd better go soon. Or at least call."

"Call," Rafe said. His wicked grin assured her that a second round of lovemaking was hers for the asking. And how she wanted to ask. Loving Rafe was everything she'd ever dreamed about. She couldn't imagine caring so deeply, giving and taking so much, with any other man.

But Beth would be worried sick. Her dad and Herman, too. And Bobby deserved to know about his reprieve. Dan had a long way to go, but with any luck, the specter of death that had hung over them all these weeks was gone for good.

"I can come back," she told Rafe as she left the bed to

find her jeans. "Anytime. Except—" she added as he started to make a suggestion "—right now."

They both dressed, pulled on their coats and walked through a couple of inches of fresh snow to the Land Rover.

"I'll call you." Rafe brushed snow off the windshield and windows with his bare hands. "About eight tonight? Does that work?"

"Unless there's some kind of emergency." Thea reluctantly started the engine. "We usually finish dinner about seven."

"Sounds good." He touched his fingers to her cheek, grinning as she squealed. "Maybe this'll be warmer," he said, bending inside the car for a kiss.

"Definitely." She was tempted to send the ranch and her dad and a day's worth of chores in the cold to hell. But with a sigh, she pushed Rafe outside instead. "Go. I have to get home and get to work. The taxpayers of Paradise Corners would probably like to see you in the office sometime today, too."

"Okay, okay." He shook his head in mock disgust and stepped back. "Drive carefully. The roads will be slick."

"Yessir." She touched his face one last time and forced herself to drive away.

Rafe was right—the roads *were* slick, with new snow layered over the frozen runoff from the day before. Thea drove slowly, out of caution and out of a desire to keep the wonder of these last few hours to herself as long as possible.

Admittedly, she wasn't paying close attention to the traffic—there were rarely other vehicles on the road in this part of Montana, especially once the snows came. The crescendoing wail of a siren didn't invade her consciousness at all until the flashing lights caught her attention. Startled, she hit the brake pedal too hard. The wheels started to slide, then the antilock brakes caught and brought her to a stop at the side of the road, only a foot or so from the edge of a deep, snow-filled ditch.

Meanwhile, an ambulance had turned left directly in front of her—underneath the sign for Walking Stones Ranch—and now raced up the private Maxwell road, straight to the house.

Holding her breath, Thea followed the ambulance tracks in the new snow and arrived as the emergency vehicle braked in the front driveway. She practically fell out of the Land Rover in her hurry to catch up with the EMTs.

"What's wrong?" She caught the woman's arm. "Why are you here?"

Before she got an answer, the front doors swung wide open. "This way," Herman told them. He looked beyond the EMTs to Thea. "Thank God, girl. We didn't know what had happened to you." He grabbed her in a tight hug, and she felt a wave of guilt. She should have let them know where she was last night.

But in the next instant she pulled back. "What's going on, Herman? Is somebody sick?"

The EMT rushed out to the ambulance and came back inside carrying a case of equipment.

"It's your dad," Herman said gently. "He collapsed a while ago, not able to breathe."

"Oh my God."

"He's a little better now, but we gotta get him to the hospital, Thea. Gotta find out what in hell is wrong and how to fix it."

She looked up at the man who'd worked with her dad for more than thirty years. Herman's own face was heavily lined, his eyes red-rimmed. Despite all the abuse her dad handed out, Herman would be loyal until the day he died.

"We will," she promised him. "We'll get this taken care

of. For the first time in his life, Boss Maxwell will have to follow orders.''

THEA TRIED REPEATEDLY to call Bobby from the hospital, but got no answer on the main line or with his private number. ''Didn't he know what happened this morning?''

''He didn't come to breakfast.'' Beth looked like a completely different person than Thea had ever known—hair untidy, forehead wrinkled in worry, her mouth tense and unsmiling, her hands twisting anxiously in her lap. ''I went back to his room once, but didn't get an answer when I knocked. And then, with all the uproar...I just forgot.''

The way Bobby had been behaving, Thea wasn't surprised that Beth couldn't get him up. The odor of beer had been pretty strong in his room Thursday night. Another problem that would have to be dealt with.

First, they had to be sure Robert Maxwell would recover.

Cassie came over from Billings as soon as school ended that day, leaving Zak at home with the woman who owned the house they lived in.

''Well?'' She came into the waiting room with her usual air of energetic efficiency. ''What is it and how do we make it better?''

After hours of waiting, Thea had run out of energy. ''Jolie was right. Dad has congestive heart failure. His lungs are filling up with fluid, which is why he can't breathe.''

Sobered, Cassie sat in the chair opposite. ''What's the treatment?''

Thea outlined the medicines the doctors had discussed. ''He should stop smoking. Work less. Watch his diet.''

''Oh, right. Why not just move mountains while we're at it?'' Her sister was quiet for a minute. ''Have you talked to him?''

"He can't talk. He's sedated and intubated to help him breathe until the fluid clears out of his lungs."

"So there's really not much point in my being here. I could have done this much at home."

"Except that it's nice to have people with you when you're waiting," Thea snapped. "Family—as you pointed out recently—has more to do with connections and relationships than just genetics."

"Well, excuse me." Cassie got to her feet. "After seven years of exile, it's a little hard to figure out when I'm welcome and when I'm not."

"You were always welcome. It was your husband Dad wouldn't abide on the property. And you knew that even before you married him. So you shouldn't have been surprised—"

Beth walked up, took hold of Thea's shoulder and shook it. "That's enough from both of you." Her low voice carried quite clearly to Thea's ears. "I'm ashamed to think I had responsibility for your upbringing, when you behave this way. And in public, with your dad sick in the hospital. What are you thinking?"

Cassie flushed, and Thea knew she had as well. "Sorry," they both murmured, and moved to different sides of the room. Except for occasional comments from Herman and Beth, the Maxwell party kept quiet for the rest of the afternoon.

They went their separate ways about eight that night, when the doctors assured them Robert Maxwell was resting comfortably, in no immediate danger. After a stiff goodbye, Cassie drove back to Billings. Thea took Beth and Herman home to Walking Stones.

The front of the house was dark—no porch light, no lamps switched on in the great room. In the kitchen, breakfast dishes and pans lay untouched where Beth had left them that morning.

She looked around as if she couldn't get her bearings. "Do you suppose Bobby hasn't been out of his room all day?"

"I'll check." Anger pumping through her veins, Thea strode through the house.

"Bobby?" She rapped loudly on the door. "Bobby, open up. If you're still asleep it's long past time to get up."

No answer. Trying the knob, she found it locked. She thought about just kicking the door in, but at the last second decided to use the universal key above the door frame instead. Less mess to clean up later.

Bobby's room was no neater than the last time she'd seen it. Just emptier. He wasn't on the bed, under it, or in the adjoining bathroom. The window was open, with a frigid wind blowing in and an inch of snow puddling on the carpet.

Thea searched the cluttered top of the dresser and chest of drawers, the pockets of the jeans lying around on the floor. His credit cards were piled on the dresser. There was no cash to be seen.

Herman stomped down the hallway. "Drove your car around to the garage," he said. "One of the ranch pickups is gone. The hands are all accounted for, in the bunkhouse or at home."

"Surprise, surprise." Sitting on her brother's unmade bed, Thea faced the facts. She'd taken a night for herself— not even a night, really, just a few hours. In that time, her father had become seriously ill.

And her little brother, out of jail on his own recognizance after being charged with drunk driving and vehicular assault, had violated the terms of his release by running away.

"Oh, Rafe," she whispered. "What are we going to do now?"

CHAPTER FIFTEEN

WHEN NO ONE at Walking Stones answered the phone at eight that night, Rafe wasn't too worried. Sure, he'd have thought somebody would be at the house by this time, but on a ranch you had to be prepared for the unexpected. They could all be at the barn dealing with a sick cow, or tending to a horse about to foal. Even Beth Peace, he supposed, might be involved somehow.

He gave himself the same reassuring talk at nine o'clock. The extent to which he believed his own words was obvious in the flood of relief that hit him when someone finally picked up the phone thirty minutes later.

"Hello?" Thea sounded frantic.

"It's me." He sat up straight, feeling the hair on his arms prickle. "What's wrong?"

"Oh…Rafe." That wasn't relief he heard in her voice, but a higher level of fear. "Did you call before?"

"Yeah, I gathered you weren't home. What's happened, Thea? You sound like you're about to fall apart."

She drew a deep breath. "I'm sorry. I—I…it's been a hard day. When I got home this morning, my dad had collapsed. We only came in a few minutes ago—we spent the day at the hospital."

Rafe could picture her face, pale with worry and fatigue. "Is he okay?"

"For now. He has heart failure and breathing problems.

But the doctors said he's stable tonight. We'll go back to-morrow to see him, of course."

"Sure. I'm really sorry about this. You didn't have any idea he was sick?"

"Oh, we did, just not how serious it is. Jolie—my sister the doctor, who was here for Thanksgiving—said that was what the problem was. We were supposed to get him checked out right away. But he refused to make an appointment."

"I'm not surprised. Sometimes it takes a real emergency to convince people to do what's best for themselves. Are *you* holding up?"

"You told me a minute ago that I was falling apart." She gave a small laugh. "I'm fine. We're…all…fine."

He waited, but she didn't volunteer any more information. "Sounds like you need some rest. I'll say good-night and let you go to bed." Rafe couldn't help adding, "Though I'd like it better if you were coming to bed with me."

After a pause, she whispered, "Me, too."

"G'night, Thea."

"'Night." Her tone was normal again…if the edge of panic in her voice could be called normal.

Rafe clicked off the phone and slouched back against the couch cushions. "Something's wrong," he told Jed, sitting next to him. "Something bad she didn't—wouldn't—tell me about."

She could be having second thoughts, after last night. But that whispered confession, "Me, too," had sounded real. Committed.

So if she wasn't regretting what they'd done and Dan Aiken was still improving—Rafe had checked with the hospital about six for an update—then what else could be wrong?

Bobby. He was up to something, Rafe would bet Jed's next meal on it. Damn the boy. Why couldn't he stay out of trouble? What had her brother done that was so bad Thea couldn't even tell him about it?

Or was it especially *him*—Rafe Rafferty, deputy sheriff—she didn't want to tell?

INSTEAD OF GOING to bed, Thea sat up making phone calls. First to Jolie in Los Angeles. Her sister didn't say anything in response to the news for a long time.

"Jolie?"

"Stubborn old fool," Jolie muttered finally. "I told him…" She broke off with a sigh. "I'll get back there as soon as I can, Thea. I don't know when, or who'll I'll find to cover for me here. But as long as Dad's stable, everything should be okay. Don't worry too much."

"Yeah, right." Thea almost laughed as she clicked off the phone. What did she have to worry about?

After a couple of hours spent calling every friend of Bobby's she could think of, hoping to find him with one of them, she fell asleep in the chair by the fireplace around 2:00 a.m. with the phone still in her hand. And with no clue as to where her brother might be.

"Thea, honey, wake up." Beth's voice rescued her from a nightmare in which she was being chased by giants.

She wasn't sorry to open her eyes. "I'm awake. What time is it?"

"Six-thirty. Herman's had his breakfast and wants to know if there's anything particular you'd like him to see to today."

"Thanks. I'll be out there in just a minute." As Beth returned to the kitchen, Thea sat up and rubbed her eyes. She needed to drive to Bozeman to see her dad. There was hay to be dropped in the far pastures, since the snow and ice were getting too deep for the cows to find grass.

And she had to find Bobby before Rafe discovered he was missing. Otherwise, in his role as deputy, Rafe would bring legal measures to bear. Including, she was sure, arresting Bobby and putting him in jail, once they found him.

Groaning, she staggered down the hallway to her bedroom and went into the bathroom to wash her face. Deputy Rafferty and Rafe were one and the same. Thea knew that. She loved him—yes, that was the word—for his honor and his sense of duty, as well as his sense of humor and his never-failing kindness. She wouldn't have one aspect of him without the others.

But the last thing their dad needed to hear was that Bobby had gone to jail. He had to concentrate on his own health problems, work on getting better, without worrying about the rest of them. She would simply have to get her brother home without help from Rafe or Robert Maxwell.

So she didn't mention Bobby or Rafe when she went in to visit her dad. "Hey, there." Thea pulled up a chair and sat next to his bed. "You're looking better than the last time I saw you. That tube in your throat had to be uncomfortable."

No longer so heavily sedated, Robert Maxwell had regained his power of command. "I need to get out of here. There's work to be done."

"We're handling it, Dad. Don't worry."

"How can you be handling it if you're here?"

"Okay, Herman's handling it." She would not lose her temper with him today, no matter how much he provoked her. "Not that anything will be done as well as if you were there," she added, "but the cattle will get their hay and all the other crucial chores will be done by sundown."

He blew out a rasping breath. "Where's your brother?"

Trust Robrt Maxwell to ask exactly the wrong question. "Um, I'm not sure right at this minute. Why?"

"I went to wake him up yesterday morning and he wouldn't answer the door. I want to know what the hell he thinks he's doing, hiding out in his room. It's time he got back to work."

"I'll tell him you said so." *When I find him.*

She left the hospital with a scribbled list of extra tasks Robert wanted done by the time he got home again.

"Obviously, we can't have him lying around too long with nothing to do." She handed the list to Herman that afternoon. "All he does is think up more work."

"Yep." The manager shook his head. "I'm surprised he doesn't want us scrubbing down the calving barn with a toothbrush."

"Don't put the idea into his head, or he will." They shared a laugh, but sobered when Thea asked, "I don't suppose Bobby's shown up?"

"Nope."

"Why would he take off like that? He has to know how it'll look to…to the authorities."

"Meaning your deputy." Herman shrugged. "I figure he hightailed it out of here the night the Aiken boy took a turn for the worse. Bobby probably figured he was about to get arrested for murder, and didn't want to stick around to face it."

Thea had come to the same conclusion. "Maybe he didn't go far. Maybe he's on the ranch somewhere, hiding out until he knows for sure."

"We can look for him, I guess. The boy's pretty good at living outdoors in all kinds of weather. He might be camped out somewhere up in the mountains."

No problem, Thea thought. There were only about a mil-

lion acres of national forest for Bobby to hide in. And that
was if he stayed in the immediate area.

But she took a recovered Sundance out for the remaining
hours of daylight and covered as much of the ranch itself
as she could, searching the horizon for smoke, the snow
for tire prints. Coming in at dark, she changed, gulped dinner and drove back to Bozeman to spend an hour with her
dad, who quizzed her about the day's work.

Tuesday morning she started out early and headed
straight for the foothills of the Crazy Mountains. Lack of
light brought her down again before five o'clock, again
without anything useful to report. She was beginning to
believe Bobby had vanished completely.

After a visit to the hospital, Cassie and Zak stopped by
for dinner on their way home. Cassie left Zak in the kitchen
making biscuits with Beth and confronted Thea in the great
room.

"What now? You all look like one of the chickens just
announced that the sky is falling."

Weary to the bone, Thea dropped onto the couch.
"Bobby's gone."

"Gone where?"

Thea shrugged. "He didn't leave a note, didn't say anything. He just…left."

"Ran away, you mean." When Thea nodded, Cassie
muttered a rude word. "If he'd ever been held to account
for any of his stupid stunts, this entire situation would have
been avoided."

"The past doesn't matter. It's the future I'm worried
about. When Rafe finds out—"

"The deputy? He'll hold off the dogs for a while, won't
he? For your sake?"

She wished she could say yes. "He's very committed to

doing his job the right way.'' Her cheeks grew hot at Cassie's skeptical gaze.

"What do a few days matter? It's not like Bobby is a serial killer. He's just a scared kid running from a bad mistake.''

"I know. But if I could find him before Rafe hears that he's gone, that would be best.''

"So what have you done?'' Thea detailed the last two days, the phone calls, the searches she and Herman had made. Cassie nodded. "That's a good start, though I doubt he would have gone to any of his friends, after what happened to Dan.'' She snapped her fingers. "Wait. Have you checked with his girlfriend? What's her name?''

"Megan Wheeler? They broke up—she wouldn't talk to him anymore. Bobby was really upset about it. He wouldn't have gone there, especially not the way her dad feels.''

"How do you know? It's worth a try, when nothing else has worked.''

"I can call her and ask, I guess.'' She picked up the phone.

Cassie put out a hand. "Wait. She might not be able to talk if her dad's home. Ask her to meet us somewhere.''

Exhaustion was making Thea stupid. "Where?''

"Someplace in town…is Grizzly's open late tonight?''

"I don't know.''

"Well, get her to meet us there, and if it isn't, we'll find someplace else—a bar if we have to.''

Thea looked at her sister. "Shouldn't you and Zak get home right after dinner? He has school tomorrow. You have to work.''

Cassie flushed. "You've been saying I always leave the hard stuff to you. So here I am.'' She grinned. "Next time we fight, you won't be able to use that weapon.''

"You always have an angle." Laughing, Thea dialed directory assistance for Megan Wheeler's number.

"I CAN'T BELIEVE you threatened her with legal action," Cassie said as they waited inside the Land Rover, parked on the street beside the closed Grizzly's Diner. "I can't believe she believed you would." She peered up and down the empty street. "And I'm beginning to believe she's stood us up. She was supposed to be here half an hour ago."

Thea curled her fingers around the steering wheel, then relaxed again. "We've got to be patient. Her dad makes her life miserable. Who knows what she has to do to get out on a week night?"

After another half hour, Thea was ready to give up, too. They'd have to reach Megan some other way, maybe confront her at work. She sat up straighter, ready to shift the car into gear, just as a rattletrap Jeep she'd seen before pulled up on the opposite corner. A girl got out and hurried across to the Land Rover, clutching the edges of her coat together against the bitter wind.

Cassie reached for the back-door handle and pushed it open. "We had almost given up," she said as Megan climbed in.

"I'm sorry." The girl was breathless, shaking. She took three tries to get the door shut tight. "I had to wait for my dad to go to sleep before I could leave. He wasn't feeling too good tonight, so it took a long time."

"He was drunk, you mean." Cassie tilted Megan's chin to the light. Thea gasped at the ugly black bruise swelling along the line of her jaw. "You've got to get out of that house."

Megan shook her head. "What did you want to ask me? I don't know anything the deputy doesn't already know."

Cassie released Megan's chin. "Have you seen Bobby recently?"

"Not for more than a month. He...I..." She shook her head, and looked out the side window, wiping her cheeks with the quivering fingers of one pale hand.

"Are you sure, Megan?" Thea spoke firmly. "It's really, really important for us to find him. Dan's getting better, but Bobby's still under arrest, and he'll be in even worse trouble for running away."

"I can't help you. I...I've got to go." She grabbed blindly for the door handle, frustrated when she couldn't find it. "Please, really, I don't know where he is."

"Megan—"

Suddenly, the young girl in the back seat burst into tears. She curled in on herself, covering her bent head with her arms, sobbing wildly.

"I wish I knew where he was...I'd go with him if I could...I don't know what's going to happen to me...when they find out..." The words dissolved in her tears.

Thea and Cassie stared at one another, then got out at the same time and went to sit on either side of Megan in the back seat. They stroked her shoulders and hair, murmured the only comfort words they knew, the ones Beth had always used. "Shh. It's all right. You'll be okay. We'll take care of you."

Megan gradually calmed down, until the sobs were fewer than the hiccups and the sniffs. Still hiding her face, she sat silent under their hands.

"What's wrong, sweetie?" Cassie used her gentlest voice, the one Thea thought she reserved for Zak alone. "Can we help?"

"Nobody can help." Megan's voice was thick, rough. "And he's going to kill me when he finds out."

"Bobby?"

"My dad."

From out of nowhere, Thea got an inkling of what was coming next. She looked at Cassie over Megan's back. "Megan, are you—"

The girl nodded. "I'm going to have a baby."

Cassie drew a deep breath. "Who's the father?"

Megan sat up straight, her face filled with indignation. "What kind of girl do you think I am? It's Bobby's baby, of course. There's never been anybody else."

SWORN TO SECRECY, Thea and Cassie watched Megan scurry across the street to her friend Racey's Jeep.

"I hate to send her back there." Thea pressed her fingers to her eyes. "If he finds out about the baby, he really might kill her."

"I don't think so." Cassie shook her head. "I think he'll use the baby as leverage to extort money from Dad. Just another little complication Bobby's brought into our lives."

Thea was angry enough not to protest the criticism. She put the Land Rover into gear and they drove home, slowly, each of them wrapped in her own thoughts. Having a baby at barely eighteen was going to be hard. Megan would suffer for what she and Bobby had done, whether he ever came back or not. The folks in Paradise Corners wouldn't be kind to one they considered "a fallen woman." Not that there wasn't plenty of unmarried sex happening in the little town. The trick was to avoid getting caught.

For the first time in two days, Thea thought about Rafe. He'd been prepared with a condom, even though sex was the last thing they'd expected to do together that night. Why couldn't Bobby have been that smart?

Maybe he had been. All birth control methods had a failure rate. Thea gave a silent chuckle as the thought occurred to her. She'd been so transported, she wouldn't have noticed if she and Rafe had experienced an "equipment malfunction." Right now, she could be...

Oh, dear God. She nearly slammed on the brakes as the idea hit her.

Cassie threw her a questioning glance. "Everything okay? Do you want me to drive?"

"No. No, I'm fine." *I could also be pregnant.*

The idea stayed with her the rest of the night, waiting for her when she woke from a restless sleep at 3:00 a.m. and four and five. Rafe's baby. What a lovely idea. She could imagine them as a family, the wonderful father he would make. He'd treat his children the way he treated Jed—with respect and caring and tenderness.

But right now she had to tell him about Bobby running away, and he would be furious she hadn't let him know immediately. She would ask him to hold off any official procedures for a while, to see if Bobby came back on his own, and that would make him even angrier.

She went to the sheriff's office as soon as she could on Wednesday, after visiting her dad in Bozeman. The scene there turned out just as she expected.

"Bobby ran away," Rafe repeated in a quiet, intense voice.

Thea nodded.

"When?"

"The day Dad collapsed—that would be Sunday."

"Three days ago, Thea. Why didn't you tell me sooner?"

"I...I looked for him myself. I thought he might have hidden somewhere on the ranch—we've got a few abandoned cabins in isolated spots, and he's always liked winter camping, so I searched the hills, trying to find him." She didn't mention that none of their winter camping gear appeared to be missing.

He ran a hand around the back of his neck, obviously furious and frustrated. "One person can't possibly do an adequate search of an area like this. It takes a team—an experienced team."

She didn't like his tone, or the implication that she didn't know what she was doing. "If he was out there, I would have found him."

His eyes narrowed as he looked at her. "You think he headed out of state?"

"I'm not sure…"

"Because that will involve the FBI."

"You don't have to tell them—or anybody—right away. Do you?" She put her hands on his arm. "Bobby might have panicked, because he thought Dan was dying. When he calms down, I know he'll come back."

"That's more than I know." He walked away from her, around the desk, and sat in his chair. "Your brother doesn't have a responsible bone in his body. He was bound to bolt. And you've made getting him back a hell of a lot harder by withholding the information."

She was talking to Deputy Rafferty now. Thea straightened her shoulders. "I was protecting my little brother and my father, who's sick and in the hospital and doesn't need this kind of stress right now."

"Family ties are important." His attempt to be patient was obvious—condescendingly so. "But justice is more important still."

"You can't possibly punish him any more than he's already punishing himself." Thea braced her arms on the desk, leaning closer to make her point. "He'll live the rest of his life knowing how badly he injured his best friend."

Using the heels of his hands against the edge, Rafe pushed away from the desk—away from *her*. "He owes a debt to the people he hurt. It's my duty to make sure that debt gets paid.''

"Your duty!" She whirled and walked to stare out the window into the street. "I'm talking about people here, and all you can talk about is some abstract concept."

"That's who I am, Thea." He didn't close the distance between them. "I made a big mistake by going easy on Bobby in the first place. If I'd locked him up when he deserved it, Dan Aiken wouldn't be in such bad shape."

"So Bobby's your scapegoat? You're relieving your own guilt by persecuting him?" She knew the accusations were unreasonable as she made them. But his detached attitude was so damn frustrating. If he would just let some real feelings through…

Instead, he stiffened up even more. "Maybe I am. At least I've learned my lesson when it comes to spoiled, self-ish, alcoholic brats. And their families, who think they can run the entire county for their own satisfaction. Next time I'll know not to trust them any farther than I can throw them."

His words hurt all the worse for being the truth. Thea couldn't think of a retort cruel enough, couldn't really speak for the tears clogging her throat. Without looking back at the man behind the desk, she just opened the door and ran away.

ROBERT HAD TOLERATED as much of this sick nonsense as he was willing to stand. When Cassie came into his room Thursday afternoon, he barely waited for her greeting. "I want out of here. Now."

Her eyes flashed with temper. "I don't remember asking what you want. You'll leave when the doctors think you're ready."

This child had always talked back. He hadn't tolerated

it when she was thirteen and he wouldn't tolerate it when she was thirty-one. He might be flat on his back, but he could still get things done. "I'm the one paying the damn hospital bill. I'll say when I leave. And that's now."

"As if Beth and Herman and Thea don't have enough on their hands, you want to go home so they can take care of you, too?"

"I'll take care of myself."

"When just walking down the hallway makes you pant? Get a grip, Dad. Why don't you read a good book? You've got enough of them piled up here." She went to the stack that had grown daily since the morning he woke up. "Techno-thrillers, Westerns, cold war espionage. Take your pick. Lie back, read, relax. You haven't had a vacation in decades."

"I don't need a vacation. I need to work." She wouldn't understand how stifled he felt, how fettered. He hadn't spent all day inside since…he didn't remember ever spending all of a twenty-four-hour period inside. He needed the fresh air. He needed to be back on his land, where he was in charge, where the orders came from him. He would rather die standing on his own property than live in this lifeless room.

"If they won't sign me out, I'll leave anyway. Hand me my clothes." Robert threw back the covers and swung his legs over the side of the bed, ignoring the dizziness of sitting up suddenly.

"I'm more likely to take your clothes away, you cantankerous old man. Get back in bed." Cassie took advantage of his weakness and made him lie down again, put his feet back under the blanket and pulled it up to his chest. "You're worth more alive than dead, Dad. Thea and Herman need your help—which means you have to stay put for now."

He hated that she was right. "Where's Bobby?" He did sound like an old man, a sick, whiny geezer with no teeth. "Is he getting back to work? Has that damn deputy announced a trial date? I hear the Aiken boy's talking okay. Can we get the charges dropped?"

When he noticed the look on Cassie's face, he felt a fist close in his chest. "You might as well tell me. I'm going to know sometime."

She looked away, then back into his face. "Bobby ran away. We don't know where he is."

Robert nodded. "I thought as much. Damn fool boy didn't believe I'd take care of him. Never could see that all the work was for his sake. That I'd do whatever it took to keep him on the land."

That fist in his chest kept tightening, blocking his windpipe, stealing his air. The pain got worse, worse than anything he'd ever known…except for losing Helen.

"Cassie—" He put up a hand, but then lost his bearings and couldn't find her face in the dark.

"Hold on, Dad." Her warm fingers closed around his, but her voice had gotten far away. "Help is coming, Daddy. Just hold on."

THEA GOT THE NEWS about their dad's heart attack when she came in from the mountains at sundown. She reached the hospital about eight Thursday night, knowing he had survived, worried nonetheless. "How is he?"

"Stable," Cassie said wearily. "The doctors were on top of it right away. He'll get better."

"I'm glad you were here. I was out looking for Bobby on horseback, trying to find him before the sheriff's department does."

"I don't know whether you should be glad or not, since I probably caused the heart attack."

"I don't understand."

"We were talking—arguing—and I told him Bobby was gone. Right after that, he had the attack."

Anger surged through Thea for a moment. They'd tried to be so careful, to keep him calm, and the first time Cassie lost her temper, she'd told him exactly what they've been trying to hide...

But with Robert Maxwell, things were rarely that simple. Thea went to her sister, put an arm around her waist and with the other hand brushed back a stray lock of red hair. "Don't blame yourself. This has been a possibility all along—the doctors told us from the beginning that one of the dangers was a heart attack. It's a physical condition, with physical causes—not emotional ones."

Cassie sighed. "I guess. It just seems like every time we talk, somebody ends up mad. I thought I was adult enough to handle him. But maybe I'll never be that grown-up."

Thea tightened her hold for a second, then let go. "I want to go in to see him for a few minutes, and talk to the doctor. After that we'll drive home, okay? You can get a good night's rest and drive back to Billings tomorrow morning early, in time to get Zak to school."

Her sister smiled. "Since when did you become the mother around here?"

Since you and Jolie dumped the job, she wanted to say. But instead, she just shrugged. "Natural arrogance taking over. A Maxwell trait, I'm told." By a man who, she was beginning to believe, would always be a Maxwell opponent.

If not a downright enemy.

A FIVE-DAY MANHUNT involving the state police, the game wardens, Search and Rescue teams, the FBI, all points bulletins—Rafe used every resource he could muster to find

Bobby Maxwell. A man wanted for evading the authorities, assault, DUI and possible poaching charges grabbed folks' attention. It was, to say the least, an impressive training exercise.

And a total waste of time. A couple of dead deer turned up, but no evidence was left to identify the hunter. Bobby Maxwell remained quite comfortably at large.

Somehow Thea showed up in town just as the teams made the decision to call off the hunt. Most of the men and women who'd come to work with him managed not to laugh in his face as they went home.

"You didn't find him." Thea leaned against the door frame, hands in the pocket of her blanket coat, one booted foot crossed over the other. She looked damn good, and completely untouchable.

"No, we didn't find him."

"They were carrying weapons." She shot the words at him like bullets.

Rafe struggled to keep his temper. "It's dangerous country."

"Did they have orders to shoot if he resisted arrest?"

"It wouldn't have come to that." If she had to hate him, he wished she would just go away. He couldn't stand much more.

"Did they?"

"Standard operating procedure, Thea. Bobby would have had an equal chance to shoot at them."

"Assuming he had a gun. There aren't any missing from home."

He shrugged. "So they wouldn't have had to defend themselves and he would have surrendered without a fight."

"You hoped."

"Yes, dammit, I hoped." Rafe forced himself to look at

her, to see what he'd lost. "I was fool enough to hope that at some point Bobby Maxwell would demonstrate the sense God gave a gopher and realize when the time had come to give up. That he'd realize a man is admired for the responsibilities he assumes, not for the volume of beer he drinks or the number of women he screws."

Thea's face went white. After a long moment of silence, she lifted one hand in a gesture of farewell. "Don't worry about the Maxwells anymore. We'll take care of ourselves. And don't cross the Walking Stones fence line again without an invitation. Or a warrant."

"No problem," he said as she slammed his office door one final time.

THEA TOOK the long way home, west and then south through the mountains across a pass that was closed for the season. The Land Rover's traction held firm on the new snow; she reached the last peak safely and with most of her tears cried away. Darkness had fallen. The trees crowding the roadway shone under her headlights in shades of gray and black and dull green. With just a couple of miles to go before reaching the back gate to the ranch, thinking only about getting home, about crawling under the covers and never coming out again, she didn't actually notice the flash of bright blue as she passed it.

But her mind caught the signal a second later. Barely breathing, Thea eased her foot onto the brake and gentled the car to a stop. She reversed slowly, farther up the steep hill than she thought she needed to, then drove forward. Again, she almost missed that bright, out-of-place splash of color.

She backed up one more time so she'd have the headlights behind her, pulled on her heavy leather gloves and a knit cap, then left the Land Rover and began to hike back down the hill. She kept one eye on her path and one eye on the trees, searching for that glimpse of blue. Between the steep slope and the slick surface, she lost her footing several times. Powdery snow coated her gloves and her jeans from rear end to knees.

Then she stepped off the road into thigh-high drifts, which strangled every stride she attempted. She had maybe thirty feet to cover. It seemed to take all night. The forest around her was quiet, yet alive. The rustle of pine needles sounded like footsteps, the occasional crack of a falling branch had her wondering whether someone was watching from behind a thick tree trunk, waiting to attack. Struggling through the snow, listening to her own harsh breaths, Thea reminded herself again and again that she was alone on the mountain. No sane person would be out here in near-zero temperatures after dark.

With her eyes blurry from cold and the Land Rover lights growing faint behind her, she fell facedown through yet another drift. Under the shadow of the trees everything was either white or black. But her outstretched hand hit some- thing hard. Big. Not a tree, not a fallen log.

A tire. The right rear tire of a pickup.

The one Bobby had taken?

Frantically she felt her way around the truck, which was coated with snow—except for the tailgate, that flash of blue she'd glimpsed from the road. She tried the doors, peered into the windows, cleared the rear bumper to see the license plate.

Then, with fingers freezing inside her gloves and tears freezing on her cheeks, Thea fought her way back to the road and the two-way radio in the Land Rover, to call on the only source of help her heart brought to mind.

CHAPTER SIXTEEN

RAFE USUALLY LIKED mountain driving.

But not tonight, on a snow-covered, corkscrew road in the dark, with Thea parked out in the wilderness by herself, waiting for him. He couldn't go fast enough. He couldn't go too fast and risk sliding straight off the mountain.

Just over the last peak he saw her Land Rover, its lights flaring out over the black tree trunks and brilliant white snow. He only realized he'd been holding his breath when he let it go.

His good sense lasted long enough to get the truck parked safely. Then he was outside and slogging through churned-up snow to get to the car's driver's door. Thea opened it as he slid to a stop.

"Are you okay?" He took her face in his hands, pushed her hat off her head, desperate to know nothing had hurt her. Just seeing, just feeling wasn't enough. Without thinking about it, Rafe wrapped Thea in his arms and found her mouth with his.

She yielded for a precious moment, then struggled to break free. "I'm okay," she said unsteadily. "Really. Nothing and no one has been near me."

He forced himself to calm down. "Good. That's good. It took so long to get here, I worried... But you're okay. All right. So..." He took a deep breath. "What did you find?"

She led him through deep snow to the blue pickup parked

underneath the pines. The space around the license plate
had been cleared of snow. "MAX 3" identified the vehicle
as one of the Walking Stones trucks.

"That's the number of the one you're missing?"

Thea nodded, her eyes dark and round in the shadows
of the trees.

Rafe followed the path she'd forged around the truck.
"The doors were locked when you arrived?"

"Yes, which would require having the key, or the re-
mote. That must mean Bobby left it here himself."

There was another possibility—the vehicle could have
been stolen, along with its keys, and hidden here by a
stranger. A glance at Thea told him she'd thought of that
scenario, and refused to acknowledge the implications.

"How many people use this road?"

"Only Bobby and me, really. Maybe some of the hands,
occasionally. It leads to the back gate of the ranch, which
is always locked. Why be here if there was nowhere to
go?"

"Hunters?"

"This is national forest land, and I don't think they open
the area to hunting. The terrain is pretty treacherous."

"Judging from that drive, I'd say so." He came back to
the rear of the truck and leaned his arms on the wall around
the bed. "We've had about six inches of snow in the last
four days, but there's only an inch or two built up in here."
He picked up a palmful, squeezed it into a ball and dropped
it back into the truck bed. "Whoever parked it did so during the last day or so. Two at the most."

"But where would he go?" Thea held out her arms and
gazed around them at the dense, dark forest. "He must have
been coming home. Why did he stop *here*?"

"God knows." Rafe raked his flashlight beam in a circle
with the truck at its center. "And I don't think we're going

to find out tonight. I'll follow you home, then go back to town by the highway. Tomorrow morning, I'll come up for a thorough search.''

''You can't leave.'' She stumbled through the snow to grab at his arm. ''He could be just out of sight. We've got to try to find him.''

''Thea, you're not thinking straight.'' He eased her grip, then turned to put his arms loosely around her. ''We could walk for hours, and Bobby could always be 'just out of sight' because we can't see. We have to wait for daylight. That's the only way we'll find him.''

He watched her struggle with the necessity of leaving this place, of driving away with the knowledge that Bobby could be nearby.

''You're right,'' she said finally. ''I don't want to accept it, but I know you're right.'' With a resigned breath, she turned and led the way out to the road and the bright lights of their vehicles.

''The gate is about two miles ahead.'' She'd taken off her gloves and was blowing on her red fingertips. ''It's bolted. I'll have to get out to unlock it, then lock it again.''

''I'll follow you, but stay well back, in case I start to skid.''

Thea nodded, her lips pressed tight together. Rafe wanted to comfort her, but what could he say? Nothing she didn't already know…or else didn't want to think about tonight.

''Come on,'' he said, guiding her to the Land Rover with an arm around her waist. ''You need to get home and get warm.''

She climbed into the driver's seat, then sat staring at her hands around the wheel. Finally, she looked at Rafe again. ''Thanks for coming. You…you were the only person I could think of to ask for help.''

Grinning, he dragged off a glove to touch her cheek with

his bare fingertip. "No problem," he said, deliberately repeating the words he'd used with her earlier. "I honestly want to do what's best for Bobby. And the rest of your family."

But that was where he made his mistake. By the changing expressions on her face, Rafe could see the problems between them flood back into Thea's mind.

She looked away from him and drew back from his touch. "We all do. Are you ready to leave?"

Rafe suddenly recognized his own weariness. "Sure. You go ahead."

And with those frosty words, they separated to make their individual ways through the bitter, snowy night.

THEA RETURNED to Bobby's truck before first light. Rafe parked just up the slope only a few minutes later. He stared at her through the windshield, obviously surprised to see her there. Leaning against the back door of the Land Rover, she waited for him to get over it so they could get to work.

He locked his truck then walked toward her, frowning, with Jed trotting along at his heels. "This is official business now. You don't have to be here."

She held his gaze. Her presence on this hunt was inescapable, and he needed to figure that out.

Finally he sighed. "Let's see what we've got over here."

Thea offered one of the pairs of snowshoes she'd brought along. "Be my guest."

Getting to the truck was easier across the top of the snow than through it. They circled from the back and met up again at the front bumper. In the growing daylight, they could see what darkness had hidden the night before.

About two hundred feet in front of the truck lay yet another headless whitetail buck—a magnificent creature, judging by the depth of his chest, his overall size and condition.

"Eight points," Rafe said, crouched near the impression of the buck's antlers in the snow. "Maybe ten. Well over a six-foot spread from tip to tip."

From a greater distance, Thea surveyed the scene. "Do you suppose Bobby saw the poacher and took off after him?" Jed sniffed around the carcass, then veered off in an uphill direction.

Rafe looked up at her. "Did it ever occur to you that Bobby might *be* the poacher?"

Her reaction was immediate. "No. Never."

"He's a good shot, isn't he? There was a gun rack in the cab of his red truck."

"Of course. But he's also a sportsman. He hunts in season, according to the rules. He would never destroy an animal so…so senselessly."

"There were no reports of poaching during the week Bobby was in the hospital, but there were some before the accident and then after he got back on his feet."

His logic increased her own uncertainty. Thea struggled to believe that her brother was not a poacher. "Because no one found them doesn't mean the kills weren't out here."

"I came upon evidence that Bobby's been up at the Walking Stones in the recent past." He told her about the sack of trash with the bloody gloves and credit card receipt dated two weeks after the accident. "Deer blood," Rafe explained.

"I figured that out," she snapped. He flinched as if he'd been slapped, and got to his feet, eyes narrowed, face sterner than she'd ever seen it. "But I don't believe Bobby killed all those animals. Where did he put the heads? I can tell you for sure they're not in the freezers in the basement at home."

"A check of taxidermists across the state and in Wyoming and Idaho might give us a clue. But we don't have time for that right now. We need to find Bobby as soon as possible." He glanced around. "Where did Jed go? Jed?"

An excited bark summoned them farther up the mountain.

Rafe went first, intending to give Thea some help as the slope got steeper, more dangerous. But every time he turned to offer a hand, she had already found her own way around—or over—the next obstacle. Gritting his teeth, he gave up on the Galahad routine and concentrated on simply getting himself up without a slip.

Jed waited on a wide, level ledge underneath a low overhang. As Rafe eased over the lip, he saw human footprints in the snow. "Watch out up here," he called back to Thea. "There are a couple of sets of prints we'll want to leave undisturbed."

"Two?" she asked, panting.

"Looks like two people were here." He leaned back over the ledge. "Give me your hand."

"I can do it." Her gloved fingers sought purchase among the crumbly rocks and powdery snow.

"Come on, Thea. I'd take a hand up from you."

She glanced at him, drew a deep breath and reached. Rafe caught her right wrist, giving her the leverage she needed to use her legs, pushing up and over. For a few seconds she lay on her stomach, face in the snow. Then she pushed up onto her knees, brushed back her hair and gave him the first smile of the day. "Thanks."

"Sure." Together they walked carefully to stand just under the edge of the overhang, studying the chunky, piled-up snow where Jed presided like a museum curator. This was the exhibit he'd wanted them to see.

After a frozen minute, Thea stirred. "They were fighting here. That's blood. Human?"

"Or it could be the deer." Rafe went around the site to Jed and gave him a thorough scratch behind the ears. "You did it, boy. Good job."

"The tracks head this way." Thea walked to the narrow side of the ledge leading farther up the mountain. "There's more blood dripping into the snow, and one set of prints weaves around the others. Somebody's hurt." She looked back at Rafe. "Bobby?"

"Or the other guy." He came to stand beside her. "The only way to find out is to follow them. They've got at least one day on us. I think—"

"You're assuming," she interrupted in a bleak voice, "that they're both still alive."

"That's what I always assume, until shown otherwise." He closed his hand over her shoulder for just a second. "And you should, too. Bobby wouldn't have taken away a poacher to murder him somewhere else—he'd have done it here, in the middle of the fight. If the poacher's plan was to eliminate Bobby, he could have done the same. But they both walked away. They're both still alive, and I'm going to find them."

She drew a deep breath. "Okay. They're both still alive."

Rafe nodded. "But I want to stay on the trail until dark and start right away at daylight."

"You mean spend the night on the mountain?"

"Or two or three—whatever it takes. I'll call backup in, of course. The game wardens and the Search and Rescue Team from Big Timber will help out, if nobody else needs them. But the farther ahead these two get, the harder they'll be to find."

"Makes sense." She was staring along the trail Rafe would follow.

"I brought winter camp gear with me, just in case. I'll go back to get it, radio SAR and start searching right away."

While Jed waited behind on the ledge, they climbed down again, which was harder than going up. Thea allowed him to help her several times over the rough spots, which made Rafe feel better…until they got back to their trucks.

She opened the rear doors of the Land Rover and pulled out an external-frame backpack, designed to carry forty to sixty pounds, easy, and went down on one knee to adjust the straps.

"What is that?" he asked, though he already knew the answer.

"I brought camping gear, too. I'm going with you," she clarified, as if he didn't understand that part.

He didn't go for the obvious "too dangerous, harsh conditions" argument—why waste his breath? "This is law enforcement business, Thea. As a civilian, you don't belong on this maneuver."

"So deputize me, and I'll be official." Her tone said clearly that it didn't make any difference to her one way or another.

Rafe tried the only other tactic he could think of. "Your dad would be furious."

She stood up. "Well, my dad doesn't know. If he did know, I'll bet a thousand dollars that *you'd* be the one he wouldn't want involved in this hunt. But if we're lucky, we'll get Bobby back before my dad finds out how dangerous the situation really got."

She was right, and he still didn't want her along. "You'll slow me down. I travel faster alone."

"So forget I'm here." With experienced ease, she

hoisted the pack onto her shoulders. "Better yet, I'll go first. If you pass me, just keep on going. I'll catch up sooner or later."

Rafe muttered a few choice words, but her refusal to argue or get mad convinced him he had no choice but to cooperate. "I'm going to radio Big Timber and get my gear. Don't—I repeat, do not—head up that mountain without me. Got it?"

Thea grinned. "Got it." To his surprise, she was actually still waiting for him when he returned with his pack strapped on.

He looked her up and down, couldn't find fault with anything, so he bowed to the inevitable. "Let's go."

FROM THE LEDGE where they joined up with Jed again, they followed the double tracks across the mountain until three o'clock, when the light began to go. It was time to make camp. The tent sites were either level and exposed to the wind or sheltered but sloped. "Wind or hill?" Rafe asked, giving Thea the option.

"Hill," she said, and he grinned. The woman obviously knew her stuff.

He got busy then, extracting his tent and spreading it out across the rocky ground below a wall of boulders to break the wind. On his knees, getting ready to insert the first pole, he looked to his left…and found Thea in the same position, erecting a tent of her own. They'd worked parallel, without noticing the duplication of effort.

"Uh, Thea?" She looked across at him, then at his tent. "Do we really need two shelters?"

"I—" She fidgeted with the aluminum pole in her hand.

"Two people in one tent would be warmer."

"True."

"Conserve fuel, maybe food."

She nodded.

"I'd be glad to share."

"O-okay." After a minute, she glanced at him out of the sides of her eyes and smiled. "Your place or mine?" Then, before he could answer, she shook her head. "I'll get mine stowed again and help you with yours."

Her agreement to share his space was the best news Rafe could remember getting in quite some time.

Thea's camp stove was slightly larger than his, so they used it to heat snow for tea and the dehydrated stew she'd brought. "You eat better than I do," Rafe told her, spooning up another mouthful. "I'm usually satisfied with crackers and butter and a long night's sleep."

"I'm warmer if I'm not hungry." She poured more heated water into a foil pouch. "Want some peach cobbler?"

Rafe groaned in appreciation and held out his plate.

Jed gobbled up his ration of dry dog food and slurped at some snow, then settled between Rafe's sleeping bag and the tent wall to snore his way through the dark night. With the camp stove still warming their space, Thea crawled into her bag on Rafe's other side. They lay on their backs, feet tilted down, staring up at the roof of the tent.

"One of them must have a weapon," she said finally. "And he's forcing the other to keep moving."

"They're slowing down, though. Not covering as much ground. We'll catch up with them tomorrow sometime, I think."

She took a deep breath. "Do you have a gun with you?"

"Service revolver. Plus an unassembled rifle. I'll put it together tomorrow morning before we start out."

"Oh…good. I didn't bring a gun. I can shoot, though…if I have to."

In the quiet, the wind swirled outside like a giant's

breath, ebbing, flowing over them. Snow shifted, cracking and creaking, branches snapped and fell.

"We'll try to make sure nobody has to." Rafe turned on his side to face her. "Nothing about this is worth somebody getting killed."

Thea sighed. "Too many people are already hurt—Dan, Jerry, Megan…" She caught her breath. "Damn, I wasn't supposed to say that."

"Megan Wheeler? Bobby's girlfriend?"

"She's broken off with Bobby." Rolling toward him, she propped her head in her hand, but didn't meet his eyes. "Her dad beats up on her, always has. If he finds out she's pregnant—"

"Damn."

Thea nodded. "Exactly. But she made Cassie and me swear not to tell Bobby. She's afraid of what he'll do."

"I'll keep an eye on that. I could press charges for abuse."

"I don't think she would let you. She's got a younger sister. Her mother would suffer." Thea covered her eyes with her free hand. "And we haven't told Jolie, because we're keeping the secret as small as possible. Why are families so complicated? Shouldn't there be one place in life that's easy, that's comfortable? That's…safe?"

"You have to make that place for yourself," Rafe said, his arms aching with the need to hold her close. "Sometimes, I think, you get lucky and find another person to build with." He couldn't say more. Given everything between them, Thea had to decide if what they could be together was worth what they would have to overcome.

Her heavy sigh joined the wail of the wind. After an eternal wait, she rolled to sit up. "Do you want the stove anymore?"

He'd lost. "No."

The dim blue flame disappeared. Thea's sleeping bag rustled in the dark. "'Night,'" she whispered.

"Sure." Rafe turned to his other side, facing Jed, and pulled the sleeping bag up over his head.

He remembered the dark, terrifying night his parents died, and the night of agony after his police partner was gunned down. But he'd never spent such a long, lonely night as this one, lying in a small tent on the mountainside only inches away from the woman he loved.

RAFE WAS GRIM and quiet the next morning as they packed up to move. Thea understood why—she hadn't taken the opportunity he'd given her to rise above their differences.

She was a coward; she'd always known that. Cowardice explained staying on to work for her dad when he denied her the chance to be a full partner. A brave woman would have bought herself some land, started an independent operation. Jolie had found the courage to leave, to put herself through college and medical school when Robert Maxwell stood in her way. Cassie had made a disastrous marriage— but at least she'd chosen her own path and now she had sweet little Zak, who could never be considered a mistake.

But Thea had stayed where she was, playing second fiddle to her younger brother, because she was afraid to take the risk of going out on her own, of failing. She'd accepted her dad's lack of confidence as the final judgement on her abilities, because that was the easy way out.

What Rafe offered—a new life, outside of Robert Maxwell's influence, or even his approval—was a hard choice. And so, once again, she'd played it safe.

By midmorning Jed had led them above the tree line. They lost the deep snow and the clear prints, relying on the dog's sense of smell. Rafe kept track of their location with compass readings recorded in a small notebook. Without those notes, they would be lost on an alien landscape of rock and ice and wind. But Bobby knew the mountains very well. Could he really have killed all those animals?

Exploring a ridge just above them, Jed suddenly halted, testing the air for scent, his long ears swaying in the fierce wind. Then, with a glance at Rafe, he dived over the ridge, out of sight.

Immediately, Rafe dropped his pack. "Stay here." He loosened the holster on his revolver, slung the rifle he'd assembled that morning over his shoulder and followed the dog.

She gave them a five-minute head start. Then Thea slipped out of her own pack and went after them.

The three of them met up over a smoldering fire in a rocky hollow two ridges farther along the mountain. Rafe watched with angry eyes as she descended the last few steps to the fire site. "Why the hell didn't you stay where I told you to?"

She threw his temper right back at him. "Why the hell do you think I came along? Because I like carrying sixty pounds up a fifty-degree incline? I came to be there when you find Bobby, of course."

"You don't trust me to bring him back safe? You think I'll drop him with a bullet and tell you he tried to escape?" Outrage and a deep hurt shook his voice.

Thea stared at him for a moment, her jaw hanging loose. The idea had never crossed her mind. "Rafe. No. I always trusted you. You're the most honorable man I've ever known."

"Yeah, well…" His cheeks were red, but it could have been the wind. He cleared his throat. "They've been here within the last couple of hours. Let's see if we can catch up."

Another hour of scrabbling with hands and feet over barren rock brought them to the edge of a nearly vertical cliff. Fifty feet below, moving into the shelter of a small stand of trees, were two men walking one behind the other. The one following held a handgun.

"Probably a revolver," Rafe said quietly.

"How did they get down there?" Thea surveyed their perch, finding nowhere to go except back the way they came. "And where are they going?"

"He must have a hideout up here, to use an old-fashioned word." Rafe didn't identify who "he" would be. "There's got to be a way down." He began to walk the perimeter of the clearing at the top of the cliff, closely studying the scrub junipers, the boulders tumbled side by side.

"Ah." Satisfaction warmed his voice. Thea turned to see him sitting on top of one of a pair of giant rocks, looking down the other side. "It's tricky, but doable," he told her. "I don't suppose you'd just stay up here and wait, would you?" He glanced over and saw her shaking her head. "No, I didn't think you would. Come on, then. Jed's found his own way down—he's already waiting near the bottom."

She took the hand Rafe extended and used it to climb between the two boulders. When she reached the top, he slid down the other side on his stomach, feet first, slowly, his toes scraping stone. "This is the hard part." He was panting with effort, his knuckles white as he clung to the rock she sat on. "And if this slab slides when I put my weight on it, then…" The top of his head dropped about three inches. "My advice is to run back down the mountain and call the sheriff. That's the only hope Bobby will have left."

But the stone didn't slide, for Rafe or for Thea. Once over the boulders, the path became a kind of winding granite staircase leading down the side of the cliff. "Probably a waterfall in spring," Rafe commented. "I bet you can't get here between March and August at all."

They descended with as little noise as they could manage, stepping carefully to avoid loose gravel and sudden stumbles. The air chilled even further as they dropped into the shadow of higher rocks and then trees. Thea shivered as she set foot on level ground again, missing the sun.

When she looked at Rafe, he was holding out his service revolver and the rifle, one in each hand, with a question in his eyes. *Which one?*

He nodded when she took the rifle, and turned away. With Jed just ahead of them, moving quietly through the needles under the lodgepole pines, Thea followed Rafe to the end of their search.

She almost gasped when she heard a voice. Rafe grabbed Jed by the collar; his silent hand signal told the dog to sit and stay. He tried the same gesture with Thea, but she shook her head. Rolling his eyes, he gave a slight shrug and eased down the slope another ten feet. When she joined him, she had to put a hand over her mouth to stifle a squeak of surprise.

They stood on a narrow ridge, camouflaged by dense tree cover, looking down on a clearing littered with rocks, boulders and huge stones. The Walking Stones.

Somehow, by a path she'd never traveled, they'd been led over the mountain onto Maxwell property, to the Indian site where Bobby and she had spent so many hours as children, where Rafe had found the bag of trash with the incriminating gloves and Bobby's credit card receipt.

A man carrying a long-barreled revolver limped into sight and stood with his profile to them, favoring his right leg. He was tall, skinny. Blond.

Thea recognized him—a cowboy they'd hired on several

occasions but always let go when the extra work ended. He had a bad attitude, never fit in with the regular hands.

Hank Reeves.

"Get over here," he said, waving the gun. When nothing happened, he pulled the hammer back with his thumb. "I can kill you there as well as anywhere else. It would be easier on me if I didn't have to move the body afterward, that's all." He disappeared, then came back, pushing another man ahead of him.

Bobby. With bruises on his face and his hands tied behind his back.

Thea took a minute to comprehend. Hank Reeves must be the poacher. Had Bobby tried to catch him and ended up getting caught himself?

Desperately she turned to look for Rafe…and found him gone. He had left her alone in the trees, moving so silently she hadn't missed him or seen him go.

Back in the clearing, a kick to the rear end sent Bobby crashing into the tallest of the Walking Stones. He slid to his knees, face scraping against the rock, and slumped to the side as if stunned.

Just at that moment, a third person walked into the sacred space of the Walking Stones.

"Hunt's over, Reeves," Rafe said clearly. "Drop your weapon and put your hands in the air."

Hank Reeves turned. "Like hell," he yelled, and fired.

CHAPTER SEVENTEEN

AT THE SOUND of Reeves's shot, time shifted into low gear, like a slow-motion sequence on film.

Rafe had dived for cover before the poacher aimed; the bullet whistled by his ear as he scrambled to his feet behind one of the stones. He raised his own weapon, ready to fire, just as a blur of black and tan raced into the clearing. With a snarl, Jed sprang at Reeves. Another gunshot cracked the air. The dog gave a small cry and crumpled to the ground.

Rafe squeezed his eyes shut, tightened his hold on the revolver.

"You know, Rafferty, you've done me a real favor." Reeves backed up against one of the tall stones, keeping both Bobby and the rock Rafe crouched behind in his sight. "I was planning to let Bobby here commit suicide—too much coming down on him, you know, what with the trial and the poaching charges and all. But it works even better if you tracked him up here and the two of you shot it out. I like that version a lot more."

Rafe thought of Thea, watching from above. He put every ounce of his will into praying that she would turn around and head back across the mountain to their packs and the radio he'd carried, to call for help. She couldn't do much for him or Bobby. But at least she would be out of the way.

"Screw you, Reeves." Bobby's voice was hoarse, painful to hear. "Nobody's gonna let you just walk out of here."

Reeves kept his back firmly against the stone. "I don't need anybody to let me do anything. You Maxwells always talk like you own the rest of us."

"Killing me won't make a difference with Megan." Bobby got to his knees, leaned back against the rock behind him, then pushed up to a standing position. "She broke up with me weeks ago. Has she even bothered to tell you?"

"Long as you're alive, she can't hope to escape, now, can she? You got the money to ruin anybody who crosses you. When you're dead, she'll be free. And she'll come to me." He turned slightly toward Bobby, giving Rafe a view of his shoulder.

"Why would she?" Contempt put an edge on Bobby's words. "You're no different than her old man. You think I don't know about the bruises you gave her when you were together? I saw you push her up against a locker at school one day, leave marks on her arm. She gets that at home. Megan's too smart to—"

"Shut up. Shut the hell up. That was an accident, I told her." Reeves strode across the clearing, shoved the barrel of his Smith & Wesson into the hollow of Bobby's throat. "She knows I'll never hurt her again."

Rafe took the chance Bobby had given him. Fast and silent, he crossed the clearing, intent on getting hold of Reeves before the man knew he'd moved. Any warning at all and Bobby would have a bullet in his neck.

Just as he came within a yard of Reeves, the air above them filled with the approaching beat of helicopter blades. Rafe swore, tried to take that final jump.

Reeves heard the chopper, looked up and caught the glimpse of movement behind him. He swung toward Rafe, arm outstretched, pistol cocked and ready to shoot.

Bobby kicked Reeves's injured right leg out from underneath him.

The poacher went down with a howl. Rafe landed on his back, reaching for the gun. Wiry and strong, Reeves twisted and rolled, keeping the primed pistol just out of reach. A sharp kick to his groin left Rafe sobbing with pain, still fighting for a grip on the hand with the weapon.

His toe found purchase against one of the rocks half buried in the ground. He pushed himself up an inch, then another, reaching along Reeves's extended arm, clawing, scratching for a hold on the thin, bony wrist. With a grunt, he pushed one more time, took hold of Reeves's hand and grasped the gun.

Rafe drew breath for a final effort…and Reeves pounded him from the blind side with a rock against his temple.

STANDING JUST A FEW FEET away, Thea bit her lip as Reeves smashed a rock into Rafe's head. Blood streamed down his face; the deputy groaned, but didn't quite collapse. Thea glanced at Bobby, made sure he'd edged behind a stone, completely out of the line of fire.

Then, as Reeves drew his arm back for another blow, she braced the rifle against her shoulder and moved to stand beside the struggling men.

"I don't think so, Reeves," she said clearly. "Drop the gun. And the rock." For punctuation, she released the bolt and slid a round into the chamber. "Now."

Rafe went still as a stone. The blond man opened his eyes, stared up at her with his lips pulled back in an ugly attempt at a smile. "You won't shoot me. You ain't got the guts."

She took another step, pressed the end of the barrel into the center of his forehead. "You might have been right a day ago, even an hour ago. But do you really want to take that bet right now?''

For a second, Reeves's grip around the pistol tightened. Thea pressed the rifle's mouth harder into his skull.

With a vicious curse, Reeves collapsed, pulled his fingers off the pistol, dropped the rock. He pushed at Rafe's shoulders, then crawled out from underneath the bigger man and sat on his knees. ''You bitch,'' he growled, gazing up at Thea. ''You're just like your daddy and brother.''

''Yeah,'' Thea said with a grin as Rafe groaned and started to move, ''I think you're right.''

THE HELICOPTER couldn't land, but lowered two Search and Rescue guys into the clearing on a rope. They handcuffed Reeves, untied Bobby and got Rafe on his feet, wobbly and covered with blood but conscious. And they discovered that Jed was still alive. Barely. The dog went up to the helicopter first, strapped safely into a Stokes litter, followed by a protesting Rafe and a terrified Reeves.

There was no time, no opportunity for a single word with Rafe. Thea stood by as he was strapped into the litter, hoping to catch his eye. But either by accident or design, they never made contact, and he was flown away from her without a chance to even say goodbye. Or thanks.

Definitely not a chance to say ''Forgive me.'' Or ''I love you.'' Thea wondered if she'd ever get that chance again.

The remaining SAR guy waited for the lift rope to come down one more time. ''You two sure you want to walk out? We can come back to pick you up.''

Thea looked at Bobby. He nodded. ''If you'll ask somebody at the ranch to meet us at the bottom of the mountain with transportation, I think we can get ourselves down there.''

''Okay,'' the guy said, strapping himself to the rope.

"Get a move-on. It'll be dark soon." In another minute, Thea was alone with her brother beside the Walking Stones.

Closing his eyes, Bobby blew a breath off his lower lip. "You want to yell now, wait till we get home, or on the way down?"

"All of the above."

"That's what I figured." He sighed. "Look, Tee, I'm sorry. I panicked when Dan died. I—I couldn't face it and I ran."

"Where were you going?"

"I didn't know. Just…somewhere. But I figured out by the time I got to Idaho that I wasn't leaving anything behind. The whole mess was sticking with me, and that made running away stupid, not to mention pointless. So I turned around to come back."

They left the Walking Stones clearing without a backward glance. "How did you meet up with Reeves?"

"He said he'd been watching for me, waiting for me to show up in town. That he'd been following me for months without me knowing it." Bobby brushed his hair out of his eyes. "I came into town planning to show up at Rafferty's office. But then I chickened out and decided to go home first. I stopped for gas on the way up here. Reeves saw me, he said, and came up to wait."

He shook his head. "I heard shots as I came over the last peak. The season's over and…and I guess I was putting off going home, so I pulled off the road, scouted around in the woods and found the carcass. I had seen that buck before, when I was out by myself. He was so gorgeous…and he should have been home free. It just made me so damn mad. I could see the guy going up the mountain, and I took off after him. Score one more stupidity for Bobby Maxwell."

"Did you even have a gun?"

"That was my revolver he was using today. I caught up with him on a ledge." He looked at her and Thea nodded. "We had a fight. His rifle went over the edge, he knocked me out and got hold of my gun, but not before I winged him in the leg. When I woke up, he had my hands tied and a plan to march me across the mountain. I went as slow as I could, hoping somebody would be looking."

"If I hadn't come by the back gate myself, nobody would."

Bobby flashed a tired grin. "I didn't say it was a brilliant plan. Nothing I've done lately has been brilliant."

He helped her over a rough spot, then stopped and rubbed his hands over his face. "Wait a minute. I should be flying back to jail with Reeves. Rafferty was hurt, but I doubt that would stop him in the execution of his sworn duties." He mimicked the formal words without malice. "What gives?"

Thea put her hand on his shoulder. "Dan survived the night you left. And he's better. Out of the coma." She saw shock and joy in her brother's eyes. She hated to dim the celebration, but he needed to know everything. "Not walking, mind you. Or using his arms, though there's hope. But he's alive. You aren't wanted for killing anybody."

"Well, hot damn." He put his hands on his hips and took a deep lungful of cold air, as if he could breathe for the first time in weeks. "The old man must be happy about that. He shouldn't have any trouble getting the rest of the charges dropped."

"Bobby…there's more news." She told him about Robert Maxwell's health problems. "He's recovering, and he'll be coming home soon. Not to work, though. Not for quite a while."

They stepped out from underneath the tree cover, into the high grass of their own pastureland, half buried now in snow. Bobby stopped and looked around him at the wide-open spaces, at the three pairs of truck headlights bounding toward them across the rolling hills.

"Good thing for him he's got some backup, isn't it? Dad can take as long as he needs to get better. Herman and I…" He glanced at Thea and put his arm around her shoulders. "Herman and you and I will make sure the work on Walking Stones gets done. That's what we're here for, right?"

Grinning, she slipped her arm around his waist and squeezed hard. "You bet. That's what we're here for."

PROPPED HIGH in the hospital bed, Robert Maxwell confronted his son on the morning after the boy's return. "What the hell did you think you were doing? Maxwells don't run away from anything."

Bobby kept his chin up and held his dad's stare. "I realized that. So I came back."

"You didn't think I could take care of you?"

"I didn't think about you at all. I was thinking about me." Hard to admit, but true.

He got the reaction he expected. His dad curled his lip and gave a snort. "That's nothing new."

"You're right." He had sworn to himself and to Thea that he wouldn't lose his temper, no matter how great the provocation. "But I'm making some changes."

"Such as?"

"Such as sticking around, helping Thea and Herman with the work. And you, when you're back on your feet."

The man in the bed blinked, as if surprised. "What else?"

"If I can—if I'm not in jail is what I mean, I guess—I'll plan on going to school next year. I don't see me in the straight Ag program, but maybe a business degree with some Ag courses. I've already called to get some catalogs mailed."

"You're just full of plans these days."

"I've been living without any plans at all and I found out that doesn't work. So I'll try the other option."

They stared at each other for a minute without saying anything. Robert Maxwell looked away first. "That Hank Reeves is crazy."

Bobby heard the unspoken message. *I was worried about you.* "He'll get what's coming to him. I doubt we'll see him around Paradise Corners in the future."

"I didn't figure you for a killer." *I'm glad the Aiken boy is getting better. I would have gone to jail in your place if they'd let me.*

The old man deserved some of the credit. "My dad taught me to take care of the land and its creatures. Not just use it."

The man in the bed nodded, brought his stern gaze back to Bobby's face. "Your drinking is out of control." No hidden subtext there.

"I know. I'm working on it."

"There are meetings and such…"

He shook his head. "I don't need the meetings. I'll be fine."

"If you say so." The powerful will, the stern control had been switched off. His dad fingered the edge of his sheet, looking older and…frail.

Bobby stepped up to the bed, put a hand on his dad's square shoulder. "Things will be okay. I've got a handle on my life now. I'll make you proud of me yet." *You and Megan,* he thought. *I'll show both of you—I can take on responsibility. I'll take care of myself and you, too.* And Megan. Especially Megan.

Robert Maxwell lifted his arm, covered Bobby's hand

with his own for a second. "See that you do," he ordered. And gave his son a rare, wry smile.

That smile disappeared when Rafe Rafferty stepped through the door. "Come to make an arrest, Deputy? You got a warrant?"

Rafe looked at the rancher and mustered up a weary patience. "I've already made the arrest, Mr. Maxwell. I'm just here to set up a hearing date."

By the bed, Bobby straightened his back, swallowed hard. "Am I going to jail?"

"The charges aren't that serious anymore. I'm expecting you to show up without a problem, though."

"So what's the point of a hearing?" Robert Maxwell sounded dangerous, but Rafe heard the worry under his growl.

"Bobby can't walk away scot-free. Judge LeVay wants to have a chance to review the evidence, hear some arguments about penalties and render a decision."

"LeVay, huh?"

"He's your friend, Mr. Maxwell, but don't count on getting anything swept under the carpet. The judge is on my side—the law's side—this time."

"Humph." Maxwell snorted, but Bobby looked relieved. Rafe had a feeling that getting past the uncertainty of his future would be a bigger relief than escaping any kind of punishment.

They discussed the rancher's release from the hospital and came up with a date that would work for the hearing, then spent a few minutes on Hank Reeves. "Taxidermy shops in three states have reported doing business with him." Rafe shrugged. "The guy can't—won't—even say *why*."

"He was always hard on the steers," the older Maxwell commented. "Enjoyed branding and castrating too much."

"He likes causing pain," Bobby commented grimly. "To people and animals."

"You're probably right," Rafe said. "He found that credit card receipt of yours on the ground outside the convenience store, by the way. You should be more careful with those things. And your trash."

"Yessir." Bobby gave him an undaunted grin. "Thea's going to be here in a few minutes."

Thanks for the warning. "I'd like to stay, but I'd better get back to work. Give her...my best." He put on his hat and winced—he kept forgetting the bandage over the sixteen stitches above his right temple.

"That was quite a cut," Bobby commented. "Must hurt like hell."

"I've had worse. You take care, Mr. Maxwell. Behave, Bobby." Rafe left the room quickly and headed for the stairs, avoiding the elevator. The damn head wound was the most bearable of the traumas he'd suffered recently.

But only one member of the Maxwell family could make use of that particular piece of information. And *she* didn't want to know.

THEA STEPPED OFF the elevator, turned toward her dad's room...and caught a glimpse of a tall man in a sheepskin coat and white hat striding down the hallway away from her.

"Rafe." She said his name aloud, too softly for him to have heard. He disappeared into the stairwell as she watched.

The breath she was holding escaped. If she ran, she might catch up with him. But what would she say if she did? And why, after the treatment he'd received from her family, would he care one way or the other?

Saving energy and her own stupid pride, she went in to see her dad.

"Good morning." She went to the bed, touched his hand lightly. "You look like a man who's ready to head home."

He frowned. "I looked like that a week ago."

"Rafferty was here," Bobby said brightly.

She thought about slapping him. "I saw him as he left. What did he want?"

"To set up the damn hearing." Her dad took a deep breath. "Looks like we have to go through with it. No telling what the judge'll come up with. The deputy as much as said LeVay's not open to persuasion this time."

Thea nodded. "That's probably a good thing. Why don't we just get this over with and move on with our lives?"

At the hearing ten days later, LeVay made that process less painful than Thea thought they probably deserved. Dan's improved condition and Rafe's recommendation persuaded him to leniency, he said. Bobby's driver's license was suspended for a year, and he would be on probation for three. He was assigned a thousand hours of community service, details to be determined by the town council in conjunction with the sheriff's department.

"Violation of any element of this sentence," LeVay said, his bushy white eyebrows lowered, his forehead wrinkled, "will result in immediate reconsideration of the entire case, with possible institution of jail time. Got that, young man?"

Bobby swallowed hard. "I got it. Sir."

"Court adjourned." The judge put his gavel down and stood up. "Now I'm headed to Sun City, Arizona. Come visit sometime."

The lawyers packed up their papers and shook Bobby's hand as the spectators filed out—half the town had attended the proceedings, including the Aikenses and the Heaths.

Tom Bonner, the driver of the other truck, and his pregnant wife were there, too.

Mr. Aiken stepped up and tapped Bobby on the shoulder. "This ain't over, boy." Dan's father had lost a lot of weight in the last two months. His hair had turned from dark brown to a speckled gray. He gestured at the families of Bobby's victims circled around them. "We all got medical bills to pay for the rest of our lives. Don't think you're getting off this easy."

The Bonners and Aikens and Heaths filed out. The last person to leave was Rafe. He stood at the back of the room for a minute, rotating his hat by the brim held between his fingers. Thea took a step toward him. There was so much to say…

But then he smiled, gave a slight shake of his head and went through the door. It swung shut behind him, leaving four Maxwells in the courtroom, with Herman and Beth Peace standing by as their only supporters.

"Well, it could be much, much worse." Cassie punched Bobby lightly in the shoulder. "You'd better behave for the next three years, or there's going to be a lynching for real. And I'm going to carry the rope."

"Let's just get home," Robert Maxwell said. "There's work to do." He walked out of the courtroom with his back straight, but the effort cost him. Back at the house, he went to bed without protest, let Beth bring soup to his room, let her fuss over him until he fell asleep.

In the days that followed, Beth became less and less the all-controlling housekeeper the family had known their whole lives. Coming in for lunch, they'd find the food prepared…but find the cook herself sitting in a chair beside Robert Maxwell, coaxing him to eat, or just talking with him while he did. The dinner dishes got done when Herman and Thea and Bobby did them. Beth was taking care of Robert. Most surprising of all, he was letting her.

Around the ranch, there was plenty of work to be done—feeding the cattle, keeping the cows in good condition, especially the ones set to calve in March, taking care of the horses, repairing the ranch machinery and vehicles for spring and summer use. For the most part, Bobby was around to help. Thea knew he'd made several attempts to call Megan, without ever getting through to the girl. Who knew if that relationship would ever be fixed? Meanwhile Christmas approached, and though there would be no big Walking Stones party for everybody in town this year, Thea, Bobby and Herman cut a twenty-foot tree in the mountains and decorated the house, while Beth cooked and served a big dinner for the hands and their families. The winter routine felt right…and completely miserable.

Thea spent more time than was comfortable, or even safe, riding Sundance across the snowy landscape. She tried to draw her sustenance from the ranch itself, from the vista of rolling pastures, the simplicity of the cattle and their needs, the majesty of the Crazy Mountains looming over them, the wideness of the Montana sky—crystalline blue on sunny days, a dense pearl gray as the snows returned.

But for the first time, Walking Stones Ranch wasn't enough. The hole in her life could not be filled with work, with the land or by her own imagination. She wasn't pregnant and she hadn't gotten herself a dog. Only one solution remained.

She went into Paradise Corners two days before Christmas. The town looked like a postcard—lights strung on all the stores, a wreath on every door, evergreen garland wrapped around street lamps, tied on with big red bows. She got a nod or two from people on the street as she drove through, and a "Merry Christmas" from Mona Rangel, sweeping off the sidewalk outside Grizzly's.

The small house just north of Main Street had been decorated with many-colored lights edging the roof and framing the windows. A swag of evergreen branches tied with a gold rope hung on the door. Evidently Rafe was thoroughly into the Christmas spirit.

Thea couldn't say the same. But she thought she might feel better if she apologized, admitted her mistakes, moved their…relationship…back to a casual footing, at least. She hated the idea that they would remain enemies. If not lovers, could they at least be…distant friends?

Taking a deep breath, she knocked on the door.

MUTTERING AT the string of tangled tree lights draped over his shoulder and right hand, Rafe opened the door. One glance at his visitor knocked the world out of orbit. "Thea?"

"Hi. Um…are you busy?"

"No." He realized he sounded doubtful, and shook his head. "No, of course not. Come on in."

She stepped into the hallway; he shut the outside door, closing them in together. A deep breath drew in her fragrance, and he felt almost dizzy. "I'd help you off with your coat, but I'm a little tied up here."

Thea smiled. "I can see that. No problem." She shrugged out of her jacket and hung it on the peg. Underneath, she wore a bright blue sweater and soft black pants. "Smells good in here—a combination of spaghetti sauce and evergreen."

"This is the official tree-decorating ceremony." He ushered her into the living room. "Jed's the supervisor. He tells me where to put the balls."

"Jed!" She dropped to her knees by the couch. "Hey,

buddy, how are you?'' Jed played invalid, wearing his most pitiful expression, rolling weakly onto his back, but wagging his tail strongly.

"Faker,'' Rafe told him. "He was chasing a rabbit in the snow yesterday morning. Didn't catch him, but that wasn't the point.''

"Of course not.'' She turned and sat on the floor, resting her back against the sofa. "That's a nice tree. How do you like Christmas in Montana?''

He pretended to concentrate on straightening out the lights. "This is the first white Christmas I've seen. Definitely lives up to the reputation.''

Thea didn't say anything, and the crackle of the fire became loud in the silence. Rafe didn't have a clue what he was actually doing with the damn light string—tying it in knots, for all he knew. Why was she here? What had she come to say?

"Rafe…''

"Hmm?'' He couldn't look at her—she'd see how desperate he was. That would put her under an obligation he refused to impose.

"I wanted to thank you.''

"You don't have to do that.'' One of the small bulbs snapped between his fingers. He went to the box in the corner for a replacement.

"You took care of Bobby, better than any of the rest of us. And you got hurt in the process.''

"Just doin' my job, ma'am.'' He imitated a TV sheriff's drawl, without looking at Thea. "Glad to be of service.''

Her husky chuckle tortured him. "I also wanted to apologize.''

"You don't have to do that, either.'' The replacement bulb wouldn't fit in the socket. Rafe thought about throwing the string of lights, the tree and all the decorations into the fire.

"You put up with insults, obstruction, lies...my family and I have treated you badly."

"It's okay, Thea. You care about each other. That's a...vital...part of life." If she'd said her piece, he really wished she would leave before he started breaking furniture.

"I care...about you, too."

Rafe dropped the light string and looked at the woman across the room. "What does that mean?"

"I don't want us to be..."

He waited.

"Enemies. Opponents."

"Which leaves us where?" His legs weren't going to hold him up much longer. Moving carefully, as if the floor were made of glass, he sat in the armchair by the fireplace.

She stared at her hands, clasped in her lap. "Um, allies, at least." Then she looked up, her green-blue gaze completely defenseless. "Friends?"

Studying her face, he saw a weariness he felt in his soul. In her eyes, he found the emptiness he'd been living with for weeks.

Most of the time he wasn't a man who made unsecured investments. This would be an exception. "Not good enough."

"Oh." Thea looked at her hands. But when she lifted her face again, the curve of her mouth forecasted a smile. Her eyes were bright. "What would be good enough?"

Rafe thought about the possible answers. "Wife," he said quietly, going for broke.

That wonderful smile dawned like summer sun. "Yes."

He stood up and she came into his arms like an arrow, straight and sure. "I love you," he said against the top of her head, her ear, the side of her throat. "I need you so much," he whispered over her lips. And then he kissed them both breathless.

Just before the kissing got out of hand, Thea put her palms on Rafe's cheeks, pushing his head back just an inch. "I get to say it, too. I love you. More than anything. Always."

The grin she loved came back. "Prove it."

Thea didn't have to be told twice.

SHE WOKE UP ALONE in Rafe's bed, but she could hear him in the kitchen, humming "Deck the Halls" only slightly out of tune. She grinned and lay back against the pillows, waiting.

In just a couple of minutes, he came into the bedroom. Instead of the dinner plates she expected, he carried a big cardboard box draped with a towel.

"Food?" she said, pulling the sheet and blanket around her as she sat up.

"Nope. That's later. First, you have to open your Christmas present."

"Rafe..." She shook her head. "I don't need a present. Nothing more than the one you just gave me, anyway."

Setting the box on the bed, he leaned over for a kiss. "No argument there. But I got this before you came today. So I have to give it to you." He took her hand and closed her fingers over the edge of the towel. "It's not hard to open. Just pull."

Still flushed with embarrassment, Thea pulled. From where she sat, all she saw was an empty box.

"Come closer," Rafe said.

Thea scooted over and bent over the container. Inside, curled up in a sweet warm circle of whiskey-colored fur, was a bloodhound puppy.

"Oh, Rafe." She cupped her hands under the dog and lifted it out. "Oh, how beautiful." Tears dripped on her cheeks as she looked at him. "For me?"

"Just for you. Jed and I call her Leona. She has a really fierce growl when she's awake, which isn't all that often. But you can change her name."

"Oh, no. Leona's perfect." Thea ran her fingertips over the sleeping puppy, down her back, across her stomach, up under her chin. Something sharp scraped her nail. "What's that?"

Rafe looked completely innocent. "What's what?"

Leona didn't open her eyes as Thea probed the folds of fur. A blue ribbon had been tied around the dog's neck.

Dangling from the ribbon was a ring.

"A Montana sapphire," Rafe explained, putting it on her hand. "I was coming out to see you. I thought you needed some time first."

"Not that much time," she told him. "I was ready to admit my mistakes the day we found Bobby."

"Well, maybe *I* needed the time." He put Leona back in her box and put the box on the floor beside the bed. Then he pulled Thea tight against him. "Time to realize that I misjudged you, and Bobby, maybe even the whole town. For a while there, I guess I saw myself as the Lone Ranger, bringing justice to the lawless frontier. But the situation would have resolved itself the right way, eventually. You could have found Bobby without my help. He was coming home on his own, he didn't have to be caught. Judge LeVay stood by the law, in the end."

Thea shook her head. "But you were—what's the chemistry word?—the catalyst for all those reactions. Without you, we might have let my father pull strings. Bobby and the rest of the town would be much worse off if that had happened. And I…"

She eased the bedcovers from between their bodies. "I would have been a thorny old maid, too sharp for anybody to get close to."

Rafe ran his hands along her bare back. "No spines. No thorns. Nice and smooth."

She kissed that sexy grin off his mouth. "And I'm counting on you to keep me that way."

The grin reappeared. "My pleasure, ma'am."

EPILOGUE

THEA AND RAFE HELD their wedding on Valentine's Day, in the Methodist Church. Afterward, most of the people in Paradise Corners—even the ones who owed Robert Maxwell money or who'd lost land to him—came out to the ranch for the reception. Only a crazy person would pass up the chance to see inside the grandest house in the county.

Robert watched the crowd, thinking that Helen would've enjoyed this day. Althea looked like…like a princess in her wedding dress. Rafferty didn't clean up too badly, himself. And he was clearly besotted with his bride. The necklace he'd given her as a wedding gift suggested the man had resources—a big, oval Montana sapphire on a silver chain, to match the engagement ring.

Even more impressive was the offer Rafferty had made for a parcel of Walking Stones land where he and Althea could build themselves a house. Robert wouldn't sell outright, of course, but they'd hammered out a lease agreement that satisfied all three of them. A real negotiator, his son-in-law.

Cassie and Jolie stood with the couple near the fireplace. They both looked nice in their blue dresses, and little Zak was proud of his first real suit. Cassie had made a mess of his tie, though, and Robert had had to retie the knot. Just one more chore a full-time dad was good for.

Strange as it seemed, after all these years, Jolie had finally come to her senses and decided to come home. At

Christmas, Thea had learnd that the city council was looking for a doctor to take over Doc Grimes's patients and had
told her sister about the opening. Just this morning, Jolie
had toured the clinic building. She'd also looked at old Fred
Walters's cabin just outside town as a place to live. The
old guy's family had decided he couldn't stay on his own
any more and had moved him into a nursing home.

Robert shook his head. A terrible fate—losing control of
one's life. A man who couldn't take care of himself might
as well be dead.

"I think everyone's enjoying themselves." Beth stood at
his shoulder, carrying a tray of plates with slices of wedding cake. "Is there something I should do?"

Robert considered her. She wore a pink dress, frillier
than her usual, and her hair was piled up on top of her
head. He hadn't realized how pretty she could be.

One of the serving staff they'd hired to help for this party
went by empty-handed. Robert took the tray from Beth.
"Give this to him," he said, suiting actions to words.
"Now go enjoy yourself." She stared at him, her soft skin
flushed. "Go on—go talk to the girls. Or that Rangel
woman. Have yourself a good time." Her eyes got a little
stormy, but she did as he said.

Behind him, the front door opened and a draft of cold
air blew in. Robert turned with his hand out for a shake,
but dropped it when he recognized the newcomer. "What
are you doing here, Wheeler?"

"I want to talk to you. Private." The man's eyes glit-
tered. He was half to two-thirds drunk.

And he wouldn't be allowed to disrupt Althea's wedding.
"Back here," Robert said with a tilt of his head, and led
Wheeler to his office. He shut the door, then went to stand
behind his desk. "So what do you want?"

Wheeler had taken a seat without being asked. "Only to see that you do the right thing."

"Which is?"

"I'm telling you straight out. Your boy's got my little girl in trouble. And I expect you to take care of it."

Dizziness washed through him, and Robert thought he was going to have to sit down. He stayed on his feet through sheer force of will. "In trouble? You mean…a child?"

"What else would I mean? She's still a baby, and now she's having one of her own. I say that's your responsibility."

He felt slow, stupid. "You want money to—to end it?"

"Hell, no. That'd be…I mean, she won't consider getting rid of it. So somebody's going to have to pay the doctor and the hospital. See the kid has food to eat, clothes, a place to live."

At last, Robert's brain started to work again. "How do you know the baby is Bobby's?"

Wheeler surged to his feet. "You calling my girl a slut?"

He kept a firm grip on his own temper. "I'm asking why I should believe you."

"Check with anybody in town. They'll tell you that boy of yours has been sneaking around with my Megan for months. It's him all right."

"I'll do just that." Though Robert knew in his gut that the man was telling the truth. "I'll talk to my son, too. Then we'll let you know what we will or won't be doing."

"I want some money. I got to feed the girl while she's carrying the brat."

Robert stared at Wheeler without a word, with such contempt and for so long that the man began to fidget. "You're leaving," he said. "Now."

Wheeler whined, threatened and wheedled as Robert escorted him through the kitchen into the backyard. "Don't ever set foot on my property again. I'll have you thrown into jail for trespassing. In case you haven't noticed—" he almost chuckled when he thought of it "—the deputy sheriff is a member of the family." Then, with a quick shove, he sent Wheeler sprawling into the snow.

In the hallway between the kitchen and the great room, he caught the arm of a waiter. "Find my son. Tell him I want to see him in my office. Immediately."

He waited at the window, thinking of lawsuits and insurance and community service and arrest charges...all the complications Bobby had created these last few months. He thought about Helen. She'd wanted grandchildren—hell, so did he. The name would have to go on. But not this way. Not with such a lack of...of...

"Dad?" Bobby knocked on the door.

"Come in."

Looking more like his mother than ever, Bobby came toward him across the room. The boy had been a real help these last couple of months. More focused, more responsible, more committed.

Robert had begun to hope for the best. Which made his question all the more violent.

"What the hell kind of mess have you gotten us into now?"

*Turn the page for an excerpt from the second
exciting installment in the dramatic saga of
the Maxwell family.*

A MONTANA FAMILY

*by Roxanne Rustand
will be available next month
at your favorite retail store.*

IN THE KITCHEN, Jolie Maxwell pulled a box of cocoa mix packets and a bag of mini-marshmallows out of the cupboard, then filled a glass two-cup measure with water and set it in the microwave to heat.

The girl was pregnant and alone, Jolie mused as she prepared the cocoa and set it on a tray. Maybe Megan was afraid to tell her family…or maybe they'd booted her out of the house.

When she returned to the great room, Jolie set the tray down on the coffee table that stood between the couch and fireplace. "Here you go, honey. A little cocoa will warm you up and help you relax."

Megan didn't move, though the blankets over her gently rose and fell with the deep, regular respiration of sleep. Firelight flickered over her delicate features, accenting the dark circles under her eyes and the bruise—faded now to yellow—that Jolie had first seen at the clinic.

"What happened to you?" Jolie whispered as she tucked the blankets snugly over Megan's thin shoulders.

The cell phone vibrated against Jolie's hip. She moved to her bedroom and shut the door before answering the call.

"Jolie? Are you all right?" Her new brother-in-law's deep voice was laced with concern. "You didn't leave much of a message."

"I've got…a girl here. She appeared at my door at midnight, alone. Apparently walked clear up to my cabin alone.''

Rafe gave a low whistle. ''Is she okay?''

''She walked in the door, seems coherent. An old, good-sized bruise on her face, wary of even giving me her last name. A runaway, maybe? Trouble at home? I don't know…she seems awfully scared.'' Jolie cleared her throat. ''And she's pregnant.''

''I'm already on my way. I'll be there within fifteen minutes. Can you keep her from leaving?''

Jolie gave a quiet chuckle. ''She's not going anywhere fast—the poor thing looks exhausted. Right now she's asleep on my couch.''

''I can take her to the sheriff's office.''

''No…please. I think she's better off here, really. At least for tonight.''

''We'll talk when I get there.''

His truck pulled up to a stop in front of the cabin minutes later. Jolie met him at the door and ushered him in, a finger at her lips. ''She's still asleep.''

At six foot four he towered over Jolie and probably intimidated most suspects with just a level stare, but Thea's husband also had an infinitely gentle side that showed in his eyes as he looked down at Megan.

''I should have guessed,'' he whispered. ''This poor kid has had it rough.''

''You know her?''

''She's Megan Wheeler.''

Jolie looked blankly up at him.

Surprise flared in his eyes. ''You don't know.''

''She didn't tell me anything, just begged for help, and fell asleep on my couch.''

''I told Thea she should say something,'' he muttered under his breath. He hitched a shoulder, cleared his throat.

His gaze shifted to the leaping flames in the fireplace. "Her father's a drunk, and those poor kids were taken into foster care at least twice before I came to town. I didn't think he would touch her again—I made damn sure he knew what would happen to him if he did—but he's been really hitting the bottle lately. She probably came to you because you're family."

"Family?"

"This is Bobby's ex-girlfriend." Rafe's voice turned cold. "Your brother has been a busy guy over the past six months, in more ways than one."

*Harlequin truly does
make any time special. . . .
This year we are celebrating
weddings in style!*

A
Walk
Down
the Aisle
WEDDING CELEBRATION

To help us celebrate, we want you to tell us how wearing the Harlequin wedding gown will make your wedding day special. As the grand prize, Harlequin will offer one lucky bride the chance to **"Walk Down the Aisle" in the Harlequin wedding gown!**

There's more...

For her honeymoon, she and her groom will spend five nights at the **Hyatt Regency Maui.** As part of this five-night honeymoon at the hotel renowned for its romantic attractions, the couple will enjoy a candlelit dinner for two in Swan Court, a sunset sail on the hotel's catamaran, and duet spa treatments.

A HYATT RESORT AND SPA

Maui • Molokai • Lanai

To enter, please write, in, 250 words or less, how wearing the Harlequin wedding gown will make your wedding day special. The entry will be judged based on its emotionally compelling nature, its originality and creativity, and its sincerity. This contest is open to Canadian and U.S. residents only and to those who are 18 years of age and older. There is no purchase necessary to enter. Void where prohibited. See further contest rules attached. Please send your entry to:

Walk Down the Aisle Contest

In Canada	In U.S.A.
P.O. Box 637	P.O. Box 9076
Fort Erie, Ontario	3010 Walden Ave.
L2A 5X3	Buffalo, NY 14269-9076

You can also enter by visiting www.eHarlequin.com
Win the Harlequin wedding gown and the vacation of a lifetime!
The deadline for entries is October 1, 2001.

HARLEQUIN®
Makes any time special ®

PHWDACONT1

HARLEQUIN WALK DOWN THE AISLE TO MAUI CONTEST 1197
OFFICIAL RULES
NO PURCHASE NECESSARY TO ENTER

1. To enter, follow directions published in the offer to which you are responding. Contest begins April 2, 2001, and ends on October 1, 2001. Method of entry may vary. Mailed entries must be postmarked by October 1, 2001, and received by October 8, 2001.

2. Contest entry may be, at times, presented via the Internet, but will be restricted solely to residents of certain geographic areas that are disclosed on the Web site. To enter via the Internet, if permissible, access the Harlequin Web site (www.eHarlequin.com) and follow the directions displayed online. Online entries must be received by 11:59 p.m. E.S.T. on October 1, 2001.

   In lieu of submitting an entry online, enter by mail by hand-printing (or typing) on an 8¹/₂" x 11" plain piece of paper, your name, address (including zip code), Contest number/name and in 250 words or fewer, why winning a Harlequin wedding dress would make your wedding day special. Mail via first-class mail to: Harlequin Walk Down the Aisle Contest 1197, (in the U.S.) P.O. Box 9076, 3010 Walden Avenue, Buffalo, NY 14269-9076, (in Canada) P.O. Box 637, Fort Erie, Ontario L2A 5X3, Canada.

   Limit one entry per person, household address and e-mail address. Online and/or mailed entries received from persons residing in geographic areas in which Internet entry is not permissible will be disqualified.

3. Contests will be judged by a panel of members of the Harlequin editorial, marketing and public relations staff based on the following criteria:

   - Originality and Creativity—50%
   - Emotionally Compelling—25%
   - Sincerity—25%

   In the event of a tie, duplicate prizes will be awarded. Decisions of the judges are final.

4. All entries become the property of Torstar Corp. and will not be returned. No responsibility is assumed for lost, late, illegible, incomplete, inaccurate, nondelivered or misdirected mail or misdirected e-mail, for technical, hardware or software failures of any kind, lost or unavailable network connections, or failed, incomplete, garbled or delayed computer transmission or any human error which may occur in the receipt or processing of the entries in this Contest.

5. Contest open only to residents of the U.S. (except Puerto Rico) and Canada, who are 18 years of age or older, and is void wherever prohibited by law; all applicable laws and regulations apply. Any litigation within the Province of Quebec respecting the conduct or organization of a publicity contest may be submitted to the Régie des alcools, des courses et des jeux for a ruling. Any litigation respecting the awarding of a prize may be submitted to the Régie des alcools, des courses et des jeux only for the purpose of helping the parties reach a settlement. Employees and immediate family members of Torstar Corp. and D. L. Blair, Inc., their affiliates, subsidiaries and all other agencies, entities and persons connected with the use, marketing or conduct of this Contest are not eligible to enter. Taxes on prizes are the sole responsibility of winners. Acceptance of any prize offered constitutes permission to use winner's name, photograph or other likeness for the purposes of advertising, trade and promotion on behalf of Torstar Corp., its affiliates and subsidiaries without further compensation to the winner, unless prohibited by law.

6. Winners will be determined no later than November 15, 2001, and will be notified by mail. Winners will be required to sign and return an Affidavit of Eligibility form within 15 days after winner notification. Noncompliance within that time period may result in disqualification and an alternative winner may be selected. Winners of trip must execute a Release of Liability prior to ticketing and must possess required travel documents (e.g. passport, photo ID) where applicable. Trip must be completed by November 2002. No substitution of prize permitted by winner. Torstar Corp. and D. L. Blair, Inc., their parents, affiliates, and subsidiaries are not responsible for errors in printing or electronic presentation of Contest, entries and/or game pieces. In the event of printing or other errors which may result in unintended prize values or duplication of prizes, all affected game pieces or entries shall be null and void. If for any reason the Internet portion of the Contest is not capable of running as planned, including infection by computer virus, bugs, tampering, unauthorized intervention, fraud, technical failures, or any other causes beyond the control of Torstar Corp. which corrupt or affect the administration, secrecy, fairness, integrity or proper conduct of the Contest, Torstar Corp. reserves the right, at its sole discretion, to disqualify any individual who tampers with the entry process and to cancel, terminate, modify or suspend the Contest or the Internet portion thereof. In the event of a dispute regarding an online entry, the entry will be deemed submitted by the authorized holder of the e-mail account submitted at the time of entry. Authorized account holder is defined as the natural person who is assigned to an e-mail address by an Internet access provider, online service provider or other organization that is responsible for arranging e-mail address for the domain associated with the submitted e-mail address. **Purchase or acceptance of a product offer does not improve your chances of winning.**

7. Prizes: (1) Grand Prize—A Harlequin wedding dress (approximate retail value: $3,500) and a 5-night/6-day honeymoon trip to Maui, HI, including round-trip air transportation provided by Maui Visitors Bureau from Los Angeles International Airport (winner is responsible for transportation to and from Los Angeles International Airport) and a Harlequin Romance Package, including hotel accomodations (double occupancy) at the Hyatt Regency Maui Resort and Spa, dinner for (2) two at Swan Court, a sunset sail on Kiele V and a spa treatment for the winner (approximate retail value: $4,000); (5) Five runner-up prizes of a $1000 gift certificate to selected retail outlets to be determined by Sponsor (retail value $1000 ea.). Prizes consist of only those items listed as part of the prize. Limit one prize per person. All prizes are valued in U.S. currency.

8. For a list of winners (available after December 17, 2001) send a self-addressed, stamped envelope to: Harlequin Walk Down the Aisle Contest 1197 Winners, P.O. Box 4200 Blair, NE 68009-4200 or you may access the www.eHarlequin.com Web site through January 15, 2002.

Contest sponsored by Torstar Corp., P.O. Box 9042, Buffalo, NY 14269-9042, U.S.A.

PHWDACONT2